Fay Weldon

was born in England and raised in New Zealand. She took degrees in Economics and Psychology at the University of St Andrews in Scotland and after a decade of odd jobs and hard times began writing fiction. She is well known as novelist, screenwriter and cultural journalist. Her novels include *The Life and Loves of a She-Devil*, *Puffball*, *Big Women*, *Rhode Island Blues* and *The Bulgari Connection*. Her most recent book is her critically acclaimed memoir, *Auto da Fay*.

Praise for *Nothing to Wear and Nowhere to Hide*:

'Pleasingly wry. Nothing is quite what it seems in Weldon's world. If there is something slightly parodic about Weldon's cast of calorie-conscious childless professionals brought up short by their hormones, it is easily balanced by the vigour and spirit of the prose.'
Literary Review

'Self-conscious and needy, the characters become their harshest critics, finally falling victim to their killer heels. We witness inner dialogues and inverted snobbery, the uses for men and money and how each and every woman is inevitably pulled back to her relationship with, and as, a parent. But far from being a depressing diatribe on what women should do, this is more an attempt to place the many different female strengths within today's framework. It is clear that shocking acts, by those whose behaviour was formerly as well-manicured as their nails, are a defiance of our ideals of beauty, success and happiness. Intelligent, tongue-in-cheek, bitchy yet mellow, these stories left me thinking of that well-worn phrase, "she who laughs last…"'
Independent on Sunday

'Written with inventiveness, verve and humour.'
Spectator

'Amuses and bemuses. There are no happily ever afters in this collection. In Fay Weldon land, the boy doesn't always get the girl, people don't always kiss and make up and the daughter doesn't always listen to the mother. But that's life. Tough. This is irreverent humour at its best.'
Ireland on Sunday

FAY WELDON

NOTHING TO WEAR AND NOWHERE TO HIDE

Flamingo

An Imprint of HarperCollins*Publishers*

Flamingo
An imprint of HarperCollins*Publishers*
77–85 Fulham Palace Road,
Hammersmith, London W6 8JB

Flamingo is a registered trade mark of HarperCollins*Publishers* Limited

www.fireandwater.com

Published by Flamingo 2003
9 8 7 6 5 4 3 2 1

Previously published in Great Britain by Flamingo 2002

ISBN 0 00 655166 1

Set in Postscript Linotype Minion with Helvetica Neue Light display by
Rowland Phototypsetting Ltd, Bury St Edmunds, Suffolk

Printed and bound in Great Britain by Clays Ltd, St Ives plc

Contents

How We Live Now

THINGS THAT GO BUMP IN THE NIGHT

Eyes in the Dark

A Knife for Cutting Mangoes

The Medium is the Message

The Site

Eyes in the Dark

Cats have souls. You know they do, because of the way they haunt houses. For a time after a cat dies you see movements out of the corner of your eye. A flash of a tail disappearing round the door, a kind of shifting blur under the table where it used to eat, yet when it was alive you got the feeling it didn't really care for you one bit, it wouldn't acknowledge you at all. I've known cats hang around the living for years, and a canary once – but that's another story. Dogs don't normally haunt: when they're dead they lie down: their graves are quiet. They're such bundles of emotion in life, they've none left over in death. The effort of communicating without words for a lifetime has altogether exhausted their spirit. Enough of that, they tend to say, that's enough, I've failed, I'm off, sorry and all that but goodbye. Finish.

This is the story of Galway, our yellow Labrador, who did stay around. I don't know if he exactly had a soul or not, but his spirit certainly outran his death. He was a sturdy, grave animal, affectionate but somehow distant, slightly disdainful, as if Olive the cat had had rather too much influence on his growing years. Olive, golden-eyed and silky black, would box his ears when he was a puppy and misbehaving, a quick one-two with either paw, and then Galway would remember his canine nature and chase her up the apple tree outside the back door, and she would sit there and sneer down at him, and he would sit and gaze up at her with doleful, rather envious eyes, as if he wanted to be like that, to be able to impose swift and just retribution, and then leap up a branch and be superior. We lived in the country then, on a smallholding: those were the good days.

In the winters Olive would sleep leaning up against Galway in his basket in the utility room and once in the morning I found my two-year-old in there as well, all three lying in a warm sleeping breathing heap, Galway, Olive and Mark. I was too exhausted to worry about parasites, or fleas, I was just grateful for a happy, sleeping child. His younger twin sisters were only six months old: if the animals would give a hand so much the better.

We had four Soay sheep in the field; what gluttons for punishment we were. Soays are a rare breed, accustomed to hardship: they have long stringy legs, they startle like deer, for which they are sometimes mistaken. Their natural habitat is the rocky Scottish coastline, their proper diet is seaweed and scrub. We gave our small flock, or herd, three ewes and one ram, lush southern grass to graze, and they took it in their stride. The ewes stopped being all rib and scrag, and turned quite plump and rounded and velvet-coated, if never tranquil, and the ram's horns grew strong, curved and proud; he learned to stamp his foot. They had an acre field to themselves, with a gate that led from our vegetable garden, and even a high point to stand on, in place of a cliff, for all it was only a grassy hump: an old burial mound, it was said. But they were always nervous of us, though we were their benefactors. We'd take them out their sheep nuts and fill their trough with water every morning and they'd dart away and stand at a distance, on their mound, staring, ready to bolt. The ram would place himself in front of his two wives and his old mother, and lower his curly horns and do a bit of stamping. But as with so many animals, they went through their rituals of flight, defence, attack, more for form's sake than out of any urgency. I never thought they took us really seriously.

And when one night unexpectedly the youngest ewe gave birth to twin lambs they were there waiting for us in the morning, the

4

four of them, proud and pleased to show us what they'd done, waiting for our acknowledgement, our oohs and aahs, before affecting to be terrified and leaping off to their mound to view us askance, the two curious, skinny-legged lambs, born ready for flight, tottering up the slope, legs tangling, following after.

The sheep fascinated Galway: he'd wriggle under the gate and lie just the other side of it watching them, while they ignored him – rather insultingly, I thought – grazing right up to inches from his nose, in sheer defiance of his canine nature, which was, quite honestly, to chase them from here to kingdom come. You could see his ears twitching from the effort of not.

One day when I was putting the washing on the line, Mark – he must have been just over two at the time, let himself out through the gate and sat cross-legged and peaceful next to Galway, sheep watching. Olive, black and sinewy, stalked through patches of nettles – they never ate nettles – to join them.

It was the first day of spring after a long hard winter; the sky was washed and beautiful: you know that line in the psalms when it says, 'And all the valleys shall be exalted,' and you wonder what it means? One of those mornings. Our robin sat on the clothesline and said, 'Well, spring's here at last!' or would have, I was sure, if he only had the power of speech. As it was, he just looked at me, head on one side, eyes glittering, for a full four beats longer than usual before flying off to the apple tree.

And I stood where I was, amazed. Because one of the lambs, dazzled perhaps by the sudden glittery sunshine, and all normal wintry rules of engagement deferred, had joined Galway, Olive and Mark. Sheep, dog, cat and child sat in a circle and stared at one another, and from one to the other, for all the world as if they were trying to decide who they were, what they were, which was the one they were like. The twins started crying in the house and I moved suddenly and the spell was broken, and they dispersed, but I think from that day on Galway decided he was a sheep; certainly after that he was for ever trying to be one of their number. The sheep didn't want that, and when he ran up to join them ran off in the opposite direction in apparent distress and panic, and Galway would run after. A process known by the local farmers as 'running the profit off 'em'. So it became our function to try and keep Galway out of the field while he tried to get in. Animals can be a terrible nuisance.

Oh, they were mischievous, those Soays, those dancing, prancing, nervy sheep from the Outer Hebrides. Once a year we had to round them up and take them to the livestock centre to be dipped against scabies. We humans would start from the corners of the field, and move in upon them from every angle, and Galway was allowed in because clearly he had the heart of a sheepdog in the body of a Labrador; he'd race round, knowing instinctively what to do, driving back any who ran for cover, and Mark at three joined in and waved his little arms in the air in the right place at the right moment, and between us we managed it. It was one of those days you don't forget, such a mixture of joy and dreadfulness. My husband fell and drove a stick into his knee and simply pulled it out and carried on. On a normal day it would have meant doctors and stitches and tetanus jabs, and all that other human ritual to do with survival.

And then that autumn when Mark turned five, Galway was run over and killed. They'd built a new bypass at the end of the lane and he was sensible enough in many ways but his life experience had not included a six-lane highway, and we had failed to protect him. The grown-ups cried, the twins howled; Mark went and lay in Galway's basket and I had to drag him out. Later, while he wailed, I swore never, never to have another animal. It was unendurable. The robin had gone, too. Some bird of prey, no doubt, or even Olive, I wouldn't put it past her. She was upset too: she marked Galway's absence by sitting in the apple tree long after dusk, waiting. Mark had screaming fits in the reception class at school; they sent him home for a psychologist's report. He wouldn't let me out of his sight, or only at dusk, when he'd go out on his own to feed the sheep.

A week after Galway's death he came back smiling and said, 'Galway's in the field with the sheep.'
'That can't be so,' I said.
'I am not in error,' he replied, his spirit back, and his colour, and with it his five-year-old pomposity. 'Galway's got into the field again. I saw him. You'd better do something.' I went out to look and there were the sheep, five ewes and a ram lined up, standing as usual on the burial mound staring, their background a red-streaked but darkening sky. No Galway. Well, of course not. We'd buried him under the mound. I went back in.
'Mark,' I said, 'I'm sorry but he's not.'
'Yes he is,' he said firmly, but happily, and went to bed on his own, refusing my assistance.

I took my husband out to the field just to check. It was almost dark by now. We had a torch with us. I could only just see the blackish blurs that were the sheep so I shone the torch and devil's eyes glittered back at me, slit eyes, yellow and gleaming, Satan's eyes, spooky but expected. Shine a torch at a sheep or a goat in the night and that's what you get. I counted. Fourteen eyes. So many eyes are hard to count but they remained remark-ably steady, lined up. I tried again.
'How many sheep?' I asked my husband. 'Quick, before the light goes altogether.'
'Six, of course,' he said, beginning to count. 'Five ewes and a ram. Why?'
'Because there are fourteen eyes,' I said.
'Oh come on now, that's impossible. They must be moving round.'
But they weren't, they were just standing there staring, as if they knew something was up. The pair of eyes in the centre of the

group were not so slit as the others, more rounded, deep green pools rimmed with white. Dog's eyes in torchlight in the dark, Labrador's eyes. I wondered if the sheep could see Galway too or if it were only Mark.

'Fourteen,' my husband said. 'Can't be.'

Now the Soays were making things difficult. They took to turning and tossing their heads, or who knows, perhaps they were winking; at any rate checking was impossible. And then they were off: the whole lot of them took to flight, and we heard the swift clippety clop of cleft hooves and then a short sharp cheerful bark as well, but you can imagine things.

I don't know. Did we count wrong? I don't think so. Mark went out alone into the field early the next morning – I couldn't: fear had caught up with me – and came back to say firmly that Galway had gone off now but he'd be back by sunset. We stayed out of the field and let matters take their course. You could just about trust Galway to do the right thing. Olive took to sitting in the nettles the Galway side of the gate instead of cursing us all from the apple tree. Mark was taken back into the reception class and forgot about it being his job to feed the sheep, and cheered up. And little by little there was less evidence of Galway being around, the movement in the corner of the eye ceased happening, the blurred flurry at feeding time, just so long as you didn't go shining torches into dark corners at night. But I do think he came back, or at any rate stayed around. It suited us all, didn't it. Galway got his way and into the sheep field, where he'd so insisted he belonged, and the sheep accepted him, and Mark was healed, and we stopped feeling guilty about Galway's death, because really you know there isn't any such thing.

A Knife for Cutting Mangoes

When I moved in his wife's belongings were still there, all around me, even to the sheets on the bed. She didn't so much as bother to change them, and very pretty, impractical sheets they were; fine white linen with scalloped edges and self-embroidery, the kind which have to be ironed after the wash. What an absurdity! Who has anything these days but drip-dry? She moved out saying she didn't want anything of the past: she wanted to start again: she was desperate to have a new life, she couldn't be her true self while married to him. I wish her every luck, but perhaps she didn't have much of a true self to begin with. It's easy to blame others for one's own shortcomings.

Using her saucepans, drinking from her coffee cups, going through the house and switching on her brass lamps as evening fell didn't bother me. Why should it? The saucepans were heavy and expensive, not the tinny things I was accustomed to: food didn't catch and burn if you stopped stirring. It made me feel quite dainty to drink black coffee from little cups with saucers, instead of from Safeways' mugs. The lamps turned out to be real antiques – student's lamps, Victorian. I found a cutting in a kitchen drawer all about them, so they were good not just for light to read by, but as a talking point when guests came.

One night she lay between the sheets, the next night I did. She couldn't have liked them all that much, or she'd have come back for them. Wouldn't she? Scalloped edges and self-embroidery and all. The things she spent money on that I never would! She was so hopelessly extravagant. She even had a knife for cutting and peeling mangoes. Mangoes are things I can do without, believe me. So messy and time-consuming. But I did quite like moving among her bits and pieces, I suppose, pushing aside her party dresses to make room for my jeans and T-shirts. All that silk and crushed velvet giving way to denim and lycra. It gave me a sense of victory. I expect soldiers feel like that when they sack and loot a town after a long war.

I've never worried about finding my true self, personally. I don't think I have an inner me and if I have I don't particularly want to meet her. And he certainly doesn't want me to waste time searching, when I could be in bed with him. Look at the trouble he had with Chloe, for ever trying. That was his wife's name. Chloe. Quite pretty, really. Mine is Jane, and very plain, but plain girls often win. And his is Jub, rub-a-dub-dub: Jub-Jub for short or for long. He says the sex between them was never very good, but men do say that, don't they.

No, of course I don't want us to get married. Marriage is for the birds. Look what happened to her, look what happened to my parents, look what happens to stay-at-home wives who have time to buy antiques and iron sheets. Divorce happens, because they get to be so dull, and end up buying mango knives. I took my father's side in the divorce, not my mother's. I wanted them divorced so I could go and live with my father and look after him and he wouldn't yawn all the time, showing his back teeth. Of course it didn't work out like that. I ended up living with my mother and my father married a real bitch of girl I didn't even know about. But all that's in the past. This is now.

Trying to find her inner self, the real her. What a fool she was. She deserved what happened. Why did she think she was more than she was? I'm sure I don't. I am the sum of my parts, of what I do and what I say, I don't add up to more. Feelings change all the time, it's part of being alive. It's dangerous to try and nail them. Define who you are and all you do is throw chunks of your life away. And what's a self anyway? Nobody knows, do they: the psychologists and the philosophers argue about it all the time. What is the brain, what is the mind, what constitutes our identity? Since we don't know, why bother. There's everyday life to get on with.

And I am so happy, and there is nothing to go wrong. The sun shines upon our love, all things are beautiful. Chloe doesn't bother me. It's not as if she were dead. I wouldn't like that, if she'd killed herself or something. Then I might get really spooked. As it is she's just off searching for her true self, after the great gesture of leaving it all behind, even to the knickers in her drawers. I guess it took all her strength, just to go.

So here I am, happy as Larry. I once had an affair with a Larry, and I can't say he was all that happy, rather depressed, in fact. I don't suffer from depression; every morning I wake up full of the joys of spring, and summer too, and autumn and winter in addition, whatever season it happens to be. You know some religions say the object of life is to be happy. That being the case I am a very good person indeed.

I tell a lie. Not totally happy. Chloe left her cat behind when she went. *Jub-Jub and Chloe together's cat.* I wasn't at all happy about it, but I took the creature on. Jub insisted. 'We are going to keep the cat,' he said, 'and that's that. No, we are not going to take it down to the vet.' I've always been perfectly kind to the animal, I never kick it or anything or keep it out all night as some people do, but it has never liked me, and I have to say the feeling is mutual. Sometimes when Jub-Jub strokes the cat so gently and carefully I get the feeling perhaps he loves me but he doesn't quite like me.

* * *

Little by little the things she abandoned stopped being hers-left-behind and began to feel like mine, and the sense of her presence altogether faded. I bought some more sheets in a summer sale last week and I took hers down to the charity shop, because I'm working and have no time to iron and I'm tired of wasting money sending them out to be laundered. The lady in the shop shook her head and said, 'Oh, they're the kind that need ironing. We'll have trouble shifting them.'

'Look at the hems,' I cried, 'look at the stitching,' and she did, and was impressed, and took them in the end. I felt quite proud for Chloe at that moment. I think my dreams have been easier since, but I don't see why they should be, I have done nothing wrong. I had only done what others do: we were both being true to our feelings, Jub-Jub and I. Why should there be punishment?

Jub and Jane, happy together. Life flows tranquilly by. If you don't count the dreams. But I take sleeping pills now, which blurs them okay. Can we grow new skins? Become different people? Or are we doomed to stay the same bawling, devious little creatures we were when we were born? Nothing singular about us, all the same? Perhaps that's why I could never feel properly maternal. When I looked at my child, I looked at me. Anyway my child's doing just fine, I'd have heard if she weren't.

Because I brought nothing out of my past either. I too wanted to leave everything behind. My husband was better than I was with our child, and the therapist said make a clean break, so I did. How strange the word husband sounds, all duty and obligation and female cowardice. 'Please don't leave me on my own.' It hurt at the time, breaking free the way I did, but I gritted my teeth and was able to follow through my feelings for Jub, rub-a-dub-dub, and this is the real life not the one I left behind. That's gone. I don't think of it if I can.

The one thing I brought with me was an alarm clock. Isn't it strange how difficult it is to find a reliable alarm clock that works and goes on working? You'd think it would be easy in this technological age. But they clatter and chatter and you don't hear them; they shriek their noises in your head and you sleep on, or else they don't go off at all. And you miss your flight and your one great chance in life.

What's so strange? Many women nowadays leave their children. As I say, I wasn't the maternal type: my husband was always more involved. I think that's what made me go off him. I just can't love a man who likes to wash dishes and gets involved with the school nativity play. I'd cringe with embarrassment at the soppy bits, while genuine tears would run down his cheeks. It wouldn't do.

A victory? Yes, I suppose it is a victory, that's how I described it earlier. To take a man from someone else. From his wife. To win his affections. Not that I set out to do it. I just was, and he just was, and there we were, and she wanted to be herself anyway, didn't she. That's what she said. Find her true self. It's been two years. I heard a noise from the back of the linen cupboard the other day: I looked, the noise drew me to it, such a little delicate clang, clang clanging, like a fairy fire bell. It was her alarm clock, I hadn't known it was there, tucked away. Such a pretty little clock, with a tiny gold bell for an alarm, and the dial had flowers painted on it. That spooked me a bit. It was hers, left over. She was still lurking in the house. Perhaps she'd forgiven me. Perhaps she was trying to warn me. More likely something had just fallen on the alarm switch, and set it off. Perhaps the cat had disturbed it, looking for somewhere safe to have kittens. She's pregnant again, that's the second litter since I moved in and I have to find homes for all the kittens. As if I don't have enough to do.

I probably didn't tell you she found us in bed together but that wasn't why she left, of course it wasn't. Something like that wouldn't be important if the relationship was good. She'd left the house before I'd even got out of bed and she never came back. She wrote a letter or two. We threw them away unopened. Why should she damage our happiness? And now I'm here. We're here. Jub, rub-a-dub-dub, I think perhaps he's rub-a dub-dubbing with someone else. The doctor's given me different sleeping pills. They're stronger. The dreams are back. I wander in a grey, still, flat landscape, without beginning or end. Some-times the dreams creep into my waking life, so I can't tell what's real and what isn't.

I think I should have taken the sheets down to the charity shop way back, but they were just so pretty and I'm so plain. I think one day I'll come back from work and there he'll be in the bed with someone else, because perhaps our relationship isn't so good as I believe, and perhaps he does hanker after Chloe, and perhaps he does blame me – you know what men are – so perhaps he'll find someone totally new. And I'll walk out of the house too, saying *I want nothing, I want to start a new life, I have to go in search of myself* and I'll leave everything behind, as she did. I don't think the new woman will like my sheets, though, nearly as much as I liked Chloe's. Mine are thin nylon, easy to wash, drip-dry, non-iron, practical, cheap.

The Medium is the Message

The ghost would have to be exorcised. Hugh had no doubt about it. Oriole had some doubts about the ghost. Ghosts did not exist. But some residual sense of the authority of the male over the female remained bedded in him: his it was to dictate the nature of the universe. She was older than he was by seven years and the family breadwinner, but never mind. He wanted to call the priest in now, now, now and so did his brother Clive, and they weren't listening to her. Hugh even picked up the telephone to call his father the Diocesan Bishop, who could recommend a good exorcist if anyone could – the Church of England acknowledged the occasional need for exorcists, though they didn't focus on the matter if they could help it – and Oriole had to pull the phone line out of its socket to stop him making the call. And then the fifth cup whistled past her ear: just rose from its saucer and hurled itself against the wall and broke. That stopped them. Silence fell. The cup, being eighteenth-century Meissen and of the most fragile porcelain, exploded rather than broke, and every tiny splinter had its own peculiar little crackle, so the ensuing silence seemed particularly dense. And again the temperature had fallen, which you only noticed after the event, when you began to feel warm again.

'Okay,' said Oriole. 'You win,' and she re-plugged the phone again and Hugh and Clive called their father. Oriole, rather than hear the conversation went to ask Sarla the help to bring dustpan and brush. Sarla was sitting at the kitchen table calmly enough, reading Shakespeare. *A Midsummer Night's Dream.* These days she had a clear complexion, a sweet smile, glossy hair, and though she still had no work visa seemed untroubled enough, and one way and another not capable of instigating poltergeist activity. According to the Internet this latter was usually associated with neurotic adolescent girls. Just as pre-pubertal boys could do Uri Geller tricks, make heavy cutlery bend and twist simply by rubbing it, teenage girls could apparently create a sufficient energy field to hurl small domestic objects around the house in a mildly malevolent way. But Sarla was into her late twenties and twice the girl she'd been when she'd joined the household two years back as a sallow, skinny, grieving refugee from Muslim Bosnia with very little English.

But even if poltergeist activity was a 'proved' fact, it didn't mean that the energy required to overcome the normal inertia of stationary objects was paranormal: just that the laws which governed the phenomenon were not yet properly understood.

In Oriole's perception the natural universe obeyed definite physical laws. You dropped things, they broke. You heated water, it boiled. People died, they stayed dead. She'd once sat next to the Astronomer Royal at a formal dinner organised by her employers, Dree Pharmaceuticals, to present the new annual Dree prize for Mathematics – and he'd told her all about the Big Bang and how it was pointless to ask what happened before, as people tended to do, because time itself only started at that moment. He'd then added that the Big Bang was only another Creation Myth, which rather spoiled things, and formal speeches had begun before she could question him further.

Nevertheless – until the matter of the suicidal cups: she still tried to joke about them – she'd had no doubt but that once put in motion the universe worked like clockwork, wound up and set going – by Big Bang or Prime Mover, who cared – cogs turning, gravity tugging, evolution soldiering on, obeying its own internal rules, and no exceptions. And now she found herself agreeing to an exorcism. Hugh and Clive had pressured her into it. She, who resented so little, found herself resenting this. If it was anyone's ghost, anyone's poltergeist, anyone's paranormal phenomenon, it was hers. *Her* ear the teacups whistled past, gold rims glittering as they flew. *Her* cups, or at any rate her deceased grandmother's, brought out of Germany in 1937. *Her* dresser: *her* whole house come to that: she might put Hugh's name on the title deeds but it was hers by moral right.

She told Sarla another two cups had broken and the pieces needed to be put in an envelope for the menders. Sarla said she'd do it when she'd finished the scene in which Titania falls in love with the ass. She was looking up all unfamiliar words in the dictionary. Sarla was developing a fine Shakespearean vocabulary. Since Oriole was paying an immigration lawyer some thousands of pounds to help Sarla qualify for citizenship it was good to see her thus dedicated to the culture of her putative new country. Nevertheless Oriole would have liked a more instant response, a springing to the feet at the behest of her employer.
'Don't worry,' Oriole said, a little more briskly than usual, 'I'll do it.'

When the first bill relating to Sarla's visa came through Hugh remarked it would be cheaper to pay someone to marry her and get her citizenship that way, and Oriole had found that somehow shocking. What shocked Hugh tended not to shock her, and vice versa. They laughed about it. Hugh was a master craftsman. He made long-necked Elizabethan lutes out of sycamore and cedar for a small specialist market. Oriole was now International Sales Director for the famous Dree pill, the new wonder morning-after-the-night-before contraceptive. She was beginning to be away from home more often than she was in it, as Hugh had sadly observed, flying round the world: so far her work had taken her mostly to Europe, but now China was opening up as a market. Neither of them looked forward to it.

* * *

Oriole took the dustpan and brush and went back into the dining room. Clive had taken the phone back from Hugh and had resumed his version of events. Clive, at thirty-four, was Oriole's age, seven years older that Hugh. But the boys, as their mother still called them, could have been twins, and were often mistaken for such. Both were tall, well-built, blond, thatch-haired, square-jawed, highly educated, softly spoken and gentle-eyed. Oriole was little and bustling, dark and petite. Clive made virginals in the Flemish style inset with ebony, an even smaller and more special-ist market than that for lutes. Oriole was famous for having a cloth ear: she couldn't tell a lute from a virginal from a viola da gamba when she first met Hugh. He was the one who could tell the true notes, the pure sound, who understood the music of the celestial spheres. She only knew from pharmaceuticals. But their bodies fitted together, spoon like: there was just the right differential in height.

'They're Oriole's cups,' Clive was saying. 'Oriole's grandmother married out, and her mother too, and Oriole herself is living out, as it were, so she's only a quarter Jewish anyway, and I shouldn't think that would affect an exorcism, would it? The ghost wouldn't have to be Christian to take notice? It could be a pagan, an ancient Roman, anyone.'

'Is your brother suggesting,' asked Oriole of Hugh, as she carefully swept the larger pieces into the dustpan, all thinly fluted crimson and gold and blue and sharp edges, 'that the phenomenon goes with the cups? Because it needn't. It could come from this house, which is old enough. It could be Sarla's neurosis, bubbling away. It could just have drifted in from outside. That's why I don't want some priest in here, nailing it into the here and now, making it real, stopping it just drifting off again, undefined, whatever it is.'

And here she was, talking about 'it' as if 'it' was real. She sat on the floor and picked up tiny splinters of porcelain with a piece of sticky tape, as the restorer advised. The first time it had hap-pened, a year ago, Hugh had used his forefinger to get the little bits, dampened by his tongue, and a sliver had pierced the tip of the finger: just a tiny drop of blood, but enough to go septic and spread, and the chemicals he worked with didn't help it heal. He'd been on antibiotics off and on ever since. She'd told him to be careful but he hadn't been.

'Besides,' she said now, 'if it gets into the local papers it will do God knows what to property prices.'

Hugh hooted with laughter and took the phone from Clive and said, 'Now Oriole's worrying what exorcism will do to property prices. We are cursed, we are afflicted, the laws of nature are reversed, and Oriole, who must be the richest self-made woman in the country, is still worrying about money!'

They were not fair to her. They ganged up on her. Money was important. They would notice soon enough if they didn't have her to spend it on them. And getting the house had been her sacrifice, not theirs, which they failed to notice. She and Hugh had been living in London. She had been travelling miles to work: he was using the garage for a workshop. She'd told her employers she was going to take a year off and have a baby, and risk losing out in the promotion stakes. Dree had come back with an offer of a house and the post of International Sales Director for their new product, which they thought was going to be big, plus a chunk of company stock.

'My!' said Hugh. 'They certainly think well of you!' He'd sounded quite surprised. 'I suppose you couldn't take the job *and* have a baby?'

But he didn't offer to look after it, she noticed. Well, he was young. He was an artist. The pram in the hall was the enemy of promise and all that. She said she thought not: the new job would mean flying round the world and uncertain hours, and what was the point of having a baby and not being around to rear it? She'd decided to stick to her resolution: she'd have the baby, not the job. They'd scrape along on her savings and him making lutes in the garage.

*   *   *

But then they went to look at the house. It was outside Maiden-head, on the Thames, and within easy reach of Heathrow. They'd taken Clive with them, in an effort to cheer him up. Clive had come to stay for three months when his marriage broke up and he needed somewhere to recover. That had been a year ago. Oriole and Hugh congratulated themselves on not being married. Look at what happened to Clive and Penny: a wedding in a cathedral, all that pomp and ceremony, and then she runs off with a banker.

'Mercenary bitch,' said Hugh, savage for once in defence of his brother.

Oriole and Hugh had been together for seven years: they were happy. She'd met him when he was just out of Oxford and she was five years into Dree. Her mother and father were both dead. Her grandmother was three years into Alzheimer's. So it didn't matter to anyone on Oriole's side that she and Hugh weren't married, there was no-one for it to matter to, and on Hugh's side she sometimes got the feeling they might even be relieved, though they would never say so, they were far too polite. They wanted Hugh to be happy, but she was not quite their sort. They were the Shires and the clergy: she was Essex and the rag trade, however fond of her they had grown.

Once she and Hugh and Clive and Sarla had seen the house, of course, everything changed. There was no way they could not have it. It was old and beautiful – some of it dating back to Elizabethan times: it even had a few of the original chimneys left – one of those houses you sometimes find down pretty country lanes, Mercedes and Range Rovers hidden behind high well-kept hedges. Directors' houses. (If her parents could see her now, how proud they would be!) And Clive could have a whole wing to himself, practically, and not get under anyone's feet, and not have to hurry in the business of starting out on his own again, working out which way his life was to go. There was a cedar of Lebanon tree in the garden, and the grounds ran down to the

Thames, and there was the barn, which could be converted into the workshop of Hugh's dreams, and Clive could share it, and contribute towards the overheads. A drop in the ocean, thought Oriole, but she did not say so. The men had their dignity. The last thing they wanted was to feel kept. It was just hard to make a profit from making old instruments, if you set about the task with love and integrity. They were above money, anyway. They were master craftsmen, artists in their own field, world-famous. TV crews came to film them working: mostly educational films, school programmes, that kind of thing. But it made her feel humble.

In fact everyone – that is to say Hugh, and Clive, and Sarla, who already in the two months since she'd joined the London household, in preparation for the so far unconceived baby, had filled out and lost her derelict look and had her missing front tooth replaced by Oriole's most expensive dentist – had looked so happy Oriole had given in. Job not baby. When Dree threw in one of the new little sporty Mercedes as the company car she stopped thinking about it. Most of the time. And perhaps if she was so easily put off she was not really cut out for mother-hood. And Hugh had his lutes for babies. And she had him for a child. And so on.

The first time it happened it was Oriole's thirty-third birth-day. The three of them were having supper in the kitchen. They'd been in the house for two months. The designers and decorators had just moved out. Sarla was off to night school. They were eating bread and cheese and pickle. Oriole's energy had for once failed: they'd been all set to go out to a celebration meal but when it came to it she just wanted to stay home.
'Don't worry about it, darling,' said Hugh. 'It's hardly surprising. Of course you're tired. Think what you've done during the last week, flown to Athens and back, and Frankfurt, and nobly stopped goodness knows how many more accidental babies being born, and dealt with the builders, not to mentioning burying

your poor grandmother.' Hugh hadn't gone with her to the funeral. That was a sore point. It was true that the poor old soul had been out of the real world for so long the transition from life to death was a formality, and Oriole herself had cut down visiting to once every three or four months – well, five or six, but what was the point anyway – so she felt she couldn't complain. She just felt bad and could have done with Hugh to hold her hand.

'And I expect it stirred up a lot of unconscious stuff about the family disgrace,' said Clive. 'Funerals are like that. Bread and cheese and pickle is fine by me.'

Oriole's father, in the rag trade, had committed fraud and been sent to prison for six months, and died there, when Oriole was sixteen, and Oriole's mother, fraught with grief, shame, and despair, had followed him into the hereafter within months of that, which was why Oriole had never gone up to Oxford, for which she had a scholarship. She'd been the only child, and had to borrow money to bury them. Which she supposed you could dispose of in the phrase, '*a lot of unconscious stuff about the family disgrace*'. He was right. The funeral had brought back into memory things better not thought about. That was why she liked to live in the present. Hugh and Clive could afford to live in the past. Way back to Elizabethan times, when their family first entered the records. It was just that musical instrument delivery dates were in the here and now and the other reason they couldn't come to the funeral was, for Hugh, that some Monteverdi specialists were jumping up and down for the new lute they had commissioned, and for Clive, that a Californian computer millionaire wanted a virginal as a wedding present to his new bride, and for both of them every hour counted. And she hadn't minded. It was just such a badly attended funeral. Herself, as the last remaining member of the family, only child of an only child, and a few kind nuns from the convent where her grandmother ended her days, all apparent links to the Jewish community gone. Because distant family had been lost too, in the camps in Germany. Another thing best not thought about. She hadn't even gone to see *Schindler's List*, the

Spielberg film: Hugh and Clive had gone and come back red-eyed, and reproached her. They thought she was heartless: she might think she was only a quarter Jewish but it would have counted at the time – and she should at least take some notice.

The temperature had dropped, although it was mid June – this year her birthday had fallen on the longest day, the solstice. Oriole went to turn up the central heating. She'd just sat down at the table again when the cup lifted off its saucer on the dresser, and hurled itself against the wall behind her, with the crack and the sharp splintery sound you somehow didn't forget, and the kind of stillness afterwards, as if everything sat extra quiet and wary.

'That cup can't have done that by itself,' said Hugh, the first to speak. 'Perhaps there was some kind of vibration.'

'I did just turn the heating up,' said Oriole. The first instinct, it seemed, was to deny that anything untoward had happened. 'The plumbers were a nightmare.'

So they had been. A steam shower had struck them as strange and unnecessary, and a Jacuzzi bath for two as insane, and they'd fitted the plumbing in accordance with the adjectives in their heads. Oriole had had to threaten them with court action. There were no pipes running anywhere near the dresser but she didn't want to think about that. Or that the cup hadn't slipped and fallen, but had somehow got out of its saucer and hurtled itself across the room in an arc that swooped low past her ear and then rose to a higher point to hit the wall.

'Could be subsidence,' said Clive.

'Could be,' said Oriole. 'If so, I'll sue the surveyors.'

'She would too,' said Hugh proudly, and because Oriole was tired went to get a dustpan and brush. Oriole said the cup would have to go to be restored: Hugh thought it was beyond repair, but Oriole pointed out that a set of six Meissen cups and saucers in fine condition – at least to date – was truly rare and valuable and you had to measure them in thousands, not hundreds, of pounds.

'Nothing should be measured by money,' said Hugh.

'I thought your parents were poor,' said Clive. 'If as you say your father stole to support the family and keep you in school uniform, shouldn't he have sold the cups?'

'They were my grandmother's,' said Oriole. 'All she had of the past. She carried them over the mountains on foot, pregnant with my mother, and kept them safe.'

'Then that's understandable,' said Clive, agreeably. 'Though I'm afraid your gran had a very *Mittel*-European taste.' Hugh said Oriole didn't much like going into family history, and one way and another in the gentle wrangling the event got lost. It was isolated. Just something that happened. Except Hugh, picking up the pieces, had hurt his finger. Oriole asked Sarla to be careful when she dusted the dresser, and not to get the cups too near to the edge of the shelf in future. Then they forgot about it. There was too much else for everyone to think about.

The second time it happened was at the autumn equinox. They were eating in the dining room. The first cup had come back from the restorers that very day, accompanied by a little note saying what a particularly lovely piece it was and if she was interested in selling the set she knew a buyer who could house it appropriately. More or less suggesting that Oriole wasn't a responsible owner of valuable antiques. So she and Sarla moved the whole set onto the sideboard in the dining room, being careful to place it safely well back against the wall. They were eating a lentil and carrot bake – Hugh and Clive had lately become vegetarians. That was okay by Oriole. These days she ate more than enough First Class protein on various airlines every week to satisfy her carnivorous needs outside the home. And Sarla bought steak for herself, which she ate in the kitchen. Clive had asked Sarla to join them in the dining room since she was now so much one of the family, but she wouldn't. She liked to read novels while she ate.

'Lucky old Sarla,' Oriole said somewhat bitterly, over the lentil bake. 'All I ever get time to read is company reports.'

'It's your choosing,' said Hugh. 'We're all free to do as we like in this world. And we are what we choose.'

Sometimes Chinese government officials would speak like that, in riddles, which somehow placed them firmly in occupation of the moral high ground, so if you weren't careful you ended up giving more than you got.

'And I'm the one who employs her,' said Oriole, 'so I'm the one who ought to ask her to join us at table, not anyone else,' and there was a shocked silence while the brothers looked at her.

'You don't own people because you pay them,' said Hugh. Tell that to Dree Pharmaceuticals, thought Oriole.

'It's just nice to have a woman around at mealtimes,' said Clive. 'And you know you're so often away. Don't be so dog in the manger, Oriole.'

And she was just thinking she might have been married to both of them, except she only went to bed with one of them, the way they both kept telling her what to say and do, when the second cup took off, a flash of gold glittering in the air, in its unnatural arc, and smashed. This time Oriole spoke first.

'If that's the one just back from the restorers I shall scream. Do you know what she charged me? Four hundred and eighty-three pounds.'

'Oh, money, money, money,' said Hugh. 'No wonder things in this house don't lie quiet.'

He was pale. The wound on his finger hurt quite a lot. It had lately given him septicaemia, and a couple of days in hospital, and Oriole found herself obscurely blamed, for not having just thrown the cup away in the first place but insisted on having it restored. Yet the brothers were the ones who valued the past. Their past, that was the trouble, just not hers.

'Perhaps this is an earthquake zone,' said Clive. 'You do get minor shakes in this part of the country.'

'A group illusion,' said Hugh. 'It must be. And we have been smoking funny cigarettes.' Well, the brothers had. Oriole didn't touch the stuff. She was allergic to marijuana: just the whiff of it could give her vertigo. They were careful not to blow smoke in her direction but didn't offer to stop smoking. It soothed their nerves after a stressful day in the workshop. And it had been rather stressful lately; Sarla had told her in her now almost perfect English, last time Oriole had arrived home from a trip abroad. At a certain stage the wood used in making lutes has to be steam-heated and softened, to be curved into shape, and the damp and the heat would cause the wound to open up again and widen. Clive had tried to take over the process from his brother – that was the point of sharing the workshop, so they could help each other – but he wasn't good at it. Virginals are foursquare and sharp-angled and straight-sided, nothing more than boxes, really. Clive was too strong and sudden: the wood felt the reproach and cracked and broke. To each brother his skill. And an orchestra called Early Ensemble were to do a major performance of Monteverdi's *l'Incoronazione di Poppea* in Athens, and were waiting for delivery, and might start thinking about another, inferior, supplier. It was not the money that mattered, it was the loss to music.

The mended cup had stayed in place. A perfect one had self-destructed. Oriole picked up the pieces.

'If you're not careful,' she said to the five cups and six saucers which remained, 'I'll put you in a bank vault to keep you safe, and you'll never see the light of day again'. And she thought she heard a kind of sighing in the air, and wondered where she had heard it before. Her blind, blank grandmother, not telling day from night, friend from foe, the bad times from the good, not any more, would sometimes sigh like that. She didn't say this to the brothers. If personalities survived, at what age did you reconstruct? Did you drift round as you departed the world, an old lady with no mind left, but supported in comfort by your granddaughter, or as the young pregnant girl who escaped from Germany, on foot over the Alps into Spain, carrying a bulky paper parcel? When the times were bad as they could be, but at least you had your youth, and a future if only you could secure it? And would her grandmother come back to haunt, or to help? Was she more pleased to have the comfort of the home, at the end, or displeased because Oriole had put her in a convent and failed to visit her enough? The nuns said she wasn't conscious of the passing of time, and didn't recognise her, she should not bother, and she hadn't, and she should have, and it was too late. She almost wished the cup would get her like a slap around the ear, instead of just missing each time. It was odd how accepting you felt at the time these things were happening. Only afterwards did fright set in. That cup too went off to the restorers: you couldn't let it get away with it, whatever either of the its might be. The brothers put it down to too much dope, and cut down.

The third time it happened was around the Christmas solstice. She and Hugh and Clive were doing the Christmas cards at the last moment, as ever. It didn't seem to matter that she now had secretarial staff and untold wealth from stock – the Dree pill, which she now took herself – was becoming a kind of world staple, like cat's-eyes in the road, and Oriole owned stock in it – you still found yourself having to do the Christmas cards at the last moment. They were sitting at the dining-room table.

'You could let yourself off a quarter of them, Oriole,' Clive said. 'Since you're a quarter Jewish you could quarter claim it wasn't your festival.' It wasn't as if the brothers went to church themselves. They went to the midnight service on Christmas Eve to please their parents and that was about it.

'I suppose I could,' said Oriole, mildly, and at that point the third cup whistled through the air past her head and broke. The second cup was due back from the menders but hadn't yet arrived. The area of plaster where the cups hit was ruffled and cracked. The builders would have to be got in yet again. This time no-one moved to sweep the pieces up. Hugh spoke first.

'So it's not a question of numbers,' said Hugh. 'It's not that it wants to be three cups and six saucers, because now it's four cups and six saucers.'

'And it's nothing to do with solstice or equinox,' said Oriole, 'because the exact solstice is tomorrow. It's every three calendar months precisely. Make sense of that if you can. Though it could still be a statistical anomaly. Too small a sample.'

They were talking quite calmly.

'It's Oriole's head they go for,' said Clive. 'It's Oriole they're angry with. I think she's got a poltergeist.'

'People don't get poltergeists as they get mumps,' said Oriole. 'And I'm too old. Blame Sarla if you want to blame anyone.'

But of course he wouldn't. Sarla was sleeping with Clive. It had been on the cards for a long time. Neither of them showed any signs of moving out. Sarla went on eating in the kitchen, and Oriole went on paying her wages. It was absurd and embarrassing. Oriole had asked Clive if he meant to marry Sarla or if she, Oriole, was meant to go on paying her lawyer's fees, and Clive had told her not to be jealous and neurotic, of course he wasn't going to marry Sarla, or live with her, she was not his permanent cup of tea, or he hers, and to suggest they should marry to save money was surely a rather shocking thing. He and Sarla just enjoyed each other. He even said he'd learned the art of non-commitment from Hugh and Oriole, which would have upset and hurt her had she time to be hurt and upset.

'I think Clive's right,' said Hugh. 'I don't think Sarla is the neurotic one round here.'

Betrayal! Oriole went to her bedroom and slammed the door. In her absence Sarla swept up the pieces and put them in the bin and joined the brothers for coffee. Oriole could hear them laughing. They were probably smoking more funny cigarettes, to combat the stress of the paranormal-which-could-not-be-denied. Sarla had found a reliable supplier at night school. Hugh came in and comforted her and told her how much he loved her, and said she mustn't show her jealousy of Sarla, it was demeaning, and she'd rather upset Clive by being so mercenary. He fell asleep. She stayed awake. That was the third time.

*　　*　　*

Oriole wasn't daft: she knew the limits of their relationship well enough. She gave Hugh what he needed, money, and he gave her what she needed, endearments. She knew she was an Essex girl made good and the brothers had been good to begin with; and that though both Hugh and she presented themselves to the world as being in love it wasn't quite that: it just suited them both. If you asked her to choose between her job and Hugh she'd probably choose the job, just as Hugh would choose making lutes rather than her. And what was love anyway? If it existed, it did so in the same way as ghosts existed, an unreasonable anomaly in a reasonable universe. Her mother had loved her father and love it was that killed her. Her grandmother had loved her country, and loved its past, and its music, and even a stupid set of porcelain cups and saucers, far too gaudy and ornate for today's tastes, enough to risk her life for, and what was her reward? Nothing. One daughter, dead before her time. One negligent granddaughter, and nuns at her graveside. Who will be at mine, wondered Oriole? And then she had to sleep too. She set the alarm for six-thirty.

The second cup came back with another desperate note from the restorer. Oriole had a glass cabinet made for the remaining cups and saucers. They looked better behind panes, and felt safer, and stayed quiet. She put the two extra saucers down for the cat's milk, in an act of defiance, and noted their continuing existence with surprise. Cats' saucers usually get trodden on, or fall from slippery hands or are knocked off steps. These ones, she supposed, were just good at survival. And the months went by and somehow they all just believed it wouldn't happen again, except Sarla, who was clearly sceptical of their claims that the cups were self-motivating, and assumed they got thrown in a family row. And perhaps they did? Perhaps they were all just firmly in denial, as the counsellor at work whom Oriole was required to see every month – firm policy, to remove stress – assumed to be the case.

*   *   *

29

And then on Oriole's birthday, her thirty-fourth, a whole year from the first occasion, the fourth cup came rattling out of the cabinet, breaking the glass as it came, nearer her ear than ever. Hugh and Clive insisted on calling their father the Bishop about an exorcist, the fifth cup followed, Oriole capitulated, Sarla refused to come and sweep up, and here Oriole was, sitting on the floor, picking up pieces again, while Clive and Hugh wondered if her quarter Jewishness would stop the normal procedures of the Christian Church.

Sarla, finished with Titania and the ass, deigned to come in to see what was going on. The sixth cup flew through the broken glass and whistled by her head and got the door behind her. Sarla began to shriek and wail. She sank to her knees; she called upon Allah in her extremis. Clive went to put his arms around her.

'Get me away from here,' Sarla wailed. 'Stand not upon the order of our going,' she wept into his manly jacket shoulder, over and over. 'Stand not upon the order of our going.'

'Pascal's wager,' said Hugh to Oriole, ignoring the noise, putting down the phone. 'Father says remember Pascal's wager.'

'What are you talking about?' asked Oriole.

Sarla stopped being noisy to say, 'Blaise Pascal, French philosopher, Pascal's wager. You might as well be a believer. If it's true and you believe you don't go to hell. If it isn't true, there isn't a hell to go to. You can't lose.'

Hugh and Clive regarded Sarla with admiration: more, Oriole felt, than they had ever regarded her, Oriole, even on the occasion when she had paid over a cheque for more than a million pounds, to pay for Hugh's new state-of-the-art workshop. She stood up and went to the phone and dialled 1471 and then 3.

'What are you doing?' asked Hugh.

'I need to speak to your father the Bishop,' she said. She did.

'This is Oriole,' she said, 'the woman you are glad is not actually your daughter-in-law, but only your son's partner while he gets through his twenties. It is not my grandmother's cups you need to send your magicians after, or my grandmother's ghost, or this house, or the memory of my father who went to prison, it is I who need to exorcise your son. If the ghost of my dead grand-mother comes to me slapping me round my ears, sacrificing everything she ever held dear, those bloody cups, why then I need her around. I am not a quarter Jewish, I am wholly Jewish, Jewishness comes through the mother's side, not the father's, and I am a direct descendant through the ages back to Israel. And I am not going to let this line stop here, after all that suffering, all that clambering out of horror, generation after generation, not for the sake of a few miserable Elizabethan lutes, some ugly Flemish virginals, or the comfort and convenience of your two idle sons. Call an exorcist around if you want, but I won't be here to receive them. I am off to find a nice Jewish boy and have a baby.'

She slammed the phone down and went upstairs and emptied the Dree pills down the loo, and took her little sports car into the night and after that they heard only from her lawyers, writing from an address in north London.

The Site

It was my cleaner Susie who first told me what was happening at the site. 'Cleaner' is the word Susie uses to keep me in my place: she seems rather more like a friend and ally, but she enjoys these social distinctions. She's the policeman's wife: she comes up to my rackety household and helps out because she's bored, or so she says, and points out that I'm an artist and not a housewife by nature, as she is. Everyone should do what they're good at in this life, she maintains. She, by implication, is good at housework: I am not.

I'm a professional sculptor. The children are with their father during term time, but I still needed help to keep domestic matters under control. I live in the village of Rumer in Kent, outside Canterbury, in a farmhouse. At the time I had two goats, two dogs, three cats, a pet hen, and an electric kiln in the barn. I did a lot of work in papier-mâché, and it tended to creep out of the studio in shreds and scraps, and was even worse than clay for mess. If there's too much mess I can't concentrate. If there's no food in the fridge I don't stop to eat: then I'm too hungry to work. Susie kept things in balance. I believe her to be some kind of saint. Calling her the cleaner is rather like calling Moses the jobbing gardener because he smote the rock. If I say this kind of thing to her she seems immeasurably shocked.

Susie's husband worked in town and though he was always kind to me, I would not want to be the criminal who crossed him. He has managed to build the fanciest bungalow in the village, and Susie keeps a perfect garden. Rumer is a pretty, peaceful and prosperous place and has won the best-kept village in Kent competition two years running, having survived BSE, foot-and-mouth, the falling off of the tourist trade – it has some good Roman ruins – and kept its village store and post office. But Susie is right: as a place it can get a bit boring. My two children, in their teens, try not to show it but are always happy to get back to town at the end of the holidays.

But nothing happens and nothing happens and then all of a sudden everything happens, in places as in people's lives, and what was to happen, what was to be described in the papers as 'The Affair of the Rumer Site', was to take everyone by surprise.

Susie had a part-time job at the local comprehensive school, as a personal counsellor. It was her task to take alienated and troubled children under her wing, get them to school if they were truanting, sit with them in class if they were school refusers, help them with lessons they didn't understand, and stay with them in the playground if they were bullied. She was not trained in any way to do it – the school can't afford anyone expensive – but there is something about her apparently stoical presence, which means the pupils seem to accept her as one of their own. She is passionately on the children's side: only occasionally does she raise her eyes to heaven and shrug. *Hopeless, why waste the State's money and my time. Let them go free.*

One Friday afternoon in mid-July she turned up with the ironed sheets, disturbed and upset. (I have never yet ironed a sheet: Susie will not make a bed without first doing so. She has an ironing press: I have not.) The weather had been very hot: drought had set in: it was in that curious inconclusive patch of time after exams have finished and school hasn't yet shut up shop for the summer. I'd been trying to finish the ceramic triptych I was working on before the children came down for the summer, and had managed it with a day to spare. I was exhausted and dehydrated, after days with the kiln, and still not quite back in the real world.

Now here was Susie sitting at the kitchen table actually crying. She said she had taken a group of her rejectees, as she called them, down to see the site. She'd thought the children would be really interested to see the unearthed graves and the skeletons still lying there, two thousand years on. But they had been indifferent, looked at her as if she was crazy to take them all the way in the heat to look at a few old bones, and one of the girls, Becky Horrocks, had tossed her cigarette into an open grave.

'What site?' I asked. 'What graves?' I'd quite forgotten. The row – about building the biggest shopping mall in all Europe on a site designated as an area of natural beauty and scientific interest, just a mile south of Rumer – has been rumbling on for so many years I had assumed it would never be resolved. But apparently it had, the developers had won, work had begun within the day and the bulldozers had been in skimming the site.

So much for the grebes and the greater crested warbler and the lesser toad and the marsh pippin: they would have to fend for themselves. As would the village shop, newsagent and post office. All must bow down in the face of progress: all must be sacrificed to the temple of Mammon. It was monstrous. Though as I sat there at the table with the dogs panting beside me in the heat, the thought of the chilly air around the long stretches of frozen-food cabinets filled me with delinquent delight.

'They've uncovered a Roman graveyard,' said Susie. 'Twelve graves still with the bodies in them. And what Pam says is a Druid's well but you know what she is.'

Pam was the local white witch: she had a mass of long white hair and a penchant for crystals and Goddess worship. She also ran, rather successfully, the local estate agency. She was widowed and had taken on the business after her husband's death, but had changed her manner of living and dressing. Now she saw faces in the running brook, heard the Great God Pan rustling in the hedges, and suspected any stranger in the village of being an extraterrestrial visitor from the Dog Star Sirius. But she could sell any property she set her mind to. I think she used hypnosis.

'I hope they stopped work,' I said and Susie said they had, but only because there was a handful of protesters still parading the site, and they'd seen a skeleton go into the skip along with the top sward, the rare ferns, the lesser celandine and lumps of sticky yellow clay, and had called the police, who came without riot gear, and were very helpful and refrained from observing how quickly they ceased being pigs and scum when anyone actually needed them.

The police had made the JCBs pull back, and Riley's the developers keep to the letter of the law and call in the archaeologists, no matter how their lawyers protested that they were exempt, and that every day of stopped work cost them at least £100,000. And there the skeletons lay, indecently uncovered – except the one rescued in bits from the skip, now at the county morgue being dated and pigeonholed – waiting for their fate to be decided. There'd been nothing in the local paper, let alone the nationals. Susie reckoned Riley's had made sure of that. They didn't want sightseers holding up the work.

'That's horrible,' I said. 'The age of a body doesn't make any difference. Two thousand years ago or yesterday, it's the same thing. It deserves respect.'

Susie said what bothered her so about Becky Horrocks, the girl who'd thrown the cigarette stub, was how little she must care about herself, if she cared so little for the dead.

*　　*　　*

That evening, when the sun stopped baking and a cool breeze got up, Matt and Susie called by and took me down to the site. How parched and dry the landscape looked! I had a bad back from heaving stuff in and out of the kiln and my hands were rough and blistered, but the triptych was ready to go off. It was a commission for Canterbury Cathedral and was part of some European-funded art and religion project. It would be touring the cathedrals of the country over the next year.

I am not a particularly religious person – not like Susie and Matt, who go dutifully to Rumer parish church every Sunday and twice on Christmas Day – but then I was not required to be: just a good artist. The theme of the work was the coming of Christianity to the British Isles, which heaven knew was shrouded in myth and mystery anyway, and my guess was as good as anyone's.

The centre panel was the child Jesus sailing into Glastonbury around the year AD 10 with his uncle Joseph of Arimathea – a tin trader – and almost certainly myth. The right panel depicted Saint Piran sailing to Cornwall from Ireland in a stone coracle – the stuff of magic, a tale drifted down from the sixth century. On the left was Saint Augustine, riding into Canterbury in AD 597 with his retinue of forty monks, sent by Pope Gregory to bring the gospel to the heathen English, for which there was a basis in history proper. The panels were in bright flower-bedecked colours, designed to glow and shine in the vaulted gloom of the cathedral: light breaking into darkness. I was really pleased with it but doing it had left me exhausted.

I thought perhaps it was exhaustion that made me react as I did. The desolation a handful of JCBs can wreak in a couple of days is extraordinary. The whole valley was down to subsoil: a great stretch of yellow-grey earth taking up the space – perhaps half a mile across and two-thirds of a mile long – between two untouched still green and verdant hills, stretching like tautened muscles on either side of the scar. I began to cry. How could I have been so indifferent as to what was going on around me? Matt looked embarrassed.

Susie took me by the hand and led me to a square patch of stony ground, more grey than yellow, which rose above the surrounding clay. She was wearing a neat green shirtwaister and lace-up walking shoes. I was in an old T-shirt, jeans and sandals. Susie always dressed up to go out: now I unexpectedly saw my lack of formality as rash. It made me too vulnerable. The living should dress up to honour the dead.

There were I suppose a dozen graves, running north to south: a few were no more than oblongs let down into bare earth, most were lined with what I supposed to be lead. In the bottom of each lay a skeleton: long strong white bones: some disturbed by animals – rodents, I suppose, or whatever disturbs the dead underground, over centuries – but for the most part lying properly, feet together, finger bones fallen to one side. Scraps of leather remained in the graves: what looked like a belt here, a sandal thong there. I was distressed for them.

'They can't just be left here on their own, exposed,' I said.
'They're well dead,' said Matt. 'I don't think they'll mind.' The wind got up a little and dust and earth swirled round the graves; already the sharpness of their edges was beginning to dull. If only rain would fall. The green surface of mother earth is so thin, so full of the defiance of the death and dust that lies beneath.

'I wonder who was here before us,' said Susie, 'laying them to rest so long ago. Young strong men: how they'll have grieved. And we don't even know their names.'

Matt was stirring the ground with his foot and turning up a few pieces of what looked to me like Roman tile. 'Reckon there's another Roman villa round here,' he said. 'That won't make the developers too happy.' But he reckoned they'd manage to get the archaeologists on their side, and forget about it and build anyway. They'd go through the motions but there was too much at stake to hold up work for more than a week at the most.

Susie and I said we'd take turns grave-watching. It didn't seem right to leave the graves unattended. I'd take the shift until midnight, then she'd turn up in their camper van and spend the rest of the night on site. Matt said we were crazy but went along with it. Indeed, he said he'd relieve his wife at six and stay until eight when he had to get to work. Surely by then Riley's would have got their act together and organised a watchman, and the archaeologists would turn up to do whatever they were required to do under statute.

I sat and watched the sun set and the moon rise, and the white bones began to glimmer in their graves. I thought I could hear the sound of Romans marching, but that was imagination, or a distant helicopter. I drifted off to sleep. It wasn't at all creepy, I don't know why: it should have been. There was a kind of calm ordinariness in the air. My earlier distress was quite gone. At about eleven Mabs turned up with a massive flashlight and a camping chair and table and some sandwiches and coffee. She'd been through to Susie on the phone. We sat quietly together until Susie relieved us: bump, bump, bump, in the camper van. Mabs took me home and I slept really soundly, though in the morning my back was bad again.

I rang the Bishop's Palace to ask about reinterring the bodies. I couldn't get through to the Bishop but I explained the situation to some kind of sub-Canon and he said they were well aware of it, and since the graves were lying north to south, they were not Christian burials in the first place, but pagan and nothing to do with the Church. It was up to the civil authorities to do what they decided was best. The University of Birmingham had tendered for the contract: the site was to be photographed and mapped – there had indeed been a Roman villa on the site, as well as a pottery and a graveyard – but take off a layer and the country was littered with them. The bones? They'd be placed in sealed plastic bags and taken off to the research department at Birmingham for medical or other research.

'Pagan?' I enquired. 'I thought we were all ecumenical, now.'

But no. Ecumenical did not extend to heathens. I pleaded without success but the bishopric was unmoved, nor would they put me through to anyone else. I thought about withdrawing my triptych from the cathedral in protest but couldn't bear to do that.

I went down to the site later in the day. The whole world seemed to be out and about in the hot sun, and not a scrap of shade. The graveyard area was roped off, there were security guards, the JCBs buzzed away at the far end of the site, archaeological students peered and measured. A handful of old ladies from Rumer had brought chairs and were sitting round the one that I was beginning to see as the master grave – it was lead-lined, decorated, and larger than the others. They were knitting. They were like Furies, or the Norns, or some kind of Greek chorus – but knitting. Well, this was Rumer. An ice-cream van plied its wares: word was beginning to get round: people were turning up in cars to stare and marvel.

Earth-moving machinery rumbled, turned, groaned and clanked in the distance, but management – you could tell them by their grey suits and pale faces, sweating in the heat – were everywhere. Pam was in urgent conversation with a grizzled man in a hat looking rather like Harrison Ford who was sitting on the end of the master grave making notes and taking photographs. A helicopter swept to and fro over the site, presumably doing the aerial survey the Canon had spoken of.

'What's with the old ladies?' I asked Pam. 'I didn't know they knitted.'

'They're from the church,' she said. 'They're making a knitted patchwork tapestry to auction for charity. They usually sit and do it in the church hall but they felt like some fresh air and all trooped around here.'

'Isn't that rather peculiar?' said I.

'No more peculiar than you and Susie sitting out here all last night,' said Pam. 'The archaeologists aren't very friendly. They're on the developers' side. Well, they're the ones who're paying. They're making a survey of the site, then they're sealing it and the shopping mall goes ahead on top of it.'

'I'll call the newspapers,' I said. 'It's a scandal.'

'The living have to exist and do their shopping,' said Pam. 'Along with the mall go sixty starter homes, a foot clinic with accommodation for six nurses, and an Internet café free for under-eighteens. Riley's put out a press release today.'

'It's still a temple to Moloch,' I said. 'And personally I have no intention of worshipping him.'

Susie came up. She had a party of A-level pupils with her, the cream of the bunch, bright-eyed and bushy-tailed, making notes as to the manner born.

'They reckon the villa dates from around the first half of the first century,' said Susie. 'And the graveyard too. I reckon it's something really special but they can't afford to admit it.'

I remonstrated with the Harrison Ford lookalike: there had to be some kind of ceremony, I said. He couldn't just pack the skeletons up in plastic bags so they lay on dusty shelves for ever. He spoke Nottingham, which was rather a pity, not Hollywood. He dismissed me as a middle-class busybody. The life of the real world had to go on. It couldn't be forever caught up in its past. Fine words, I thought, for an archaeologist. A *trahison des clercs*. Even the academics had forsaken us, and bowed down before Mammon. We had quite a row, which he won. When I got to the station to meet the children I was still quite pink with anger.

They had bought computer games with them. I took them down to the site: they were moderately interested, out of politeness, but not much.

'They're just old bones,' they said. 'Chill, Mum,' and went into a chorus of *dem bones dem bones dem dry bones*; I supposed they'd seen piles of bodies on TV in their time. I always looked away at the horrors. I turned on the news to find out what was going on in the world. An official drought had been declared. Hosepipe bans had been imposed in most parts of the country. That would put paid to the lettuces, already struggling, and the gooseberries would be tiny and sour.

Their father was going to marry again. That was okay be me, and by them. They seemed to like her. We were all on good terms. It's always rather a shock, though. The children said I should marry again; it was easier for them if there was someone to look after me. I said I didn't need looking after and they laughed hollowly.

That night we stood around the special grave, the master grave, the grave of the tallest soldier, in the moonlight. There was Susie, Pam, Carter Wainwright and I. Riley's didn't run to a night watchman. Carter was a hippie silversmith: he made the kind of jewellery Pam loved to wear: crystals set in silver: a kind of feng shui approach to the art of jewellery. Beads that brought you luck: earrings to focus the chakra required. I couldn't stand that woozy kind of thing, really, but he was a nice enough fellow. Even quite good-looking for a pagan. And not married.

'I don't see how we can be sure he wasn't a Christian,' I said. 'People travelled a lot in those days. For all we know these are the bones of the centurion John Wayne played in the film, the one who took Jesus' robe after the crucifixion and was converted. Why are people so sure such things can't be?'
'Because it's so very unlikely,' said Carter Wainwright. I bet he

was christened something like Kevin Smith and changed his name when he came down here. People do. But he had a nice deep voice.

'My point is, Carter,' I said, 'if they found an early Christian cross in this grave tomorrow, they'd have to believe.'

'But they're not going to find any such thing, are they,' he said.

'They might,' I said. 'You never know. If you come back to my house tonight I can show you all sorts of early Christian references. If you add mercury to the silver mix they always assume it's old silver. Should anyone take it into their head to do any testing.'

'I know all about that,' he said. 'I had a job once faking old clock faces. "Restoring" they called it, but from what they charged, I called it faking. I came down here to Rumer to live a more honest life.'

'Two wrongs don't make a right,' said Pam, primly, but she didn't sound very convinced.

'I don't think we'd better tell Matt,' said Susie. 'He's such a stickler.'

'You can't do this,' said Pam.

'Yes we can,' I said. 'Then they can give these bodies a decent burial and we can all get some peace and some sleep.'

I bent down and picked out of the grave what looked like a sliver of wood, or had once been wood, in a blackened kind of way. And I gave it to Carter Wainwright and he put it in his pocket.

'Give it the trace of a wooden frame,' I said, 'just to confuse the issue.'

I noticed my blistered fingers were getting better. Touch had been quite painful and cooking the children's chicken dinner had been hell. Carter Wainwright came back with me for the books and a certain amount of canoodling did take place, I must say, before he took his leave. I didn't want to be a burden to my children: a silversmith and a sculptor could live fairly amicably together. And he swore his name was truly Carter Wainwright and I believed him.

In the morning my back was better and my fingers unblistered and smooth. This is what a little sex can do for you, I concluded. And amazingly, it started to rain. You could practically see the lettuces breathe the moisture in, and their hearts swell and curl and firm. All the animals went out into the wet, which was rather unusual for them, and skittered about in pleasure. The ground was parched, how it drank in the rain.

I went down to the site with the children. Now that there were news teams and cameras and journalists with notebooks, they took more interest. Apparently a Christian cross, a Chi Rho, made of silver and wood, had been found in the grave of one of the centurions. They reckoned the sudden rain had loosened the earth, which was why they hadn't seen it before. No-one had expected rain; it certainly hadn't been forecast, and it was only local.

Harrison Ford from Nottingham was in a foul mood. This was the last thing he had wanted. Pam reckoned he was on some sort of performance bonus. He was in conference with his friend from Riley management, Marcus Dubiddy; I saw the Chi Rho lying on a piece of plastic by the grave while they argued. Both men looked thoroughly cross.

The rain had stopped pelting and now drifted in a kind of warm gentle misty shroud over the site. Those of us in jeans and T-shirts were at an advantage over the suits, whose ties began to look flabby very quickly. My son Joel even consented to join the dustpan and brush brigade, volunteers rounded up locally to help the Birmingham students sieve the ribboned-off sections of the site. They had at least five minutes' training before setting to. At least there was stuff to find: oyster shells, bits of metal and broken Samian ware, all of which were being catalogued, plastic-bagged, and logged. Faster, faster, urged the overseers. They must cover more ground, more quickly. I felt protective of him, as if he were being whipped to build a pyramid.

Joel eavesdropped on Dubiddy's conversation – I had been marked out as a troublemaker. The Chi Rho was to be sent by courier to the British Museum and they'd date it as a matter of urgency, and value it.

I must admit we panicked, Carter, Pam, Susie and I. We were to be discovered. The silver would be traced back to Carter: my involvement would be suspected. We had forged an early Christian cross. They would think it was some elaborate plan to make money out of the tourist trade. They would not believe our motives. Who nowadays would put themselves out to get a few old dry bones a Christian burial?

We drank too much Chilean red that night, round at my place, to quell our nerves and celebrate the removal of the triptych to Canterbury Cathedral. The carriers had come that day. The more we thought about it the more delinquent our forgery seemed, and indeed impertinent. The Roman legions came from all over the world: the centurion could have belonged to any of a dozen faiths. Many worshipped Mithras, the Sun God. Susie said she didn't think he was a Mithraic, see, it was still gently raining; surely Mithras would have honoured his own? It was fine enough over the rest of the country: only our graves dwelt in this gentle, moist, life-giving Christian mist.

Matt, usually so wary of Pam, for his sort and her sort do not usually agree, came up and drank with us, and they told each other jokes. Susie became quite pink and giggled: Carter decided he had fallen in love with me; the children persuaded me to take in a stray cat who kept trying to live with us, while I tried to let her know, tactfully and firmly, that it was not to be. That night there was a terrific thunderstorm and lightning struck the village shop. The postmistress said it was the spirits of the unburied dead up there on the site bringing bad luck.

The British Museum sent an e-mail to Harrison's laptop the next day. The Chi Ro was genuine. Two thousand years old, give or take a decade or two. Riley's put out a press release. Carter was beside himself with pleasure. Not only had he had found me but he was one of the greatest forgers alive.

The next day the press turned up in force. Priceless, or at any rate in the region of several million pounds. We could say nothing, and we had won nothing. It was too late. Riley's put guards on the site and strung a barbed wire fence around it. But still the bones were to go to Birmingham the next day. And within hours after that the skimming would continue and the vast screed would be laid, and that would be the end of our history, not to mention the nesting sites of the greater crested warbler, et cetera.

Then a Canon from Canterbury rang me to congratulate me on the triptych, and I think he meant it. I bought up the matter of the graves.
'If they've found a Chi Rho in a Roman soldier's grave,' I said, 'and the British Museum has validated it, then can't we just accept that the dead soldier is a Christian? Sure, he might have stolen the cross, but for that matter he could have been present at the Crucifixion.'

It was amazing with what equanimity I could lie. I put it down to being in love. The Canon hummed and hawed and then all of a sudden cheered up, and said of course. He would be happy to do some kind of service of reconciliation, before the bones were bagged. He'd get through to the Rumer parish priest. I said they'd have to be quick. He said the Church could be if it had to be.

* * *

And sure enough early the next morning, while a restive Harrison Ford and his team stood back, and the JCBs stood silhouetted against the skyline with the young sun behind them – the storm had cleared the air – the knitting women set up a trestle table with a white cloth and a pot of wild flowers on it: and the Canon, an eagle of a man, turned up in his little Volkswagen, even bringing with him a Bishop from a neighbouring diocese – he had his crook with him and his gold embroidered over-vests, or whatever they're called, in the back seat, and all those concerned and interested turned up, and a few journalists as well.

And the priests performed a service of reconciliation: and we sang a few quavery hymns, lost on the breeze – *O God our help in ages past* – then the table was folded, and the altar cloths, and we drifted off, and peace descended on the valley. All of a sudden it was a place like anywhere else.

Then Harrison and his team darted in like a team of vultures to take their pickings away, and their vans moved off. The JCBs surged down the hill to get to the part of the site they'd been denied, and a hundred cement mixers queued up on the new roads waiting to get in. Goodbye, marsh pippin, goodbye. The future knocks on the door, and if you don't let it in, it simply batters it down.

But peace and prosperity has descended upon Rumer as if it were blessed: visitors come from all over the world to see the knitted patchwork tapestry, which won an international art prize and now hangs behind the altar, instead of being auctioned. To our relief the mall traffic was rerouted away from the village: a free bus service runs three times a week there and back for those without cars. Our flowers win at Chelsea: we grew a record carrot and its photograph was in the *Mail*. We keep the post office and the village store, and the little school was even reopened: the young stay instead of going off to the big city: why live away from paradise?

*   *   *

As for the mall itself, that prospered mightily. The fruit was always fresh and the bread stayed cheap. The charity shops were given concessions. The Internet café sopped up the alienated young and has given them purpose and achievement. Becky Horrocks took up computer studies. Matt was promoted to crime prevention officer and could work locally, to Susie's pleasure. The mall even boasted a little museum, endowed by Riley's and the University of Birmingham, where you could see photographs of the site, and the outline of the villa and the graveyard, and a replica of the Rumer Cross. I could not find out what happened to the original. It was probably bought by Bill Gates or Steven Spielberg to enrich their collections.

I married Carter Wainwright (in church, of course). My hands stay smooth and strong the better to continue to work. So do his. We are both employed these days doing restoration work, mostly for cathedrals. Carter replaces stolen silver plate (there's a lot of that to do) and I forge, fashion and bake metal, stone and clay, making good whatever the weather undoes.

We don't say it to each other, but we can both see in retrospect that what was going on at the site was miraculous, outside the normal order of things. It would not surprise me if it were indeed a sliver of the true cross I picked up that day and which Carter worked with: and that it leaves its blessed traces behind. I think we will be forgiven for our deceit: we were meant to do what we did.

THE DEVIOUS
AND DELECTABLE

A Summer Person

What the Papers Say

Smoking Chimneys

Percentage Trust

A Summer Person

I'm a summer person, and she's a winter person. Her name is Jennifer, mine is Kate. She's twenty-five and I'm twenty-four. She used to be my best friend. Now she's my father's girlfriend, and soon he'll marry her, once he's divorced my mother. Then she'll be my stepmother. We're all good friends. These things have to be done amicably, for the sake of the children: that is to say me. My mother and I are in therapy, and dealing with our negative emotions very well, but the other two don't seem to need it.

Jennifer and I were at college together. We've known each other since we were fifteen. Now we both work at the same travel magazine, going all over the world trying out holiday destinations for our readers, which is a pretty terrific kind of job. We earn well and travel well, and we're both ambitious: I even got promotion to deputy editor recently, and Jennifer was happy for me, or seemed to be. She is, was, my best friend.

When I say she's a winter person I mean she's very fair and delicate-skinned, and burns easily, and likes to stay out of the sun. If she's in it too much she goes red in the face and sweats. She's the Iceland expert at the magazine. She goes for the cold destinations whenever she can: mountains and glaciers: I go for the hot places, lying around on beaches. If a mosquito bites her neck her whole face swells up, and her eyes go tiny, red and puffy so she can hardly see out of them. She gets hay fever and sneezes a lot in the pollen season, and has to dose herself with so much histamine she hardly makes sense when she talks.

But she looks fantastic at a Christmas party, her skin pale and almost translucent, her eyes big and haunted, and the blonde bob fragrant and silky, and wearing cashmere so pale pink it's almost white. Wrap her in a winter coat and she looks sexy and vulnerable.

Me, I bloom in the summer. I have an olive skin and tan easily and love lying in the sun. I am at home on a beach and have a bikini figure – long-waisted and athletic. My hair is very thick and curly, and at its best looking as if it's just been dunked in the washbasin and left to dry in a hot wind, as befits Nature Girl. I shiver all winter and get goose-pimply, eat too much chocolate and get spots, and put me in a winter coat and I look like a sausage wrapped round the middle with a piece of string. I like high heels, but they're not good on ice.

I was wearing a plaster cast at the Christmas party at which Jennifer ran off with my Daddy under my mother's nose. He doesn't want me to call him Daddy any more. He wants me to call him by his non-parental name, Francis.

You'd think when people got to their fifties, like my parents have, they'd be past all that emotional nonsense, but no. My mother says Jennifer is welcome, what does my mother want with a husband anyway: she runs a radio station and has enough trouble without a man about the house, losing his socks and his temper all the time, filling the place with testosteronic vibes. But I know she's upset and I hate that. Not that I ever got to see much of my mother after I was about five: it's a twenty-four-hour news station, and my mother's a career sort of person, not the maternal type.

It was a smart networking party, mind you, all caterers and canapés, rather than a friends and family party, and my mother was schmoozing a network controller from the BBC, who she thought might be useful, rather than paying much attention to my Daddy, but never mind. She came across him with Jennifer on the bed in the spare bedroom where she kept all the books on digital radio and wavelengths. She wanted to look something up for the man from the BBC.

You'd have thought Jennifer would have had some consideration for me, and not done it, but no. I had taken a couple of boyfriends of hers in the past, it's true, but no-one she wasn't better off without. And this was my father. My mother came out of the room in hysterics.

I ran out into the snow, as best I could in my plaster cast, without my coat I was so upset, and everyone had to run after me. I got a terrible cold in the nose, and ran a fever: my poor mother got flu – we're all summer people: winter doesn't agree with us one bit – and by the time we could concentrate again on what was going on my father had moved into Jennifer's studio flat and was talking about true love for the first time in his life and so on. I scrubbed and scrubbed away at the plaster cast to get rid of Jennifer's name where she'd signed it – *To the new deputy editor with my love* – but it seemed somehow embedded.

Jennifer didn't have a resident father of her own – so few have, these days – but this was no reason for her to have mine. I try not to think like this, it's so negative, but resentment keeps breaking through. Perhaps I'm just a mean sort of person.

'I don't see why you two have to get married,' I said to her on Valentine's Day, when the happy couple announced their engagement and the divorce papers came through for my mother to sign. 'Isn't that all rather old-fashioned? Why don't you just live together?'

*　　*　　*

Jennifer and I, over many a glass of Chardonnay after work, had sworn we would never get married.

'Marriage is crap,' I remember Jennifer saying to me once. 'Nothing but a legal tie, madness for any woman who's likely to earn more than her husband. If he chooses to run off with a mistress she could end up having to pay alimony to him for ever and handing over half her pension rights as well. Who wants to be some man's free meal ticket for life? No thank you!'

And I'd agreed. She was so very definite in her opinions. No marriage. No children either. The world was overcrowded as it was, and how could a woman concentrate on her career when she had a baby to hold her back. In the travel world you have to be free of domestic obligations: you never know what's going to happen next. A mother just can't give her job her best shot – unless you're my mother, of course, and superwoman. But I'm not, and nor is Jennifer.

And now look at her. Flicking through fashion mags picking over wedding gowns. The full Monty, veils and trains and figured satin. I felt betrayed. Not that she was likely to end up sharing her pension rights with my father, who owned an advertising agency, I could see that. It would quite definitely be the other way round. He spent well but he saved well too. Jennifer's always thought quite a lot about the financial practicalities of life. It couldn't be, could it, that she was marrying him for his money and half my mother's pension rights?

'But I love your father so much,' said Jennifer, 'I want to be his wife, not just his girlfriend. I don't want him ever to get away. I want to do it properly, with lifelong vows, in church, with peals of bells and tradition behind me. He married your mother in a registry office, and see what happened. I want to be married in white, to prove I'm starting life afresh, and so does he.'

*   *   *

54

My father does have a white suit: he sometimes wears it to meetings to impress the clients with his integrity. I wouldn't put it past him to wear it to his own wedding, to show his own life was starting afresh with Jennifer. She'd have put the phrase into his head.

She's even asked me to be a bridesmaid but I haven't quite said yes. If I do I'll wear black. He is exactly twenty-six years older than she is. They share a birthday. They think this is destiny. I know that according to the laws of probability it's not all that extraordinary. I share a birthday with my mother. I daresay they'll ask her to be matron of honour, just to show the press how amicable everything is. We've been doorstepped quite a lot by the press: Jennifer quite likes that but my mother hates it. Bad for business.

I don't want them to start having babies, I really don't. They wouldn't be so crazy, would they?

But summer's coming at last and with it comes hope. Perhaps when the really hot weather comes – and it's meant to, in August, to make up for the miserable winter and spring – her sneezing and sniffing and runny eyes will put my father off, make him see the real Jennifer. He'll understand that it was a winter infatuation and it's over. And he'll go back to my mother. I expect she'll pay him more attention now and they'll live happily ever after.

What's more, my father – sorry, Francis – wants us all to go on holiday just to show there's no hard feelings. I was doubtful but my therapist says it's a really good idea. It's destructive to harbour anger, and I ought to be through that stage by now. She'd impressed me at the beginning by saying that the cold and the flu was weeping with the nose instead of the eyes which made a lot of sense, and that was how my mother and I dealt with grief. But jealousy could hang around for a long time and was a very dangerous and undermining emotion to have. It wasn't exactly jealousy, I said, it just made me feel yuk!

Bad enough that my mother and father still had sex, apparently – I'd rather thought they only did it the once, when I was conceived – but my mother had a different story. Now the bouncing bedsprings, which marked my father's and Jennifer's nights, were just too much: if we went on holiday I'd have to make sure I wasn't in a room next to theirs. My therapist said but surely I was well in with the tour operators, and that could be easily enough arranged, and I was putting obstacles in the way of my own recovery, which was true enough. She said she didn't think I was the kind of person who was easily embarrassed, and I lied and said no, I wasn't. And so it was agreed. We were going on holiday together. My father, my best friend soon to be my stepmother, and me.

My father wanted a holiday with a difference. It was to be a pre-honeymoon extravaganza, after all. Advertising was having a bit of a hard time and he really shouldn't take time out at a time like this, but life was for living. He would cash in a life policy and get the very best. That Jennifer and I were accustomed to the best hotel suites and the best sea and mountain views in the world, and for free, and that he'd have his work cut out to impress us, passed him by.

He wanted to go to Libya, of all places, to see the spectacular Roman cities they'd recently excavated – he was a bit of a Rome nut, my Daddy – and I watched Jennifer go pale when he suggested it. Hot sand, dust storms, no air conditioning in the hotels, let alone the tour vehicles. It was her idea of hell. But she didn't want my Daddy to know. He was a hot weather person, like me. He loved striding around in shorts, showing off his legs, which were long and slim, and, apart from the hair, would have suited many a girl very well. He had very blue eyes and his hair bleached to blond very quickly and he always looked good in the summer.

We were a summer family – summer people and winter people shouldn't holiday together, and she knew it.

'I'm not so sure about Libya,' I couldn't resist saying. 'Jennifer's not really a hot weather girl, are you, Jennifer, and besides, aren't there terrorists and landmines?'

Jennifer gave a little shriek and looked daggers at me. 'I'd adore to go to Libya,' she said. 'I love all that Roman ruin stuff.' Liar.

Now I don't know what sort of biting, stinging insects there are in Libya – probably not enough. You get them more where there's less wind. So I let her off the hook and suggested Antigua. She's not much good at long haul fights either. It sounded pretty good to her, after Libya, and she waxed all enthusiastic and Francis gave up his ideas of Roman ruins and I booked first-class seats through the magazine.

Jennifer had already given in her notice, and told everyone about her marrying my father. She could at least have kept it quiet. People kept looking at me curiously, and laughing, and saying I should never have accepted the deputy editorship, this was Jennifer's revenge. Which was of course absurd. I just went on saying that my parents' marriage had been in name only and my mother was happy about the arrangement. Ha ha ha.

We were to stay in those little beach cabins attached to the big hotels. The beach is glorious, white, smooth and long, fringed with palm trees, coconuts drop at your feet, and there's mango juice for breakfast and fresh pawpaw. There's water sports of every kind, which my father loves. He's a champion water-skier, as I am. And we love to go deep-sea diving.

Jennifer's idea of a holiday is to sit in the shade and catch up with her reading, and go to a bar for an espresso followed by a visit to a museum and a historic building or so, but all Antigua has to offer is great gloomy prisons, and if you leave the coast and go inland you feel you need to look after your wallet. And you don't go alone. Daddy went with her a couple of times but the sea kept calling him back. She didn't protest, or show her disappointment, she was too canny for that, and just smiled sweetly and rearranged her wide-brimmed hat, and watched from the hotel balcony and admired him for his strength and virility.

It's not in my nature to interfere with the course of events. It seems ignoble to me. But when I overheard her talking about the possibility of getting my mother out of the marital home – she lived on her own, what did she want with all that space – and she, Jennifer, wanted to have at least six children, and how she, Jennifer, was already pregnant – I knew this wasn't true, she'd just borrowed some Tampax, being someone who would never buy if she could scrounge – I decided to take direct action. This was not true love. This was unscrupulous manipulation.

I did three things. I suggested to my friend Maria, who was the water-skiing instructress, that she paid my father rather a lot of attention, and pointed out to Jennifer, watching from the veranda, just how well they seemed to be getting along. Jennifer took the point and the next day when my father asked Jennifer to go water-skiing with him she did. Of course she was hopeless at it. That meant her thighs were black and blue by evening and no amount of sun block could keep the ultraviolet from getting through to her shoulders. The spray just washes the block off. She kept uttering little cries of pain through dinner, which irritated my father, and I didn't think the sex would be all that good that night. It was sex that kept him unthinking, I knew that. All he needed was a chance to recover.

I moved a very large ugly land crab, which had taken up residence beneath my cabin – I don't mind what I pick up – and put it in her suitcase – they like sheltered spaces – and waited for the screams.

*   *   *

I trapped a very large mosquito which was bashing itself against the insect screens, using a glass and a piece of card as if it were a spider – no easy matter but desperation made me patient – and put it into their bathroom. It got her chin the next morning and by midday her face looked as if she'd only just escaped from a hotel fire. Mosquitoes always left my father well alone. They like a nice white soft winter skin on which they can wreak real damage.

When she fell asleep on her sun bed while in the middle of reading her improving book – Gibbon's *The History of the Decline and Fall of the Roman Empire*, my father's favourite read – and the sun moved round so she was no longer in the shade, I didn't wake her. I let her burn.

That night they had the most tremendous row, which woke most of the cabin guests, and involved a lot of her screaming, hurling chairs and breaking windows, and he saw her as she really was. I knew, I had seen her in action against recalcitrant tour operators, airlines and hotel management when she didn't get exactly what she wanted. My father hated being embarrassed even more than I did. In the morning he drove her to the airport in silence and came back to join me on the beach. He didn't say much to me other than, grudgingly, 'Lucky escape'. And a little later, while we dined *à deux*, a suggestion that I make friends among classier people. The nerve of him! And if he did go off with Maria for the rest of the holiday – what one starts, unwittingly – at least he didn't plan to marry her. And my mother did have him back. I knew she would. She's a realist, too, like Jennifer.

What the Papers Say

New York was hot and soggy and you couldn't smoke, so they checked out of their hotel where the air conditioning groaned and shuddered, and took the train to Boston. Damask thought the journey would be pretty but it wasn't. Just indeterminate August trees, and the only spot of romance was the whoo-whoo of Amtrak, as they'd heard it in a hundred black-and-white movies, floating back from the engine. How painfully slow and bumpy anything seemed these days that was not air travel, and after you'd been in Concorde, apparently even ordinary air travel irritated. Ariel had flown in Concorde, although, because he'd had to go stand-by, only in the rear section where the noise and vibration is already beginning to catch up with you. Anyone who's anyone knows to travel in the front. Stand-by on Concorde! Damask marvelled. She was always marvelling. That was what he said he loved about her, so she did it a lot.

Ariel was fifty-two and called after the archangel, not the blithe spirit of Shakespeare's *The Tempest*, nor the soap powder, as Damask, who loved him newly and passionately, would tell everyone who didn't already know (and quite often even if they did) from the press cuttings. Ariel King, Irish film star, Oscar-winner. Married. Not to Damask. Ariel was meant to be in Hollywood for promotional purposes but had managed to take a week out in order to show Damask Vale-Eden America. His wife Elspeth was on holiday with the children in the Seychelles. Elspeth King liked a flat, watery place with a known circumference. Elspeth marvelled at nothing, grieved at everything. Elspeth was Ariel's conscience, and Damask his delight.

Damask was a model of the plumper kind, though thin enough by ordinary standards: she was the one they liked to use when accused too savagely of heroin chic. Damask was twenty-two, and smoked like a chimney.

Boston was even hotter and soggier than New York: the clam chowder was good, if oddly grainy, and Damask tried to light up in what she assumed was a bar area of the hotel restaurant. An angry woman in a blue sequined dress snatched the cigarette from her mouth and accused her of murder, and said she was a slut and a whore. The woman was crazy, everyone agreed, but it was a nasty incident, so Damask and Ariel flew down to Chicago where the Catholics cluster and the sense of sin is not so great – it being traditionally purged by confession and so having no way of accumulating over long periods – and the rich and successful are allowed to be fatter and happier than anywhere else in the States. You could smoke, mostly, but after you'd been to the Art Institute and the John G. Shedd aquarium and walked in the parks and taken a boat out on the lakes, there didn't seem much to do. How could anywhere be so hot and windy at the same time? They couldn't go to grand hotels, in case Ariel was seen by someone he knew: so they went to the run-of-the-mill kind, where there wasn't a concierge to tell you what was what, and they had to depend for their entertainment on tourist traps, as if they were just anyone. The hotels were okay, but there was no swanning about, no half mangoes with giant strawberry for room service breakfast: and sex felt oddly perfunctory: not overwhelming, now for once there was time for it. Ariel was guilty about Elspeth, so his performance led them to joke about Viagra, and Damask was, frankly, not all that keen on anything that tended to take her by surprise, making her screw up her face: she didn't want to get wrinkles. But that was okay. 'This thing,' as they assured each other, 'is about more than sex.'

*　　*　　*

After Chicago they went to Washington DC and on a guided tour of the White House, and even caught a glimpse of Bill Clinton himself, in the midst of a posse of security men, whose necks seemed wider than their heads.

'Isn't he handsome?' marvelled Damask, and a fellow tourist remarked, 'Well, yes, a girl like you would think so.' Damask did have Lewinski-like qualities, it is fair to say: a kind of buoyant overflowingness, spontaneity, and a rich, loose, red mouth. She had been named Damask by her mother, with just that same kind of spontaneity, only somehow messier. Damask was one of five sisters, by four different fathers, none of them ever resident. The family had lived in Cornwall in a pretty bohemian house on a cliff top, but rising seas had eroded the coastline and they'd had to leave when Damask was sixteen: such eccentricity no longer suited the times, and even the ocean knew it.

Damask and Ariel left Washington DC and went to Nashville on South West Airlines, an August-only deal, just $42 a head, and by coach to Memphis and Gracelands, because Ariel had a thing about Elvis Presley, and where it would be a very good idea indeed if he wasn't seen. Ariel had won his Oscar for playing Beethoven in *Prometheus*. And in his new movie, *Pure of Heart*, he played a Christian Scientist prepared to lay down his life for his faith. The studio had high hopes for it: the sequel, *Heartlands*, was about to go into production. Ariel was indeed seen at Gracelands, as it happened, by a passing fashion photographer, who recognised them both and double took, in every sense of the word, but when it came to it neither Damask nor Ariel noticed his presence. Lovers always tend to believe they are invisible.

Back to Nashville for a night out at the Ole Opry, which Damask couldn't stand. New men in black hats and girls singing twangy therapist songs. She was an acid house girl herself: she couldn't bear lyrics.

'Did you know,' said Ariel, 'that if they want to preserve fish from getting sucked into grilles they play acid house into the water. The boom, boom, boom, drives them to the far end of the pool.'

Yes, this relationship was cooling off. Neither wanted to admit it, but both knew it. He from experience and she because she knew perfectly well he was too old for her and in taking up with him in the first place had only been trying to annoy her mother. It is not nice to find yourself with no home, albeit it is the ocean's fault, at sixteen, and to have to go to live with an aunt, along with your twin sister Velvet, with whom you do not get along though everyone thinks because you are twins you must. And your mother, though remaining fond, seems to have simply given up on her role, and no longer sees it as her responsibility to provide board and lodging. She has to be punished, just a little, as the years go by.

Velvet had recently become pregnant by a Rastafarian, which was a far more drastic kind of thing to do than merely going off secretly with a man thirty years older than herself, as Damask had done. But Velvet had always taken things to extremes: she was alleged to be Damask's identical twin but during their grow-ing years was always fatter or thinner or taller or shorter than Damask: Velvet too had tried to start a career modelling, but was too inconsistent in shape and behaviour, too scatty in atti-tude, and the rich red lips seemed to look bad-tempered rather than to pout; how two people so nearly alike could be so different in photographs was a marvel to their mother Caledonia. Velvet and Damask Vale-Eden. School had been a torment.

'Take no notice,' said their mother. 'They're just envious, all the Annes and the Joans and the Marys. The Browns and the Smiths and the Joneses. Don't try to be like other people, girls, because you're *not*.'

Perhaps Ariel and Damask got together not just because sudden fame went to his head, and the brave must surely deserve the fair, and not just because she rated a man who won Best Actor about as high as Lewinski rated the President, which was just about as high as you can get, but because of this question of the *names*. Ariel's father was an Israeli out of Germany, a socialist of the pre-war kibbutz movement: his mother a nice girl called Anne from Dublin, but they'd had no more mercy than had Caledonia. How mixed up everyone becomes!

The soft green grass and the fireflies and the low, full moon of Nashville made outdoor lovemaking tempting: they walked back to their hotel from the Ole Opry and into what was either a park or someone's front garden, what did they care? They fell upon the ground and embraced, and he sang 'Moon River' and she wished he didn't. The photographer had followed them all the way from Gracelands, patiently, pitter-pat. Lawn sprinklers suddenly started, security lights flared, dogs barked, the errant couple started up in surprise, Damask's fine cotton dress, drenched, clung to her body, all her fine bosom revealed, his cotton chinos to his manly form; the couple fled into the dark, rearranging clothes as best they could. That was Nashville.

They flew to San Francisco but there was no air conditioning. Really, August is not the best time for cities. Then Hollywood lost patience with its errant star and tugged the cord and Ariel obeyed, and it was time for Damask to fly back to Heathrow. She would arrive back first thing on Sunday morning, ready for a shoot her agent arranged for the Monday. She looked forward to it. Swimsuits for the *Living Family* magazine and its mail-order catalogue: but a classy catalogue for once, and the more unclothed Damask was, the better she always looked. The creamy curves of her shoulders and arms, the smooth stretch of long full legs – she would never be totally chic, everyone agreed, but chicness in itself was beginning to feel unfashionable. Once skinny, attitudey chic reached the high streets, things had to go the other way.

*   *   *

At the British Airways Terminal of LA Airport Ariel and Damask kissed and hugged each other goodbye.

'I'm no Humbert Humbert,' Ariel said. They'd seen the remake of *Lolita* in Chicago. 'I can't do this to you. This week has been the happiest of all my life, and it breaks my heart. But I renounce you, I set you free, find the man you love, my darling, be happy always. And call me when you can. Use the mobile number.'

Mobiles are best for clandestine phone calls. You can switch them off in your spouse's presence, switch them on when privacy is available. Damask resisted the temptation to whinge and sulk. To be happy, she knew, is always the best revenge. It is only natural for a girl to want the man she's just spent a week with to yearn passionately to spend the rest of his life with her, but she could see it was unrealistic. Had she already been a well-established world figure she might have had a chance; to share headlines keeps a relationship afloat – look at Mick and Jerry. But if they tilt either way too sharply and suddenly, there's bound to be trouble sooner or later. No, let him go back to Elspeth, who'd never had a headline in her life but only made body text, and was two stone overweight, three by the best people's standards, and pale and plain and reclusive and terribly, terribly serious. Damask had her future to think of, and besides she was a good, kind girl and knew how to behave. 'I shall never forget you,' Damask said softly to Ariel, 'never. Whoever I'm with for the rest of my life I'll remember you: the best and tenderest first lover in the whole world. My mother always says I'm lucky and so I am!'

A nice girl indeed, Damask, though of course Ariel wasn't her first lover, but it was pleasant for him to think he was and that he had made such a fine and lasting impression on her. Damask became a little fidgety and wanted to go off to the smoking area, so she did not hold him back when he kissed her for the last time, and left, leaving her with an hour to catch her flight.

*   *   *

On the flight back – club class: Ariel had paid – she thought of him with affection, but no longer with love. She felt more mature and more experienced now: that was the thing about older men; you osmosed worldly wisdom from their bodies. She hated using condoms. Such a waste. Everyone knew – alas, there was no word for it that didn't put you off – that coital bodily fluids were the best thing for the complexion, whatever orifice was engaged. So she used an old-fashioned cap. The pill made you put on weight, and she couldn't afford to, her size being so finely tuned to the needs of the market – enough for wow! But not enough for yuk! – as her agent put it. Damask was not afraid of AIDS; she believed in a benign fate; all she wanted was not to be pregnant and not to have to take time off for a termination, which would interfere with her bookings.

Velvet, her twin, had had two abortions, each more traumatic than the last: the previous Christmas when the whole family had for once gathered together, in a borrowed house, there was Velvet, the youngest by twenty minutes, making everyone miserable by weeping and groaning and lamenting. What a sight the family made! Six pairs of red lips around the table, clear skins, wide blue eyes, firm chins – Caledonia had had a face-lift – so like one another some swore the mother must have given birth by parthenogenesis – there really should have been nothing in life to complain about. Only Velvet was given to fits of misery: the others felt she lacked style. All the girls save Velvet were doing well: Chenille was a practising lawyer, Satin, who these days called herself Joan, was an analytical chemist, Georgette was doing a PhD on the influence of the Napoleonic Wars on figurative painting, and Damask's modelling career seemed to be taking off.

But now it was the end of August. And Velvet was pregnant again, though this time happily, if drastically, and engaged to be married. Having got rid of the genes of a racing driver and a professor, as Georgette had crossly observed, she had settled for those of a Yardie. A Rastafarian rock star.

*   *   *

67

'All men are equal, none of my girls are racists, I am so proud of my Velvet,' Caledonia had crooned when they'd all got together at Easter, and she'd taken another whisky, and inhaled marijuana for her nerves, but her eyes looked slightly cross-eyed with the effort of not worrying about the polyglot nature of the future. It was an embarrassment. When young white women run off with beautiful black men it is seen as if lust is uppermost in their minds; and lust is not ladylike. Such a difficult line to tread when bringing up children: you want them to absorb your own intellectual, sexual and artistic messages in the proportion in which you yourself enjoy them, and which works well enough for you, but the children never quite seem to get the proportions right. Velvet interpreted a joyous sexuality as the alrightness of being sex-mad. Encourage Satin to read a book and she ended up a misogynist scientist. One rash overnight visit for the mother, taking Georgette along to a painter's studio, and the girl spends the rest of her life among paintings, knowing everything, but so far as Caledonia is concerned appreciating very little. Preach forgiveness and Chenille spends her life protecting the criminal classes from their just deserts. Only Damask seemed to get everything just about right: the balance worked in the daughter as it did in the mother. So what if Damask went off on holiday with a married actor, at least you knew she'd be back in time for work. Of the twins, it was always Velvet who had the unluck and Damask the luck. A single slip-up from Velvet and she'd be pregnant and you'd know in advance there'd be a power cut and a botch-up should she be whisked into hospital for some emergency operation. Whereas Damask – Damask rode the crest of any wave going: Damask would be swept along on the tide of popular taste: the *Living Family* catalogue today, but tomorrow's Ms Versace, as bosoms and smiles became the rage, and there was no more profit in poky ribs and puncture marks. Yes, Damask, second to last, was the most successful, the most balanced, of Caledonia's daughters.

Caledonia, herself the younger daughter of a former Foreign Secretary, now deceased, and executor of his estate, was involved in a long-running lawsuit with the publishers of his biography, a book full of disgraceful and humiliating tittle-tattle, most detrimental to his memory. The estate claimed damages for various posthumous insults to the elder statesman's reputation. It would make a legal precedent if it succeeded: the past claiming damages from the future, as it were, rather than the other way round. It was at a sensitive stage. The family hoped for half a million at least: Caledonia would at last be able to buy a proper new home. For five years she had been house-sitting for absent lovers, or staying with friends, or one way or another putting off her domestic duties.

And Damask? Damask just wanted the family to be happy and all together. She was a good, sweet girl. And now she had sensibly parted from Ariel, and allowed him to go back to his serious wife, as a good, sweet girl should.

And that was that, or so Damask thought. She loved the flight back with its endless unnecessary servings of dainty snackettes, and its little movie screens, and Ariel was on one of them, playing the faithful husband of a faithful spouse. He always played the good guy, the old-fashioned hero: Harrison Ford the younger. Me, me, she thought, that man on that screen loves, loved, well, something, once, me. It was thrilling. She slept.

When she came out into the light at the end of the Heathrow tunnel it was into a mob of paparazzi, news crews and journalists: grabbing and snatching, pressing forward like the surge of the waves which once carried her home away: crashing into her happiness. What can be happening, she wondered, what's going on, it can't be *me*. But it was. Photos of Damask coming out of Arrivals, stunned and staring, jaw dropped, looking far from her best, not even any eye shadow, made the front pages the next day. And alongside Damask, re-runs of Saturday's pics of Elspeth back from holiday, two stone the lighter and for once looking fabulous, if of course grieved. And the captions ran the gamut from *Fury Wife Chops Out AK* to *Daffy Damask Steals the King* to *Face of a Marriage Breaker*. Elspeth was suing for divorce through a PR firm, and claiming untold millions. And there were the two sweet blonde King kiddies too, weeping all over the pages, front, middle and back. And everywhere, everywhere, was the pic, which had got Elspeth going. Damask drenched to the skin, bosom half-bared, rising like Venus out of long grass, fireflies glittering her hair, from her horizontal embrace in the Nashville night with the clothed Ariel King. Picture of the year. It made the photographer half a million. It ended the King marriage. *Cheesecake sur l'herbe*, as it was known, after Manet, and became the trigger for great media debates on everything from the selfishness of parents, to adultery as sin, to the merits and otherwise of lovemaking out of doors and the life cycle of fireflies. But that was later, and only after what Damask had said at the airport, and when Georgette had made her rash comparison to *Déjeuner sur l'herbe*. None of the sisters was to be left alone. Pitter-pat, pitter-pat, went the sweet tough newsgirls after the lot of them: do you have any comment, don't you want to put your side of the story? We'll be nice to you, the others won't. You, the five beautiful sisters with four different fathers (and if the last two hadn't been twins no doubt it would have been five), do we blame you, pity you? Can you just tell us where your mother is? Caledonia? What kind of name is that? Caledonia's father was once in the running for Tory Prime Minister: haven't we some old pics of some old scandal: hasn't the daughter got some ongoing lawsuit? And there were the biographer's calumnies all over the literary pages again and the book selling like hot cakes but the profits to the biographer. Out came the therapists, the geneticists and counsellors: the infidelities of the father visited unto the second generation: compulsive marriage-breaking in the genes. The media couldn't believe their luck.

Because of course at the airport Damask, instead of reacting with appropriate shock, horror, confusion and apology to her uncovering as a bad girl, had coolly observed, 'Why blame me? Why not blame him?' And had fled to take refuge with Velvet, press pursuing. Otherwise it might all have died away sooner.

On the Sunday, Damask and Velvet prowled up and down in their besieged apartment in Parson's Green in south London. Damask had made her escape through the kindness of a couple of journos from *The Mail* who had whisked her into their car, evaded the following pack, and delivered her to Velvet's place for what they had hoped would be a quiet interview. But Damask had managed to slam the doors in their faces before they could follow her in. They shouted at her through the letterbox: all they wanted to know, they said, was what Ariel was like as a lover? How did he rate? Did she wish to comment on Elspeth's statement that she'd have been happier with a dildo? Didn't Damask want to comment on that? Eventually they went away. Damask and Velvet pulled the curtains, locked the doors, took the phone off the hook, and smoked a couple of joints.

In the middle of Sunday night Velvet started to miscarry, and had to go to hospital in an ambulance. The press were still there outside. Velvet – when finally she wrote the story of her abortions for a miserable £5000: *I Murdered My Unborn Babies* – attributed the disaster to the shock of it all, though actually she had been bleeding on and off for days, and no-one in the family knew, frankly, whether to be glad or sorry, and anyway concern for Velvet's emotional state was not currently at the top of the family's agenda. *Velvet Loses Rasta Baby* had almost become a *so-what*. Though it gave rise to yet more column inches – dire warnings from health experts saying that for every two abortions, expect one miscarriage.

It was as if the nation had gone to sleep one night careless and randy, as usual, and woken up the next in such a fit of respectability you couldn't believe it. Cruel Damask, the media reported, couldn't even be bothered to go to hospital with her own sister:

perhaps she was too busy making phone calls to married men? Oh yes, they knew her sort!

Caledonia had gone into hiding but broke radio silence by getting through to Georgette, also under siege, and saying of Damask, her one-time favourite, 'Darling, it's so vulgar for a woman to have her name in the paper. I can never forgive Damask for this.' And then, relenting. 'But don't tell her so, Georgie. She has enough to put up with.'

On Monday morning early, Damask called a taxi and fought her way through the ravening cluster on the steps and got to the studio with only a small crowd following. She was met there by her agent and the client. She was no longer needed on the shoot. She was notorious, and notoriety was not needed on *Living Family*: they had a young, wholesome image.
'But the magazine won't come out for a month,' pleaded Damask. 'It'll all be forgotten by then.'

The client shook his head. He knew better. Her dewy implorings counted for nothing. She wasn't looking her best. Jet lag, shock and terror at her new image as perceived by the world, had rubbed the bloom off her. A nice damask plum. Her agent raised sceptical eyebrows. Versace had been on the phone first thing. They didn't want the association. Sure, ribs and drugs were on the way out, and health and sex on the way in, but why use a model the whole world hated? Her bosom was way too big anyway; they'd assumed it was silicone and could be easily diminished: but real flesh? It might go wrong and she'd sue. So thank you, Miss Vale-Eden, but no thanks. And only twenty-two, poor girl, and trusting. She who'd once believed in her own good luck.

Stories are spun out of nothing and sink back to nothing, leaving a few ruined lives behind, living sacrifice in the cause of headlines, being there first, getting the exclusive. Or else see it as a horse race, a starting point and a finishing point, when the editor finally says enough of that: and a mad gallop in between. *Who's to blame, the man or the woman?* And they're off, like horses from the starting post, ripping up the turf as they go! Others see it as feeding frenzy: piranha fish at work. Nothing once it's over but the bare bones of the victim, glimpsed on the river bed, whitened and bleached and thin.

On the other side of the Atlantic, meanwhile, from coast to coast, Ariel was the brute, the monster, the seducer, Damask the young victim. Wrongly described in one paper as being sixteen years old, facts picked up like Chinese whispers, she ended up little more than a child. King the paedophile, though nobody quite used the p-word in case he sued. *The New Yorker* ran pieces on the media as the new morality and the innate helplessness of New Woman in the face of her own sexuality. *The New York Times* linked the scandal with Clinton. *Great Lives, Silly Loves, Poor Wives*: CNN did a special out of Atlanta. There was a report that Elspeth King had sold her story for $500,000, and had met up with her (married) PR agent while holidaying in the Seychelles: but it suited nobody to know that. That story quickly died. The studio stopped production of the new Ariel King movie *Heartlands* out of sensitivity to public feeling, throwing away $30m and a dozen new hopeful film careers on the way.

On the Heathrow side of the Atlantic Damask became the hate figure, the girl all other women fear (or are said to), the stealer of husbands, the marriage breaker, the careless, selfish, dangerous bitch. The media dug up family photos, decided her upbringing was not to blame. Caledonia was exonerated. Blame the daughter, not the mother! Caledonia, lone mother, doing her best in the face of personal disaster. A series of wicked abandoning men. She'd brought up a family, hadn't aborted a single one (or none that anyone discovered) and had never been a charge on the State. Caledonia, pursued, gave herself up to *The Mail*, offered them her story if they'd only keep the others off her back. She gave the £100,000 to the Prince's Trust charity. Bred a lady, always a lady, the papers agreed. So long as it's the aristocracy, bad behaviour is allowed to turn into a delightful eccentricity. So much remains of noblesse oblige. Caledonia was off the hook. Except the law then swung against her. She was a public figure, wasn't she? How could she claim loss of privacy? She got damages of one penny and the biographer laughed all the way to the bank.

All this because of one lovemaking observed and interrupted among the fireflies and the green grass of Nashville, Tennessee, after a night out at the Ole Opry. A longing look from Damask, English Rose, a bosom unconfined, a lusty clasp from Ariel, film star out of Hollywood, and pow!

Someone looked up Ariel's birth certificate back in Dublin. Barry turned out to be his given name. '*If I'd known it,*' Elspeth was reported as saying, '*I wouldn't have married him. It was Ariel, archangel, which so enchanted me.*' A hundred new features were spawned. The power of the name! The Israeli father turned out to be a fantasy. The true father was an absentee builder. Elspeth sues him for $8m he hasn't got.

An Oscar he may have, but until *Prometheus* he hadn't been a huge earner and now *Heartlands* was being withdrawn. His agent advised, '*Lie low for a year or two, restart a career as a villain, what are your options now? When will you guys ever learn?*' The agent shook his head but he was just going through the motions. He was on Viagra, he had his own problems: in love with a twenty-year-old who wasn't responding, Viagra or not. He couldn't be bothered with a client who'd fucked up, and would in all likelihood never earn any money again. Ariel tried to change agents but only the real shysters would take him on. He thought back to the day he'd first met Damask. It had been at some fashion show in London: it was the mother who'd interested him until the daughter showed up: '*A titled family*' someone had told him, though being fierce egalitarians, they never used the title.

Dubious motives, Ariel suddenly saw, brought with them their just deserts and more. It was wrong of him to have taken advantage of the sexual pulling power of an Oscar. He was ashamed of himself. He was a more serious person than he had imagined. Perhaps the studio knew what it was doing, typecasting him the way it had. He began to feel not so much oppressed by the Devil as saved by God, taught a necessary lesson. When Damask got through on the mobile, weeping, he was kind and fatherly. All things pass.

For two and a half weeks the story ran before the editors said enough, within which time lives and fortunes changed. Then someone showed up in LA from the Seychelles – a beach guard. He came with snapshots, which could not be denied. Elspeth in déshabille on holiday, embracing her PR man on the beach. He was slipping a slice of pineapple from his lips to hers, and they were not pretty lips. Behind them one of the little girls had her hand to her mouth in horror. One final outburst, the manic squeal of a balloon deflating, shooting round the room. And the life just went out of the story. The goods and the bads became blurred, and that was a disappointment. And another story broke: an air crash and a royal divorce, and no-one cared about the Vale-Edens any more. The thick, wedged envelopes from the cuttings agencies became thinner, thinner, slowed to a trickle through the family letterboxes, stopped.

Caledonia reappeared. While in hiding, she had found a new rich lover, twenty years younger than herself. A Scottish landowner, a laird of lairds, bored by fog and cold, wanting warmth and central heating, too grand and rich to be afraid of publicity. He came south with her; they married and set up house together.

Velvet and Damask went home to their mother; Velvet developed ME and had to be waited on by Caledonia hand and foot. At the end of the year she got better and after the horror of *I Murdered My Unborn Babies* became first, a serious feature writer, then an almost intellectual columnist, and actually married a banker. All the sisters came to the wedding. Satin had become spokesperson on ethics for an international drug company and earned a fortune, Georgette had given up detecting art forgeries and ran a gallery, and Chenille had given up law to write legal thrillers. The lot of them, in fact, were in the media. If you can't beat them, join them.

One day Damask got a phone call from Ariel. He was in Scotland, playing the lead in a major Hollywood special effects movie. He was an alien on the run; a kindly being who could control the weather. It meant big money. His agent had been wrong. He had a week off. They went to Edinburgh together and saw the castle and ate Arbroath smokies, and to Glasgow to see the Mackintosh chairs, and to the Isle of Skye to taste the home-made whisky, and to Dundee where they stood on the Tay Bridge and recited McGonagall, and as far down as York to visit the Roman Museum there. They shared a bed for warmth and companionship but nothing else. Damask had stopped smoking, and was training as a photographer. Ariel kept dropping in at Catholic chapels for a quick *Ave Maria*, but Damask didn't mind that. Once he'd put up with her smoking: now she put up with his religion. They had a wonderful week and when they got off their respective flights, he at Aberdeen and she at Heathrow, no-one took the slightest notice.

Smoking Chimneys

I am by nature a solitary person. If I were to advertise in a newspaper for a partner – and who hasn't at one time or another been tempted? – the entry would go something like this: *Reclusive blonde young woman (thirty-two), workaholic, sharp-tongued, hates company, children, loud music, country walks, wining and dining, likes crosswords, seeks similarly inclined male. No smokers, no Viagra users.* Nevertheless, when Marigold asked me to Badger House for the Christmas weekend I was glad of the invitation. Aloneness, that normally enviable and superior state, can around Christmas feel suspiciously like loneliness.

'You don't have to talk to anyone,' said Marigold. 'You can sit in a dark corner among the pine needles and wrapping paper, and pretend to be the au pair. My family won't even notice you, I promise.'

Well, I thought, don't be too sure of that. I can make people notice me if I put myself out. I share an office with Marigold: fortunately she, like me, is a silent person. We are both the offspring of noisy, ducal families, who, having taken to drugs in the sixties, dropped babies like flies and failed to make proper arrangements for their upbringing beyond sending them off to boarding schools. Now, for both of us, just to be in a quiet room alone is bliss: I for one seek it perpetually. In the same way, my mother says, those children who were kept short of butter in World War II grew up to slaver it on their bread for ever. Thus she excuses her own obesity.

*   *   *

77

My mother decamped with a movie maker to California some four years ago, and one by one my younger siblings drifted after her – I was the oldest of five. I could have gone out to join this new ersatz family of mine for the festive season but I declined. I mention this so you don't feel sorry for me or see me as the kind of person who is short of places to go to at Christmas. It's just that I sometimes fail to want to go wherever it is on time, and then end up miserable. I do like to feel I have removed myself from company, not that company has removed itself from me.

I also need, I think, to point out to you that the benefits of my temperament are such that my confinement in this prison cell is not in itself onerous. Don't feel pity for me on this account. I have faith in justice and assume that I will be found innocent of a murder I did not commit, and in the meantime I rejoice that I won't be expected to go to some party to see in the New Year. I understand that here in Holloway we just all sit silently and separately in our cells on the dreaded night, and contemplate the past and the future. Suits me.

No indeed, sir, I did not murder Lady Hester Walpole Delingro. Let me tell my story in my own way, as is normally done, from the beginning. Or are you in some great hurry? Perhaps you Legal Aid solicitors are on piecework? No? When I hear from my mother she'll have the best lawyers in town take over my case: it's just that she's staying oddly silent, so you will have to put up with me for the time being.

Badger House! My heart sank on seeing the place, at the wrong end of a two-hour standing journey on a crowded train, which smelt of alcohol and mince pies. Marigold had showed me photographs of her family home. It looked lovely enough in the summer, with rampant nature creeping up to its door, but in midwinter, standing isolated and denuded of foliage, you could see it all too clearly for what it was. One of those badly sited, dull, ostentatious houses built at the end of the eighteenth century by people with more money than sense. For one thing the house was situated too near the brow of the hill – downdraught would be bound to make the fires smoke – and faced north. Wall the sloping kitchen garden as you might to keep off the bitter wind, there would be endless troubles with drainage and slugs.

Badger House – badgers prefer valleys, actually, but I daresay occasionally wander – was the property of Marigold's grand-mother, Lady Hester Walpole Delingro. (Delingro had the money, she had the title; the marriage – her third – lasted six weeks.) But she kept the name, if only because it stood out in the gossip columns, and she loved a smart party, as did all the family. It was here at Badger House, every Christmas, that the whole vast, noisy, extroverted, once-Catholic Walpole family assembled to celebrate if not exactly the birth of Jesus (they had all long ago forgotten Him, except perhaps for Marigold's ninety-three-year-old great-aunt Cecilia, who was a nun, but whose convent, these days, let her out for Christmas), then their survival as a unit for another year.

The taxi let me out by the great front door: it was half past five on Christmas Eve, heavy crimson damask curtains had been closed, but there was an urgent sense of movement and life behind them. I rang three times and no-one answered. I pushed the door open, and went inside. What noise, what brightness, what Babel! I would have turned and left at once and taken my chances on a train back to the city but the taxi had already gone.

In the great hall someone played a grand piano, honky-tonk style, and a group of adults gathered round to sing Christmas carols out of tune: rivalled only by a cluster of teenage children singing the pop world's seasonal offering, *Have Yourself a Hip-Hop Xmas and Other Tunes*, and jigging about in ecstasy frenzy. Decorations were plentiful but without discrimination, organisation or style.

Dull paper streamers, of the kind made by earnest children, hung droopily over great distances from wall to wall. Vulgar tinsel draped old family portraits, and cheap Woolworth's magic lanterns in gold, silver, scarlet and green hung from chandeliers and doorways wherever the eye fell, without order, without symmetry. Little children ran around to no apparent purpose, the girls dragging Barbie dolls around by their hair, accessories scattering far and wide on the oak floors and never picked up: little boys panicked and shrieked, pursued by clanking and fashionably cursing computer toys they seemed unable or unwilling to control. Fires had been lit in all the rooms and as I had predicted, smoked. I was obliged to pull my scarf up to cover my nose and mouth and breathe through that to save myself from the worst of the fumes.

As I stood dazed and horrified I was approached by Lady Hester. I recognised her from the pages of *Tatler* and *Hello!* (Yes, she stooped to *Hello!* I assumed that there were financial problems.) Lady Hester was a woman well into her eighties, still tall and gaunt, bright-eyed and vigorous for her age. She wore black leggings and a waisted silver jacket, which would have looked better on a cheerleader. Old legs are old legs and look skinny, not slender, and that's that.

'You must be Marigold's friend Ishtar,' she said. (My parents had been deeply into Indian mysticism around the time of my birth.) 'Welcome! I'm sorry about so much smoke. Very cunning of you to think of the scarf. As soon as the fireplaces warm up, it gets better. It's a problem we have every year. Part of the ritual!' And just as Marigold came running up, I was saying, 'Personally, I'd abandon the ritual and put in central heating,' which Lady Hester obviously did not react well to, if only because it was sensible advice. But Marigold hugged me and said, 'Ishtar, please don't tell the truth, remember it's Christmas. Let us have our illusions, if only for the weekend.'

*   *   *

I had never seen Marigold like this, as if she were six again, tippy-toed. Her usually pale horse-face was flushed and she looked almost pretty, tinsel in her hair, wearing a low-cut black top which left a bra strap showing, knocking back the punch as if it were Diet Coke, hotly pursued by the Seb she sometimes talked about, a young man with tendrilly-golden curls clinging to a finely sculpted head.

'This is Ishtar,' she was saying to Seb. 'I share an office with her. She had nowhere to go for Christmas, so we've all agreed she can be this year's Outsider.'

Well, thank you very much, Marigold. Who wants to be labelled as an Outsider, an object of pity, the one invited to the Christmas festivities because otherwise they'd be on their own? It seemed to me a gross abuse of the laws of hospitality and if thereafter I did not behave like a perfect guest who can be surprised? Nor had I liked the way Seb's eye had drifted over me and away, even before he heard me described as the Outsider. Prada, to the uninformed eye, can sometimes look too plain, too dowdy.

But what did I do, you ask me, to justify some twenty people and a host of sticky little children bearing false witness against me? Firstly, remember that the Walpoles as a family are notoriously mentally unstable: they have become so through generations of mismarriage, drug-taking, miscegenation and eccentric social mobility. Rest assured that a girl who goes to the best school in the country is more likely to end up with a Rastafarian or a truck driver than a stockbroker or a prince. Secondly, although Marigold maintained that what kept the family together was their adoration of Lady Hester and their reverence for the Christmas ritual, it seemed just as likely to me that all were simply hoping to be first in line for a legacy. Or is this too cynical of me? I hate to be thought cynical, when all I am is realistic.

What did I do to annoy so much? Very little, by my standards, but what I did I made sure was noticeable. Shown to an attic room with three makeshift truckle beds in it, with twigs and soot tumbling down into the empty fireplace every time the door slammed – the chimneys were not even netted against the rooks – I explained that I would have insomnia if I did not have a bedroom to myself, and that I needed sheets and blankets, not a duvet, and after much apology and discussion ended up sleeping in Marigold's room, and her on the sofa under the Christmas tree, so that Seb was unable to join her that night – I am sure that had been their plan – and the children did not get their normal sneak 2.00 a.m. preview of the presents. People should not invite guests if they cannot house them adequately.

Earlier I'd found a gold dress in Marigold's wardrobe and put it on. Well, she offered.
'Isn't that one too tight?' she asked. 'The navy would be more you.'
'Oh no,' I said. It was tight, of course, and incredibly vulgar too, but what does an Outsider know or care? I draped myself round Seb once or twice and pole-danced round a pillar for his entertainment. Then I let him kiss me long and hard under the mistletoe, while everyone watched. Marigold fled from the room weeping and flinging her engagement ring on the floor. People who put up pagan mistletoe at a Christian ceremony must expect orgiastic behaviour.

Before going to bed I used the machines in the utility room to launder the damp towels I had found on the floor of Marigold's bathroom. I had searched the linen cupboard for fresh ones but found none; what else could I do? The washing machine was faulty – there was no warning note to say so: is one meant to read the mind of machines? – and overflowed and caused some kind of electrical havoc to the kitchen electrics, so the deep freeze and the fridges cut out. This was not discovered until well into the next day. People who stuff turkeys with packets of frozen pork and herbs deserve what they get, and must risk E-coli if the power goes off.

*   *   *

On Christmas morning, leaving Seb in the bed, I rose early when only small hysterical children were about, and restrained the ones who assaulted me too violently, or made me sticky, and escorted them by ear to where their parents slept in their drunken stupors, and asked them to take charge of their offspring. People should not have children if they do not have the moral wherewithal to control them.

I spent the morning assuring enquirers that Seb was nothing worth Marigold having, and in all probability, was not her cousin but her half-brother, and preserving the Christmas presents from the ravages of the children, standing up to their wails and howls. Then came the adult giving ceremony. The custom was for every adult Walpole to bring what they called a tree present, a gift acceptable to all ages and genders, to the value of £15, to place it under the Christmas tree, and when the time came to take another out for themselves. Thus everyone came with a gift and left with a gift. It was a system fraught with dangers: simply by taking one out and not putting one in, I caused mayhem. The nun Cecilia, being slowest on her feet, was left without a gift and made a terrible fuss.

Lunch did not happen until three. Some thirty people sat in a triangle formed by three trestle tables. The table setting, I must admit, was pretty enough, and decorated with Christmas crackers and the heavy family silver had been taken out of storage. But thirty! How this family bred and bred! I had been seated at the jutting end of one of the tables, as befitted the Outsider. This did not improve my mood. I declared myself to be a vegetarian just as the three turkeys – one at each side of the triangle – were being carved. People who have thirty to a meal must surely expect a certain proportion of them to be vegetarians. I mentioned the deep freeze débâcle and a number of the guests converted to vegetarianism there and then – all of these, I noticed, had married into the Walpole Delingros; those born as family were hardier.

*   *   *

Next to me was Cecilia, rendered incontinent by the morning's upsets. When all were finally served I enquired of everyone what the strange smell could be. A faulty drain, perhaps? Or one of them? A few rose to their feet and the children, seeing the adults rise, found the excuse to leave their chairs and run hither and thither, sniffing around under the table, overexciting the dogs, and pulling crackers out of turn. People should look after the elderly properly and make sure they do not drink too much or lose control of their bladders.

It was at this point that Lady Hester Delingro rose to her feet and, pointing across the festive triangle at me, arm fully extended, asked me to leave her table since it was clearly so unsatisfactory to me. I too rose to my feet.

'Thank you for making me your Outsider,' I said, 'at the annual feast of the Walpole Delingros. I would hate to be an Insider.'
Which was no more than the truth. Lady Hester's noble horse-face contorted, reddened and went into spasms. She grabbed her heart; her hand fell away, she fell dead into her plate. It was over in five seconds. She can hardly have suffered. Rage and pain get confused. Nevertheless, it was a shock. Silence fell. Even the little children returned to their seats and sat silently.

And then something to me even more shocking occurred. A group of male Walpole Delingros carried off the body to the next room, without so much as checking for a pulse, and stretched it out on the sofa under the Christmas tree. They closed the door, returned to the table, and behaved as if the death had not occurred. Lady Hester's plate was removed, her daughter, Lady Rowan, Marigold's mother, filled her chair. Everyone moved up one, even Cecilia, leaving me isolated, but with one damp, smelly chair next to me.

'Shouldn't someone call a doctor, an ambulance?' I asked. No-one replied. 'You can't just eat Christmas pudding as if nothing had happened.'

*　　*　　*

But they could: curtains were drawn, lights put out, heated brandy poured over hot Christmas puddings to be set ablaze and carried in with due ceremony. I was offered none. It was as if I had ceased to exist. Only after coffee had been made and served and crackers pulled – those the children had left – and the dreadful jokes been read out and scorned, and the ritual been declared complete, were the doctor, the ambulance and the police called.

And that, I swear, is what happened. Even if thirty, not twenty, Walpole Delingros allege that the death happened after dinner, and that I took Lady Hester's head and deliberately banged it into the edge of the marble fireplace during the course of an argument about the cause of smoking fireplaces, so she fell dead, suffering a cardiac infarction on the way down, I cannot help it. This was not what happened. If there is, as you say, a nasty dent on the side of Lady Hester's head why then one of the family did it while she lay dead on the sofa, with a blunt instrument, the better to incriminate me. The Walpole Delingros are famous for sticking together, and I would be the first to admit I got up one or two people's noses, even to the extent of their feeling that prison hereafter would be the best place for me. And others might feel that by being so rude to Lady Hester I had caused her death, and natural justice should prevail. It is not the first time people have borne false witness against me. Or again, perhaps one of their number, finding the old lady was still just about alive, and simply wanting to inherit, finished her off and the others closed ranks and decided to get me, in passing? Or is that too cynical a view of human nature?

It won't work, of course, one of the children must surely blab, or perhaps Marigold will remember she is my friend. I believe she is back with Seb. In the meantime, while I wait for my mother's call, I am happy enough in this cell. But perhaps you could arrange to have *The Times* sent in, so I can do the cross-word? And if you could ask the Governor, or whoever he is, to stop people playing their radios and TVs so loud? Or at any rate to tune them to the same station? I am feeling a little insecure. I am accustomed to having enemies – the honest and righteous always are – but it was my bad judgement to make so many, in one place, and in that particular season. It is never safe to disturb the ritual, however much fun it may be.

Percentage Trust

He came to her out of the desert, like Valentino, wearing not robes but a well-cut coat in camel cashmere. He had a solid gold pin in his lapel, in the shape of a Lear jet. His cravat was pure silk, deep red and bright blue, and his black shoes were pointy and highly polished. She met him at Heathrow; she was waiting and waiting for an uncle from Johannesburg to come out of immigration. He was waiting, similarly, for a business colleague from Lagos.

His face was narrow and his nose aquiline, as if carved by hot winds driving over an arid land. He was perhaps fortyish, but when people are from foreign parts you can never quite tell. He was a member of a Saudi Royal Family, he said; a cousin of the king, but he chose to live in Rome. Though he had offices in London. He loved the way she laughed, he said. The world did not contain enough laughter. His teeth were perfect.

He asked for her telephone number. A girl needs only about 60% trust to part with that. Trust that the man isn't a nutter, and will simply go away if you decide not to continue the acquaintance. She wanted to hear more of the voice. It was soft, and delicately, sweetly accented. She wrote her number down for him, before he was whisked away in a limo with the colleague from Lagos, who was tall, impressive, shiny black, beautifully tailored, wearing rather a lot of gold. She did not really believe he'd call. What would a man who could have, and probably did have, girls with legs up to their navels, big blue eyes and masses of blonde hair, want with her, Elspeth Gray, children's book illustrator, late thirties, living alone and happily in a flat in Camden, if having a problem with the rent?

'Love,' he said, when he called the next day. 'Love. I fell in love with you at first sight. I loved your laughter, I loved your grace, I loved the elegance of your ballerina neck.' A ballerina neck! What her mother had always called, 'your neck the giraffe'. Of course she melted.

'Now how can I help you?' Aziz asked Elspeth. Elspeth's uncle was not to be allowed into the country. His visa was not in order. Aziz said he would take the matter up with the authorities, and did. But her uncle decided to go home anyway. Elspeth felt apologetic to have put Aziz to so much trouble, for nothing.

'My dear,' said Aziz, 'anything in the world I can do for you, I will.' They were having supper at a little Italian restaurant round the corner from where she lived.

A girl needs only 65% trust to have supper with a man; trust that his table manners will be good, his conversation lively, he'll pay his share of the bill and not put her under any kind of future obligation. Elspeth insisted in advance that they both pay their own way, and chose Chez Luigi, where it was cosy and quiet and the food was okay.

'I love this place,' he said, 'I love it because I'm with you. Who wants grandeur, chandeliers and caviar when they can have the simplicity of happiness?'

He ate with care and delicacy; spaghetti wound perfectly round his fork, helped by his spoon. If you lived in Rome, as he explained, you got good at spaghetti. His marriage to an English girl, a sports-shoe heiress, had failed three years back. He had two teenage sons who lived in Canada: he saw them whenever he could, but he was so busy about his cousin the king's business, it was not often enough. Import–export. 'Of what?' she asked, and he laughed, a little, complicit, sexy laugh. 'Not drugs,' he said. 'Don't worry. Gold, diamonds, precious stones.'

He was in disgrace with his family, of course he was, living away from home the way he did, marrying outside his religion, his children lost to them. But he preferred the Western way, though it could break your heart. He had thought after the end of his marriage he would never love again, but now he had met Elspeth. Her laughter had rippled through the Heathrow halls like streams through the stately pleasure domes of Kubla Khan, and worked its magic. Her head had turned, so gracefully.

He made love with the practised care, delicacy and enthusiasm with which he ate. You can always tell from the meal how it will be.

A good girl like Elspeth needs 80% trust to go to bed with a man on the first date, that's if she doesn't love him. Trust that he won't turn out to be a serial killer or try to rape her; that he's not doing it for a dare, or to be revenged on a wife, or to prove to himself that he isn't impotent: in other words that she's unique, that she's somehow involved in this transaction, that she's not just a woman, all women. Trust that he'll be in touch afterwards. Of course if she loves him trust can fall even below 60% and still she'll do it.

Elspeth loved Aziz a little bit before and a lot more after: but for some reason the trust never soared to 95–100%, as you'd expect. As it has to be if you mean to marry. Trust he won't leave you, won't live off you, isn't after your money, your name, your nationality; trust he is what he says.

Not that marriage was mentioned. Good Lord, they'd only known one another a week, and who got married these days anyway? He took her to dinner at the Ritz to celebrate. He paid, with a platinum card. She let him. They ate oysters. He waved to an affluent-looking man two tables away who waved back and smiled.

She introduced him to a friend or so, back home.
'You look so well,' they said, 'and happy, which is the main thing. But he is rather *foreign*.'
'He's very helpful and so polite,' said Elspeth's daughter Angela, who was nineteen and in college, living in York. 'If you married him what fancy relatives I would have! I suppose he is on the level.'
'Why shouldn't he be? Is there any evidence that he isn't?'
'But is there any evidence that he is? Have you met his family, his friends?'

Well no, she hadn't. Nor seen where he lived. Nor been to his offices. He travelled so much. To Paris, to LA, to Hong Kong. He'd call her from these places. Hurry to meet her on his return, to slip between her cool, ironed sheets. Elspeth ironed her sheets. She was a good girl. Her work went swimmingly. She paid off her credit cards. Sexual satisfaction cast a glow over all she did.

But he'd make a date and then just break it without warning. She hated that. She'd leave messages for Aziz on his office answerphone. He'd call back from wherever, full of apologies.
'He has a wife tucked away somewhere,' said her friends, 'that's what it is.'

Trust wavered, and fell to somewhere between 55% and 60%. She almost broke it off. She tried; he wept. He'd been so busy, about his cousin the king's business. And in his country the rules were no different. A woman waited for her man, if she loved him.

'He must love you,' said Angela, 'or why would he bother? It's not as if you had money to steal, or a title to offer, or were a raging beauty. You're just a middle-aged, poverty-stricken illustrator of children's books.' Oh thank you, daughter!

But trust rose again to 70%. He was back in her bed. He'd brought her legal documents, bonds, to prove he was who he said he was. There was his name; there were the columns of figures, descriptions of jewels, pharmaceuticals, so many noughts everywhere, littering the stiff formal pages. She wanted to trust, so she did. She laughed at her own suspicions and he rejoiced in her trust. He borrowed her mobile phone. He'd left his in Rome. The office was so busy: simpler to borrow hers than organise another.

He took her to stay the weekend at Claridge's. They drove down Bond Street in a limousine, and he bought her elaborate designer clothes, evening gowns, low-cut, and a little jewelled bag for £1200. He said it was a cheap throwaway thing.
'But where will I wear these things?' she said.
'I like to show you off,' he said.

That night at dinner at Claridge's she wore a deep red heavy silk gown with a strappy top and no sleeves. People looked at her in admiration.
'You're really meant to wear sleeves when you dine,' she murmured (she'd been so well brought up), but all he said was, 'You have perfect skin; the more you show the better.' And it was true, she realised: she had a skin so white it seemed to glow. She'd covered it up all her life: in dull greens and browns, cotton and denim, anything that was virtuous, not flash. Dull, in fact.

An American crossed over from another table to say hello. Hogan McBride from LA, dealer in fine jewellery.
'Meet my fiancée,' said Aziz, and Hogan kissed Elspeth's hand. 'Perfect for diamonds,' he said. 'White background glow, like white sound on a tape. Such truly pale fingers.' Elspeth could see that her hands were perfect, now that a Bond Street salon

had attended to them: creamed the skin and polished the nails. 'Your hands the claws,' her mother had said.

'I'll certainly think about that,' said Aziz. 'But perhaps better a necklace, to show off the perfect neck.' Hogan nodded and smiled and went on out.

'Fiancée indeed! I haven't said I'll marry you,' said Elspeth. Trust was running at 90%, but a man shouldn't necessarily know it. 'And now I have to get back to real life and finish a commission. I'm late as it is with my deadline, and I have a tax bill to pay.'

Aziz went to see the concierge: something about a limo. Elspeth went upstairs again to collect her coat. He'd left the mobile phone on the bed. It bleeped. Elspeth pressed okay. It was her phone after all. She told herself for all she knew it might be a call for her. But really it was the 10% between 90% and 100% which bothered her. Perhaps it was the wife or girlfriend calling: the one where he was when he wasn't with her. But it was a man's voice: a rich man's voice: she could tell by now. The voices of the rich have an easy confident flow.

'Aziz,' the voice said, 'pick me up at ten tomorrow for Paris. Take the Mercedes, we'll go by Chunnel. I'll need you for the day.' And that was all.

Trust bottomed out at perhaps 35%. She put the phone into her pocket, and when Aziz returned kissed him goodbye as if nothing had happened. Everyone has a different way of dealing with emergencies. Elspeth's was to smile and hold her fire while she worked the parameters of danger out. Screaming and shouting was simply put on hold. Aziz arranged to meet her for lunch the next day, at Chez Luigi. She had a 25%-ish kind of miserable idea it would be one of the occasions when he didn't turn up and made his excuses later.

She went home and finished her commission. A sweet story about a little girl and a computer with a heart. Then by judicious punching she got the mobile phone to read out the caller numbers over the previous month. They ran at the rate of five or six a day. She checked out their area locations. She marked the map of London; a drawing pin for every number. They were not random; the gold points circled within the wealthier areas of the city. Well, naturally. She tried a few numbers. Secretaries, receptionists, housekeepers, answered. 'Can I speak to Aziz?' met with a polite non-response. She switched off the phone. If she responded to the bleeps he'd know it was in her possession.

She went at lunchtime the next day to Chez Luigi. Aziz did not turn up. She ate her spaghetti alone. She realised how often she did this. She went home, got on with her work and waited for him to call.

The next morning he rang her from a phone box to apologise. He'd had to go to Paris unexpectedly: a diamond deal. He'd call round that evening. He loved her. Trust almost soared again: desire can have that effect. But she made her excuses. If he couldn't come round to her place, he said, much disappointed, would she come to the Dorchester that weekend? Of course! He said, by the by, he'd lost her mobile phone: he was dreadfully sorry. It must have fallen out of his pocket.

She traced the number he'd been calling from. Dial Okay and 1471. A call box in south Hampstead. For its own mysterious reasons, the phone company would not tell her its location. She called the box again and again until a passer-by succumbed, picked up the phone and told her its location. She went and stood outside the phone box and surveyed the street. Across the road was a car-hire firm, called Classy Cars. A fancy place. Limos were parked in the yard. Chauffeurs came and went. Elspeth hung about the phone box for a couple of hours. About the only place in a city where loitering women attract no attention. Presently a car drove up and Aziz got out of it. She almost didn't recognise him at first, in his chauffeur's cap. She went home.

He had a honeymoon suite booked at the Dorchester. He had her new clothes in the wardrobe. She realised he never took her to the same place twice. Since the credit cards were stolen that of course would be unwise. But if you knew the punter's travel plans you could assess the risks. And whoever curtailed a conversation because the chauffeur might be listening?

They were to meet Mr Hogan in the downstairs bar at six-thirty. So she got to the Dorchester late, at six not five, the better to stay out of Aziz's bed. With trust at 10% desire altogether fails. And that 10% is there only as a kind of generalised burnt offering to faith.

She wore the white silk dress, simplicity itself, that had cost £2200. 'You might spill something on it,' he said anxiously. 'I won't,' she said. This dress too was strappy and low-cut. Her neck was so long and elegant and pale, she could see that now. Beautiful, not freakish, just right for diamonds! She understood now why he'd chosen her; of all the women in the world he could so easily have charmed and cheated. She was a good girl, above suspicion, and she had a perfect neck. She felt just a flicker of warmth for him.

They sat and waited for Hogan McBride in a quiet corner of the bar. Hogan strode in; he had just time for a quick drink. His limo was waiting outside, he said; Classy Cars no doubt, thought Elspeth. He put his briefcase on the table, and with his back to the world drew out, layer upon layer, a gold and diamond necklace of great magnificence. He fastened it around Elspeth's neck. Both men breathed deep in admiration.

'Your wedding present,' said Aziz to Elspeth, and to Hogan McBride, 'It hangs about an inch too low. I thought so.'

'It goes back to the workshop at once,' said McBride. 'Leave it to me. Perfection demands perfection!' And he leant forward to unclasp the chain, but with a little gasp Elspeth spilt her red wine all down her white dress, and had to rise and run, benecklaced as she was, burbling about cold water quick, to the ladies' room – and ran straight out the other door, into the lobby extension,

and had the doorman hail a taxi and went home. She changed
into her homey dress and was an altogether different person at
once. Herself. Unrecognisable, as fiancée to a king's cousin. She
switched on the mobile phone. Within the hour it bleeped.

'Bitch, bitch!' he said. 'Where are they?'

'Not in my pocket, not in yours,' said she. 'In a safe deposit in
the bank. I'll go fifty-fifty, but only because I need your help to
sell them on, before I learn the trade.'

'What do I do about Hogan McBride?' he whined, all the stuffing
knocked out of him, taken by surprise. Defeated by a girl!

'Just get out of there quick,' she said. 'And don't go back to
Classy Cars. We'll make new contacts. Do the disappearing trick.'

As a partner in crime she grew to trust him 90%, and the other
10% was just a burnt offering to the Fates, who don't like too
much confidence. But she never went to bed with him again.
The percentages were too fickle. Crime is one thing, love is
another, and much more sensitive.

MAKING DO

How Donna Came to Win the Lottery

Trophy Wife

Live Like a Dog, Alone

Well, I Said

How Donna Came to Win the Lottery

Bad things happen in threes. Good things do too, but we don't notice. 'That's two up and one to go,' we say, after the loo has blocked and the car won't start, 'better be careful!' And then we trip and break a leg. But after two things have gone right, after the gas bill is lower than you expected, after the cat has come home after four days missing, do you wait for the third good thing that day? No. We're not fair to our guardian angels, who do turn up from time to time just to see how we're getting on in their absence. They're like social workers: too many people to look after, too little time to do it in, but they wish us well and do their best.

Donna did try to be cheerful. It wasn't easy. Her boyfriend had dumped her. She was nearly fifty-two and he was sixty-three and you would have thought both would have settled down by now, but no. It had taken her eight years to find him, too, as she told her friends. Now what? Married at eighteen, divorced at thirty-eight (still young and hopeful), on her own for nine years, then at last finding Harry, Harry the retired science journalist, nuclear specialist. Now after four years he said that was enough. No more cinema once a week, walks on Sunday, bed on Saturday. What was wrong with her?

Nothing wrong with you, said her friends, it's him. He was ever so dull, he wasn't right for her, she was too lively for him: she wanted emotion, and passion, and commitment. She loved going out, and all he wanted was a quiet life and to look after his old mother in peace. 'Easier when it's you who does the breaking,' they told her. 'He just got in first so you're smarting.' Yes, she was smarting. She worked for an engineering firm as top book-keeper with eight staff under her and loved it, loved getting everything right, having things exactly so, but even that had suddenly lost its savour.

So the good things happening had to start from a pretty low base, it was true. She was smoking twenty cigarettes a day again, but that hadn't stopped her from putting on ten pounds, and her ankles had begun to swell in the evenings. She would never win a glamorous grandmother competition now, even if her only daughter Margaret wasn't living in Melbourne and swore she didn't want children, even if such things as glamorous grand-mother competitions still existed. They probably weren't politi-cally correct any more. She knew nothing, she was out of the swing of things, she was just too old. She'd been dumped, no man would look at her again.

Come on now, said her friends, cheer up. There's more to life than men. It was wonderful how friends rallied. But why did they say that? Why didn't they just say you're still Donna the Wild Card, Donna the Heartbreaker, Donna the Too Beautiful and Picky for Her Own Good? Could an extra ten pounds do all that to you? Well, perhaps more like fourteen, it depended where you stood on the scales. Ten days now since Harry had broken it off and not a word.

On the eleventh day Donna got up early and bravely and sang 'Somewhere Over the Rainbow' as she made coffee and wondered where her guardian angel was. She'd seen him once as a child, mystic, wonderful, standing at the end of the bed smiling, radiant in white, and the next day she'd got into the grammar school. And again when she was seventeen the night before she went to the party where she met Walter whom she was destined to marry and have Margaret with, and live with for twenty happy years until he had an affair and the friends said she had to divorce him and she did. She'd had fleeting pains in her heart ever since but the doctor said it was indigestion: it happened when you got older.

She had a feeling her guardian angel had been around the night before. She'd woken up around midnight and there'd been a kind of flickering white sheen at the end of the bed. But when she mentioned this to her friend and colleague Alison, who was sleeping over after a failed hot date, Alison had laughed and said surely she knew about the laser show.

'I went to bed at ten,' said Donna.

'Trust you,' said Alison. 'The sky was brilliant until midnight, the whole city was lit up, and then the closing fireworks would have woken you up, and by the by I called the hypnotherapist yesterday and he has a cancellation at five-thirty this evening: you can leave work half an hour early, for once.'

'Why do I need a hypnotherapist?' asked Donna, in some surprise. They were eating breakfast and she'd made a lot of toast for Alison, who was thin as a rake and always hungry. To keep her friend company she put butter instead of low-fat margarine on her own toast and spread it thickly with lemon curd.

'What do you want to cure me of? A broken heart?'

'Come off it,' said Alison. 'Your heart isn't broken. Your pride is hurt, that's all. Harry just got in first. He wasn't any good for you, he was much too dull and old, everyone knows. No, it's your smoking. Now that's really a worry. Tony the hypnotherapist cures the smoking habit. Everyone we know goes to him.'

'What does it matter if I die an early death?' asked Donna. You could tell what kind of mood she was in when she stopped singing. Alison raised her eyes to heaven and Donna remembered that it was Alison who had been the friend most determined she shouldn't put up with Walter's infidelities and must be strong and true to herself and get a divorce.

*   *   *

But you can't blame friends for the advice they give you. It's you who take it. They have your best interests in mind, it's just they're not *you*. And perhaps they do want you for themselves and men do get in the way. Most of Donna's friends were divorced or single or had passing affairs with people from abroad who were just passing through or hoping for asylum. Who had great bodies even though you only understood half of what they said. Which was all to the good, everyone agreed. The friends had given up hope of romance long ago, as Donna could never find it in her heart to do. She thought they rather envied her, even while they mocked her.

Oh Donna, they said, you are sweet. There's no such thing as true love, written in the stars. Most of us get over that at twenty. When they mocked, her stutter would come back, just a little. She'd had the stutter since she was seven when the elastic of her knickers snapped and they fell down round her ankles at the bus stop. And a group of boys had noticed and pointed and laughed and it had got round the class. Most embarrassing moment.

She'd never told anyone that, not the doctor who tried to treat the stammer at the time and certainly not her parents. She never quite addressed the memory head-on. If her mind got anywhere near it she'd feel herself growing hot and quickly send her thoughts off in another direction. Little sections of the brain you learn how to bypass! As if she was a child in a dream fast turning into a nightmare, managing at the last moment to turn it in a positive direction, give the thing a happy end. She could do that when she was small – control her own dreams.

'I suppose I might as well go,' said Donna. 'But supposing I get even fatter because I stop smoking? Suppose he seduces me and then hypnotises me to forget all about it? And remember Angela who went to him and had to be carted off to the loony bin.'
'Excuse me,' said Alison. 'You mean the psychiatric ward, but only for a week, and then care in the community.'

'Sorry,' said Donna. 'Okay, not loony bin.' They were all a bit like that, the friends. Determined to have the right thoughts at the right time. They'd let nothing incorrect pass.

'I always thought that was because of the hypnotist,' she persisted. 'Sure, Angela stopped smoking but he told her it was easy, so when she got depressed and anxious and twitchy she didn't believe us when we explained it was just nicotine withdrawal, and thought she was going mad and tried to top herself.'

'It was a cry for attention,' said Alison. 'Not a serious attempt and nothing to do with the hypnotist, and don't you think that's a bit brutal? Top herself?'

'Sorry,' said Donna.

Then the post came and with an A-level result. Donna had got an A in Art History. What with Harry and one thing and another she'd forgotten all about the exam, and the results coming through. When you were young summers took for ever. When you were fifty-three and your sixty-three-year-old boyfriend dumped you they whizzed by. But that was nice, getting an A and the most tremendous luck.

'That's wonderful,' said Alison. 'Think of that, an A. But what are you going to do with it? I mean, what's the point?'

'Dunno,' said Donna. 'Some people like catching butterflies, I like collecting A levels.'

'I don't know anyone who likes catching butterflies,' said Alison. 'What a cruel and irresponsible thing to do. So many species are becoming extinct, as it is, what with insecticides and pollution.'

Donna ate another slice of toast thickly spread with lemon curd and Alison said you'll never get thin that way, and off they went to work together in Donna's little car. Donna could tell Alison was a little peeved about the A level, though Alison would have got a starred A-plus any time if she wanted, not just an A like

Donna. They left the car at the garage next to the office for its MOT, and Alison said it will never get through, that old wreck of a thing, it's positively anti-social. You need to buy a smart little runabout. Like mine, red and sexy and undefeated.

'P-p-p-perhaps I will,' said Donna. The stutter still put in an appearance every now and then if she was upset, or there were things she wanted to say but couldn't quite bring herself to say. The ps were the worst and the ks. K-k-k for knickers, she sometimes thought.

The car passed its MOT when she collected it that evening. Guardian angel, thank you. I knew it was you at the end of the bed.

'Great little car, that,' said the mechanic. 'Don't even dream of getting rid of it, it will go on for ever.'

She went to the hypnotist and he gave her a session telling her how horrible smoking was, and how disgusting and all the things she knew anyway. He was hopeless. She could have sworn she didn't go into any kind of trance. She remembered very clearly him saying do you want me to do something about your stutter while I'm at it? Stutter? Had she stuttered? For some reason he took her back to the time at the bus stop when her knickers had fallen down and she had neatly stepped out of them and put them in her pocket.

She got home at eight and there was a message from Harry on the answerphone saying he'd really missed her and could they start again? She called him back.

'Okay,' she said. Not even o-k-k-k-kay. Half a love affair is better than none.

'I'd really like us to get married,' he said.

'We could be partners, I suppose,' she said, cautiously, and not even p-p-p-partners.

'We could give living together a try.'

That evening she won £10 in the lottery. Three good things, and one extra for luck. That was no laser show last night, she thought, that was my guardian angel. We all have them, they're just over-worked.

Trophy Wife

I spent two years in a Greek prison for the impulsive sin of hatred, not for any real crime. It was not too bad: it was even a rest. The hours which once I spent on my hair, my figure, my complexion and my make-up were at last available for introspection. I had lost my title as trophy wife.

Most of us have someone we hate. It shouldn't be so, but it is. With women it's usually some rival in love, someone they once saw as an inferior – older, perhaps, or fatter – who has nonetheless managed to steal their man. With men it's some low-grade business rival or a dullard bank manager who once had the nerve to stop them making the millions they deserved. But while hate is reserved for the inferior, all bow down to the leader of the pack. I've known men happy to hand their wife over to the big boss for the night, and bear no grudge. A size 16 woman will bow gracefully out of the mating contest when a size 10 comes along. To those that hath shall be given, as the Bible says. It's the reversal of the proper order of things that so upsets.

Max and I managed to upset each other quite dreadfully one midsummer night, on the occasion of the office party. Max's recent acquisition of the Greenwich Dome demanded a celebration. Max was my wealthy husband, I, Marianna, was his fourth, and trophy, wife.
'I'll give the staff a party,' Max said. 'It's cheaper than giving them bonuses.' Rich men are rich, I sometimes think, because they are mean.

'Let's use the yacht,' I said. 'It's been sitting on a marina in the Aegean for more than a year, burning up money to no purpose. We can fly everyone down for the weekend in the private jet. We can finally take *Marianna* out to sea.'

Ocean cruising has never really been my idea of fun: people who like lying about on decks tend to be on the dull side. The women are routinely narcissistic, the men routinely lecherous and the conversation tends to be more about cosmetic surgery or how many tentacles an octopus has than Rilke or Kierkegaard. But if Max felt he needed to own one of the more expensive yachts in the world, then I'd go along with it and not complain. I was trophy wife. The yacht was called after me, but otherwise was nothing to do with me: it was Max's property and Max's alone. My financial rights were strictly limited by pre-nuptial agreement: his experiences of three divorces had been bitter.

Being a trophy wife is altogether different from being a bimbo. The bimbo can be as noisy, sluttish and silicone bouncy as she wishes – in fact the more the better. A trophy wife on the other hand must keep her own likes and dislikes to herself: she must be socially adept, always well groomed, talented and charming, never bored, always gracious. It helps for her to have a measure of fame in her own right, or a title, or a family name others recognise. I had no title or celebrity name, but before my marriage I had been a successful portrait painter and once even painted the Queen of England. That was enough for me to qualify as trophy wife in the highest circles in the land.

Life is a matter of reciprocal rights and duties. Max provided money, security, and the sexual charisma of power, albeit he was old, pudgy and squat. I provided beauty, charm, entertainment, aesthetic competence and comfort to his old bones. It seemed to me to be a more than satisfactory arrangement. We liked each other and were, or so I'd thought, good enough companions.

As to sex, there was some token activity between us, but for the most part we went our own ways. Max spent an illicit night here and there, with one beauty or another. What rich and powerful man does not? Surely that is why he has become what he is, to be top dog, to have first sexual pickings? As for me, I'd choose a personal trainer here, a film star there, young muscled men, but more for form's sake than any real passion. Max liked to feel I was appreciated by the pick of the crop. The notion fed his vanity.

The stars glittered in a navy sky as the yacht slithered through the Aegean waters. All went well until, on the Saturday night, we ate at long tables placed round the deck, alfresco, the table-cloths made of paper, deliberately casual. The usual thing – lobsters, champagne, nothing original: some of the guests were sadly unused to wealth: website designers and secretaries sat next to financiers and arms dealers. It was, after all, an office party. One puts up with them. The scent of flowers drifted across the ocean. It was unfortunate that a consignment of blooms brought on board just before we left port was found to be swarming with tiny spiders. Since some of the poorer guests were Buddhists or environmentalists and could not bear to see little creatures squashed or sprayed, the spiders ran riot. The rich, left to their own devices, are not so squeamish.

Max sat at the end of one of the tables and I sat next to him. On Max's other side sat his senior secretary, Vera Monkavitz, a rather obnoxious young woman, famous throughout the company for her efficiency. She was fleshy and pallid and wore a revoltingly low-cut red velvet dress. She had a soppy winsome smile and looked up at Max with trusting devotion. She helped him crack a lobster's claw which he could perfectly well have done for himself and then hooked out some of the flesh for him as if he were a child. He had a silly smile on his face and smacked his lips together. The boat took one of those lurches boats sometimes do and the waiter stumbled and the hem of the tablecloth was swept up and I could see my husband's hand creeping up between his secretary's cellulosed thighs. Had Vera Monkavitz been beautiful, elegant, or titled, I could have forgiven the offence: had she been Orlanda the opera singer or Bambi, the Count's bit of totty, both on board that night, I could have endured it, but Vera Monkavitz from the office! How badly it reflected upon me! His hand was equidistant between Vera's thighs and mine and he had chosen Vera's. The tablecloth fell again, but I had seen what I had seen, and felt a fury and upset far beyond anything this dull and tawdry situation demanded. That creeping hand of Max's was mine by rights, not hers, she was not worthy of it.

A trophy wife cannot afford to show her jealousy. It is beneath her dignity. So I did what I could. I rolled the menu into a spill which I then lit in the flame of a candle. As if by accident I brushed the lighted spill past Vera's hair before setting it to the edge of the tablecloth. The weather had been hot and dry. The tablecloth flared up and flames raced down the table between plates and glasses, to little cries of alarm and surprise from the guests. It was all most satisfactory, though alas, Vera's husband, a weedy computer nerd called Paul, had rushed to her side all too soon to put out the flames in her hair. The crew very soon had the fire under control, but some damage was done to the deck, and in some places nasty black smoke lines stained the paintwork.

'What on earth did you do that for?' asked Max, when all was quiet again.
'Such a dull evening,' I said. 'I thought your staff deserved a little entertainment.'
'You've done at least $50,000 worth of damage,' he complained, though what was $50,000 to a man like Max? I was upset and hurt, for all the careless tossing of my head, and said so.
'A spider had run up her leg,' he said, all injured innocence. 'And my hand was following it, to catch it for her, that was all.'

That was so absurd it might even have been true, but I had my grievance and I would not weaken.

'You love your boat more than me, and you love Vera more than your boat,' I said. I who had never used the word before now wanted him to say it, but of course it is never said when most you want it. Love, love, love. We all want what we can't have. 'See that she's fired,' I said, and she was.

She came to me the next day as I lay in my deck chair by the pool, with the Aegean islands drifting by, and begged to keep her job. Something about length of service and insurance, and being pregnant, but I didn't listen. She was put off at the next island to make her own way home. I insisted that her dull little husband stay on board or lose his job too: someone had to look after the computers. That night I took him into my bed, just to show her who was who round here. He was too dazzled by the honour of my invitation to refuse.

Max came into the cabin, looking for me, as I knew he would, and found us together. He dragged me out of bed. I thought I was perfectly safe: trophy wives cannot be seen with bruises. I assumed, in any case, that the full blast of his rage would be directed not towards me but towards Paul, so very much his inferior. That was the way things worked.

'You'd better be careful,' I said to the wretched creature as I left. 'Check your brake cables before getting into your car: don't stand too near the edge at the Metro, or your little wife will be a widow.' A rich man's enmity can be dangerous.

But Max surprised me. I was not to get off so lightly. We were alone on deck. How beautifully the sea glimmered in the moonlight. I let down my red hair and Max accused me of being like Circe, who turned men into brute beasts and would not let them feel love.

'Why Paul?' he asked. 'You can't have fancied him, so why? So you can tell his poor bloody wife about it?'

'I wouldn't stoop to tell her,' I said, 'but I'll certainly see she finds out.'

'You know who you remind me of?' he said, his face black. 'My mother. You are turning into my mother. You are spiteful, vicious, and full of hate.'

I remembered then what I had forgotten – that Max hated his mother. Now when a man hates his mother he hates the source of life itself, and no normal rules apply. He marries you because you are not like his mother, sets about turning you into his mother, and when he's succeeded he leaves you, and tries again with someone else. Before I married Max I was a perfectly nice person, and now I was not, I was horrid.

Fire is a cleansing thing. It propitiates the Gods. In the night Max laid a trail of fuel and set fire to his own yacht. The guests were brought screaming from their beds and had to take to the lifeboats. A fire at sea is a spectacular sight. A funeral pyre for everyone's fine hopes.

'How did this happen?' asked the policeman in Athens, when finally, rescued at sea, we hit dry land.

'My wife did it,' Max said, pointing at me. 'She's unbalanced, obsessively jealous. She has a history of this kind of thing.'

And of course everyone had seen my first impulsive act of hate, setting fire to the tablecloths. Who was going to believe me? What a scandal! The newspapers loved it. I, who'd once painted the Queen of England, an arsonist! Burnt down my own yacht! *Marianna Medea*, they called me, though thank heavens there were no children involved. I did not even try to defend myself. It would have been hopeless. I received a two-year sentence and served it in Greece. Max divorced me in my absence, the pre-nuptial agreement nullified because I now had a criminal record. He saved himself millions, and moved on to his fifth trophy wife, the opera singer Orlanda. Such a nice woman, but I don't know how long for. He claimed on the fire insurance for the yacht. What an opportunist that man was! I had to admire him, but I was better off not married to him.

Live Like a Dog, Alone

She thought about what he had just said. 'Now I live like a dog, alone.' It seemed, as a statement, unnecessarily gloomy. But then so did he. His shoulders hunched over the wheel. The back of his neck was dirty. It was five in the morning. He slammed his taxi round corners, not slowing down at the approach, as driving instructors liked to think people did, but speeding up. He enjoyed the squeal of tyres well enough, it seemed, the making of his mark on empty streets, just not enough to compensate for the way his fate had brought him to this end – a refugee, living alone in a strange land. She decided not to put it to him that actually dogs did not live alone, but with human families. Perhaps the poor beasts he was accustomed to, in Kosovo, did indeed all skulk in sheds or live on the street. Certainly, from his analogy, dogs did not enjoy much honour in his homeland.

'But you could look at it another way,' she said, from the back of the cab. 'You could say you lived alone, like an eagle. In a mountain eyrie, proud, triumphant, lord of all it surveys. It doesn't have to be like a dog.' She felt duty-bound to cheer him up. She wondered what he looked like. She'd taken no notice when he turned up to collect her from Casualty, summoned by the grimy FreePhone in reception. He was just the cab driver, darkish and short, an identity tag hung around his neck, calling out her name. Now she had only the back of his neck to go by, and the single, casual, long-fingered hand on the wheel; one hand, as if he would not accord these empty city streets the privilege of his full attention. Fortyish, she supposed: thin black hair, greasy and in need of a wash, a dreadful shapeless thick sweater in grey knitted nylon. A sad sulky voice, a broken accent. He went through a red light. She fastened her seat belt, taking care to be quiet about it. She did not want to offend his feelings by the click, the suggestion that she did not trust him to get her home safely.

'But every eagle has a mate,' he said, not at all persuaded by her smile. 'A family, a nest, eggs. I have no-one, Miriam. You have to believe me. I am no better than a dog.'

How did he know her name? She realised she was still wearing her name badge. She'd been take into Casualty by ambulance, straight from the conference hall, duty done – she'd been the keynote speaker – *Stress, the New Pandemic* – her heart racing in overdrive, 170 beats the minute, requiring medical intervention before it could calm down again. Too much adrenalin.

She was a regular at the hospital: a matter of routine to the staff and herself. It happened every few months. She'd get there, normally by taxi – it was others who insisted on ambulances – they'd not waste time, whisk you through triage, strip you off and lay you bare on a trolley, wire you up, thrust in a canula, inject into a vein – the drug stopping the heart for a few nasty, choking seconds, letting it start up again in its proper, regular, steady beat. Then they'd let you go, back into the world, or as soon as the duty doctor could be re-found to sign you out. Only healthy hearts did it, or so they said. Only healthy hearts could stand the strain. But tonight a new doctor had been over-scrupulous, wouldn't take her word for anything: they'd done blood tests and she'd had to lie on her trolley for hours waiting for results to come back from wherever. It was well after four in the morning before she was out, then twenty minutes waiting for the cab. And she had to be at a meeting by ten in the morning. A couple of hours' sleep and that would be it.

*   *   *

She took the name badge off and put it in her bag. Such an enforced informality: people you had never met required to address you as if you and they were on first-name terms: as if they had some existing relationship with you when they had not. It was part of the general feel-good conspiracy, thus to turn colleagues into family and friends. So you never felt alone in a crowded room, and all evenings were enchanted. Only it wasn't like that. You used the names and disremembered their owners, and ended up in hospital.

'Okay then, not an eagle,' she conceded. 'Try saying live like a lion, alone.' But that wouldn't work either: anyone from anywhere would know lions lived in family groups. 'Live like a tiger, alone,' she quickly amended. No-one knew much about the social life of tigers: or at any rate she didn't. This was an absurd conversation. They screamed round the base of the Telecom Tower. She lived in St John's Wood in an elegant house, as he would soon discover. While he lived, as he'd told her, in a single room in Hackney. Like a dog, alone. He'd been in Britain for three years: he'd left Kosovo just before the war, seeing what was about to happen. She hadn't liked to ask him if he were Muslim or Christian; how could she understand the complexities of whichever answer he gave? The question would be an impertinence. Nor did she like to ask him if he was in the country legally. Probably not. He was taking fewer and fewer red lights seriously. She could see the quite acute need to keep him calm and happy. They might meet quite a lot of traffic on the Marylebone Road, even at this hour.

It was her instinct to cheer people up, in any case. Pollyanna to her bones. The habit had driven her husband mad: she suspected it was the real reason he'd left. Dire events, illness, redundancy, impending bankruptcy – and Miriam's only reaction, he'd complained, mimicking her as he slammed out, was to be positive, brave, make the best of things, take a long-term view. He couldn't stand the stoic common sense a moment longer. What he'd needed, it seemed, was drama: the rending of garments and shrieks and wails of despair at every terrible new turn of events as he created them. He'd run off with an English actress, hysterical, volatile and beautiful, with a drug problem she told everyone about, and left Miriam penniless. As soon as she was in a position to make money, she had. Now she ran a successful nursing agency, and had been voted Businesswoman of the Year. How he'd mocked that: Miriam the looker-afterer. He'd gone back to the courts, asking for alimony now she was so rich and famous. Miriam's friends had been outraged, but all Miriam said was, 'Sauce for the wife must be sauce for the husband. These are the days of gender equality,' and had paid up.

The driver said that tigers lived in prides, like lions. A tiger was only alone when stalking his prey. She said why had she never seen film of it, then, and he said perhaps tigers were more dangerous to get near than lions. He asked her if she lived alone, and she said no, she lived with her husband. She wasn't sure why she lied, other than this mountain man from Kosovo might suggest he came in for a coffee when she paid the fare. 'He'll be waiting up for me,' she added, unnecessarily.

'And I have no-one.' He was reproachful.

'But you have friends, surely.' She wanted to shake him.

'Oh yes, I have friends,' he said. 'But it's not the same.'

'Look,' she said, 'one day someone comes along and everything changes, just like that.' It did too. And changed back pretty quickly in her experience, but why burden him with detail. 'You'll meet some girl and the good times will begin.'

'Girls don't like me,' he said. 'They come near and then they bounce away as if we were magnets with the same pole.'

She thought that was rather poetic. For all she knew back home with the lonely dogs he'd been a professor of physics. Then she felt irritated. 'Wash your neck,' she almost said, 'clean your nails, stop going through red lights, take off that depressive sweater, put on a clean shirt and look cheerful, and you'll find no shortage of girls in the land. If you live like a dog, alone, it's no-one's fault but your own.' But she didn't say it. A minicab driver is a minicab driver. You can't let them into your life though a lot of them will try. And to give people instructions for their own good is to let your life into theirs, and theirs into yours. He could be fresh out of a lunatic asylum.

She said how beautiful London was in the early morning, and he agreed. She said she was tired and had to be up at eight and he sounded surprised and asked if she was still working.

'Why?' she asked, taken aback, 'do I look as if I am past retirement age?' She was fifty-five but most people assumed she was in her forties. If you live alone you can take care of yourself. If you have no children you can afford a face-lift. You have time to read the papers and keep your mind alert and the cut and thrust of business life gives you no time for self-pity. It is self-pity which ages a person. Her husband had always looked older than he was.

The driver said he was no good at judging women's ages, but she could see that in the scale of things he did not place himself beneath her, and he was letting her know it. He might be the driver and she the driven, she might be able to tell him where to go and how to do it, she might be the citizen and he the immigrant, but in basic life terms she was older than he was and she was only a woman. He stopped at the next red light, if only to be able to turn his head and smile at her. He was better-looking than she had imagined. His nose was straight, his eyes were dark and glowing and intimate. His teeth were just fine. The dirt behind his ears could have been nothing but shadow misinterpreted. He took his identity tag from round his neck, and laid it on the seat next to him. He turned off the meter. They continued on their way.

'No creature in nature lives alone,' he said, firmly, 'except a dog.' 'That's absurd,' she said. 'What about moles?' Moles are among the most anti-social of animals. They live underground in single-person households; the young leave home the minute they are able, the sooner to dig themselves in and be solitary. Males make annual reluctant excursions, paddling away through earth with human-like hands, to find a female. They meet, they mate, they fight savagely and quickly return to their own quarters, licking their wounds and their mutual antagonism. They heave up people's lawns just for the hell of it. Miriam said so to the driver. He said he did not believe her.

'This is a nice street,' he said, when he turned into it. 'These are nice houses.' She could see how it would go. She would ask him in, there would be sex, they would end up married, thus he would stop being an illegal and get citizenship. He would use her capital up and turn himself into an arms dealer or some such and then run off with a girl from his own country of his own age.

'Shall I come in for a cup of coffee?' he asked. 'I expect your husband's still asleep. I would never let any woman of mine go to hospital on her own.' It was her weak spot. Only in the hospital, her heart stopping and restarting, did she feel the weight of her loneliness.

She said actually she didn't have a husband, she had just said that, and he parked in the drive behind her little red sports car and they went on into the house. That was her other weakness, wanting to know if her own prognoses would come true.

Well, I Said

'Well, I said to her, well, I said.' I keep finding myself saying this about Laura to our mutual friends: some people just drive you to gossip. She also keeps making me say, 'I told you so,' though I despise myself for it.

For example, over coffee with Nikki I'd find myself saying, 'Well, I said to Laura, "Well," I said, "I told you so. You were just plain stupid about this street person. You cannot take people you don't know into your house just because they look hungry and cold. Of course they're going to run off with the cash for the milkman taking your camcorder with them." What did she expect?' And my voice would get higher and higher with exasperation as I spoke. We all loved Laura to bits but she was just so bad at looking after herself. She would trust other people.

Laura, Nisha, Nikki and I all live in Mortimer Crescent, which is just off Mortimer Street. We all have children at the primary school and part-time jobs and three of us have husbands, and two of us are getting college diplomas which is just about par for the course, these days. And if one or the other of us is ill or upset or in trouble the rest of us close around to help, bend an ear, collect the kids from school, walk the dog, smoke out a wasps' nest, fetch the dry cleaning, that kind of thing. We're lucky, I suppose, and long may it last, it's just that sometimes Laura needed more help than the rest of us: if only because she's so very trusting, believes in the essential goodness of humanity and so on, and it can end you in trouble.

* * *

It was shortly after Laura moved in that I'd found myself saying to Nisha, 'Well, I said to Laura, "Well," I said, "what did you expect? If some woman keeps ringing you up to tell you she's your husband's wife, the least you can do is investigate, not just give her the phone number of the Samaritans and hang up. Problems just don't go away because you don't want to look at them." I told her so but did she listen? No!'

The police had turned up and arrested lovely Stuart for bigamy and taken him away and he got a suspended sentence and went back to the first wife, leaving Laura in a kind of limbo with two children under five. Love and loyalty can take you so far but no further, Nisha and I agreed. Stewart had bigamously married Laura: it wasn't Laura's fault and Stuart, who is charm itself, managed to persuade her, and the court, that it wasn't his either, he just hadn't wanted to hurt anyone's feelings.

He kept giving the children presents – which was why there was a camcorder in the house – but he couldn't actually be persuaded to buy a pair of socks, or pay the mortgage, and had ways of getting round the CSA that you wouldn't dream of. One way or another money in Laura's household was always tight, tighter than it was in ours, and we'd take her children clothes shopping along with ours, so little Carla and James did not feel left behind or left out, and we'd buy plants for her at the garden centre. She was a glorious gardener: she was a good person and anything that grew seemed to know it and repaid her by producing flowers, fruit and vegetables in glorious abundance. Her garden put ours to shame.

So when Stanley Combs moved into the area and started up his new trendy business as a landscape gardener, and Laura got a job fronting his shop in Mortimer Arcade, we were delighted for her. Laura just loved talking gardens to the clients, and brought him in a lot of business with her enthusiasm. The hours were a little difficult for someone with children – ten to six and Saturdays and half-Sundays as well, but she could take any two days she liked off during the week, when his wife Alison would take over. A forty-six-hour week at £4.50 the hour meant £207 a week and Laura could walk to work so there were no fares, and she was off benefit altogether, which is always a great relief. You feel you're in the land of the living again.

And Laura juggled and she managed, as we all do, and Stanley didn't mind, should there be a domestic emergency, if Nikki or I took over the shop on occasion, though we weren't nearly so good at luring the customers in as Laura. We'd have to force the enthusiasm, Laura never did. She really wanted everyone to live surrounded by a dream garden, no matter how expensive these were, and Combs Gardens, let's face it, were.

The thing about Stanley was he was such fun: he was around forty and bulky and had a beard and wore faded old clothes and looked in general arty and special. He'd whirl into the shop in a gale of energy, and laugh and joke and tell stories about his customers, who mostly came from the rich end of Mortimer Road, where all the big houses are. Though he wasn't above doing a humble roof terrace for a little old lady, not that little old ladies are given to roof terraces, but you know what I mean.

He had the gift of looking you in the eye and you'd trust him with your life story, whereupon he'd trust you with his. He told me about how Alison couldn't have babies and it was a tragedy but how they'd made gardens their children. You'd start them off growing and sometimes they'd obey and sometimes they'd go their own way, but you loved them and they loved you. Don't get me wrong, he was never over-intimate, you never got the feeling he was making a pass, you were just glad to have him as your friend, or perhaps like some new big brother come happily all of a sudden into your life.

*   *   *

Nisha and Nikki, Laura and I, all agreed on this. Our husbands didn't mind him either – he was safely married, and properly domestic – except oddly enough Stuart, the bigamist, who insisted on going round to interview Stanley to see if he was a proper person for his non-wife to be working for. And even Stuart came away charmed and satisfied.

Alison was a really pleasant woman a little older than Stanley: an artist of some kind. They'd rented a big town house centrally while they looked round for somewhere to buy. They had a great big bounding Afghan hound with soulful eyes and a way of leaning his head on your knees which would break your heart. They had real paintings on the walls and lots of books on the shelves, and Alison's brother was a famous folk singer with his own weekly TV show, so when you were with the Combses you always felt a little as if you were brushing up against the famous, which is a silly way to think but there you are.

Stanley would do minimalist, cottage, wild or trendy, small-town or park-grand at your pleasure, and with the aid of a computer and some very nifty graphics indeed, show you what your place would look like in two years' time. His self-confidence showed in his lavish premises, which my husband Alan, who's an estate agent, told me were the most expensive in the Arcade.

We had rather a row, Alan and I, over Stanley, and we hardly ever had rows.

'I assume he pays you when you stand in for Laura?' he asked. I'd put in about five hours for her the previous week. James had had trouble with his new teeth coming through and Laura had been back and forth to the dentist. I was obliged to admit that no, I wasn't paid.

'So Laura pays you?' he asked.

'Well no,' I said, 'because she gets paid by the hour and if she's not there she doesn't get paid, does she?'

'So he gets his staff for nothing?' Alan asked. I said I was just helping Laura and Stanley out. I wasn't exactly staff. I loved being there anyhow. Stanley had about fifteen other employees working for him now – gardeners, concrete layers, fencing people and so on, and we were really busy.

'Then perhaps Laura gives you some of her commission?' he asked.

I said I didn't think she got any commission. In fact I knew she didn't.

Alan said that was disgraceful, we were being conned.

I really hate conversations like this. I want everyone just to like one another and be happy.

'You're as bad as Laura,' he said, 'You live in Munchkin land.'

I said I didn't think he was a bigamist or did he have something to tell me?

He said I wasn't allowed to work for Stanley unless I got paid.

I said it was many decades now since husbands 'allowed' wives to do this or that, and if I wanted to work unpaid I would.

Then I began to laugh and he began to laugh. We agreed Stanley was on the mean side, but on the other hand he was an entrepreneur and just the kind of person the country needed, and he was providing employment at a time it was most vital, and he was just starting up so we had to forgive him. And as for Laura we had to do everything we could for her.

Nikki said she'd had pretty much the same conversation with her husband Trevor. None of us were daft, we knew what was going on, we just wanted to help Stanley and Alison and Laura out.

Nisha and I went round to Laura's on Sunday evening to see if we could help: she was ironing the children's clothes for the next week and freezing the packed lunches – Sunday evening is often the busiest time of the week for the working mother, and she's full-time while we're just part-time.

*   *   *

She was singing along happily enough to a CD of Scottish folk songs made by Alison's brother, which Stanley had just given her for her birthday, but she was worried. Stanley had asked her to take a cut in wages to help him through a difficult patch, it was just temporary, he'd make it up to her as soon as the next big commission came through, which was any moment now. We agreed it sounded reasonable enough. And a pleasant job is hard to come by.

And sure enough as soon as he could Stanley made up her back wages and Laura felt so rich she actually went out and bought herself a new winter coat instead of going to the charity shop. The central heating at work had broken down and she needed a good coat. Nisha took them round an electric fan heater to use until the central heating was back on line, and Stanley accepted gracefully. He asked Nisha to walk the dog for him for a couple of weeks because Alison was poorly – more fertility tests at the hospital – and Nisha did. God, that dog had energy! She didn't get paid but she was given a CD of Alison's brother.

In wintertime not so many people want their gardens done. They think about summer holidays instead. Spring's the peak time for new commissions: winter's the hard work time, digging, preparing land, concrete mixing and so on. Stanley held a meeting of the staff and asked them if they'd all work on reduced wages till the spring when he'd make it up to them. They agreed, they wanted to help out. Stanley made them feel they were all in this together.

Stanley gave a great Christmas party for everyone and Alison's brother came and gave a great performance of Scottish folk songs, complete with bag-piper.

But I wish Alan hadn't said, 'Funny he can give that great party and not pay the staff. Lobster canapés don't come cheap.' And

I wish even more he hadn't said, 'A pity he's behind with his rent too. In fact he hasn't even paid the first instalment.' I should have taken more notice but all I said was, 'He's got in some sort of muddle, I expect. Or perhaps it's just that Laura's in charge of the accounts,' and Alan groaned and said he wouldn't be surprised, Laura again! And then the rent did get paid, or some of it at any rate. He'd been changing banks or something and the direct debits hadn't gone through.

So we all kind of waited for the trouble to pass, and the spring to come and money with it. Laura even got up early to go with Alison to the hospital once or twice, while I got Carla and James to school. Alison really trusted Laura, it seemed.

Nisha wanted her fan heater back even though the central heating hadn't been fixed but didn't like to ask. We dreaded to think what Stanley's quarterly electricity bill would be like. We were well into January now.

Then when we went round one Sunday evening, I saw that Laura had a whole pile of papers from the CSA and the Benefits Agency. She said that Stanley hadn't paid her at all since October, and she'd been obliged to go back on benefits and most of the staff were in the same boat, but he'd promised to pay them all the back amount in March. Everyone was working for free.

I didn't like to tell Alan: I knew what he'd have said, and it wouldn't have helped my repeating what Laura said, about how the crocuses were already showing and spring was on the way, and the trouble with the world was it didn't trust enough. It worked with me but might not have with him.

But I did find myself saying to Nisha again, 'Well, I said to Laura, "Well," I said, "don't blame me if it all goes wrong."'

*   *   *

127

In March the firm got a few big commissions in, and the deposit money was in the bank and the staff were waiting for their back pay, which amounted to several thousands a head, when instead of Stanley turning up to hand it over the official receiver came instead. Stanley had declared himself bankrupt. He was a limited company, which meant he didn't have any obligation to his staff. If they'd worked for nothing more fool them.

Alan went over to the Combses, of course, but they'd already gone, with a month's rent owing. Gone, fled, along with the paintings, the books, canapé dishes, the lot, even the dog bowl. Even the light bulbs. Flown the nest.

We told ourselves that he hadn't meant it to happen. He'd just panicked and ran when he found he'd let us down so badly. He just couldn't face us.

In early April a whole lot of plants which should have started surfacing in gardens up and down Mortimer Street simply failed to do so.

In late April we heard Stanley had opened up another landscape business in a town a hundred miles away just in time for the seasonal rush. He made a habit of it, we weren't the first, we wouldn't be the last. He was just a ruthless operator.

And I found myself lost for words, for once. I could not even say to Nikki, or Nisha, or Alan or the husbands, 'Well I said to her I said, "Well Laura, what did you expect?"' I could only barely say, 'I told you so.'

Because you have to believe like Laura that there's good in everyone and it's better to trust than not to trust because otherwise how do you live your life? Love and loyalty can't go too far, even though sometimes they're abused. It's the exception not the rule, and this year Laura's garden is so lush and wonderful – all that rain early in the season – we're all really proud of it, and her and us. And we may be fools but we're nice fools and we'd rather be us than him.

MAKING GOOD

Freeze Eggs, Freeze Eggs!

Cold, Wet Nose

Wild Strawberries

I, Boadicea

Freeze Eggs, Freeze Eggs!

Pauline read a science fiction story once, in which the human race had so degraded the planet that even air was hard to come by. People lived under the water and sucked air through straws. 'Grab air, grab air,' went the refrain of the storyteller: it served as charm, chant and admonition. Now she stared at her beautiful daughter, product of years of toil, perseverance and much putting-up-with, so alive and alert and happy in the New World, though far too creased with tiredness around the eyes, and found herself murmuring, 'Freeze eggs, freeze eggs.'

'Is your mouth just moving by itself, Ma,' said Dee, in her charming, husky voice. 'Or is there something you want to say to me?' Children know their mothers' faces well. They stare at them a lot, trying to work out what is really being thought, what is about to happen. 'Nothing I want to say,' said Pauline.

They sat in a tapas bar after the show and ate little bits of things and drank rather sweet white wine, and Pauline wondered if she should warn Dee about what seemed to be pepper pips embedded in the tough rounds of toast. Her own mother had lived in fear of pepper pips: they lodged in your stomach lining and gave you ulcers, or appendicitis, Pauline couldn't remember which. She decided against saying anything, and just scraped them to one side. The young had digestions like iron. They ate raw leaves from under hedges, in wilted salad, but feared meat. They had sensitive brains and got meningitis but seldom these days appendicitis.

*   *   *

Dee had dragged her off to the theatre saying, 'It's Christmas, we have to do something, I can't come home because I'm on duty, you'll love this show, it's won every award under the sun.'

Or out of the blackness of hell, thought Pauline, as those on the stage tortured one another, gouged out each other's eyes, tore at each other's testicles, and male and female raped each other on stage with little more than a gesture towards simulation, for all of which they seemed to require understanding, pity and even admiration from the audience, and from the standing applause at the end even got it.

'Wasn't that totally wonderful?' said Dee, as they came out. 'I'm still trembling.' Well, start them off with *The Exorcist* and what did you expect? 'The author's only twenty-three, but she had a very hard beginning.'

Hard beginnings, thought Pauline, you should know from hard beginnings. Dee was thirty-four, born on Christmas Day, without anaesthetic, which is fine for baby but not for mother. It was at the height of the natural childbirth movement and Pauline had fallen for it.

'But your mouth is still going, Mother,' Dee said, as they looked for a table. The place was crowded: lots of glass and mirrors and noise. 'I know there's something on your mind. I wish you'd just spit it out and we could get it over.'

Pauline could see she would have to offer something. It couldn't be the truth, because the truth always caused endless trouble. She looked for a least worst option.

'Why do the girls go round with bare midriffs in midwinter?' she demanded, as if Dee was responsible for an entire generation. 'To show off their skinniness,' said Dee. 'So as not to be burdened with clothes. So as to save their mothers' washing machines. To offer sex to men and then withhold it. Because wherever they go there is central heating and they never have time to chill down. Because they're on ecstasy and expect any minute to be drenched with sweat. I don't know. Take your choice.'

They'd found an empty table. Dee pulled back the spindly chair for her mother and took her coat. Men's eyes followed her. She was astonishingly beautiful, considering how plain her father had been. Pauline had gone to live with him not quite out of pity, but in the kind of romantic belief that if she was good to him somehow his luck would change: he'd find a proper job, his grey teeth would whiten, his sad eyes go bright, his thin hair thicken: and for a while it seemed to, and then she couldn't leave him for years because she felt responsible for him. Now Dee wouldn't do a thing like that. Dee wasn't in the business of saving men's feelings at her own expense. None of her generation were. They waged a war of attrition against men and victory was so sweet they didn't mind spending Christmas alone, mulling over the year's spoils, that is to say the anecdotes they could tell their girlfriends about the crassness of men. They had lots of girlfriends and the girlfriends had their mothers, and occasionally but not often fathers too, and they'd go 'home' for Christmas. As Dee would have, Christmas and birthday both, if she hadn't been on call at the hospital. She worked an eighty-hour week, in a dire hospital in a dire area, and loved it. She was kind to the sick and the ill and the disturbed, and kept her outrage for the able-bodied, smooth young men who courted her. She loved what was rough and tough and unsavoury, perhaps because these things had never entered her own childhood. Pauline had seen to it that they didn't.

'This is the life,' said Dee, happily, sipping her Chardonnay. 'You start to think it begins and ends in a hospital ward. Now tell me what the matter really is. It isn't girls exposing midriffs. I know, because your mouth is at it again. Silent working.'
'You shouldn't be taking your mother out at the age of thirty-four,'

said Pauline, bravely. 'You should have your own household and a Christmas tree of your own.' She wasn't talking husbands, they were both beyond that, but good daughters should turn into good mothers, not work themselves to death for not enough money.

'I have got a Christmas tree,' said Dee. 'It's small but it's pretty.'

'And by this time I should be coming to you for Christmas, not you to me.'

'But I'm not a turkey person, Mother, and you'd hate eating on your knee.' Dee's flat was so small you had to choose between a desk and a table and she'd chosen the desk. Of course. 'Eat up your nice tapas. I'm just fine.'

'You know what I mean,' said her mother.

Dee's bleeper went. 'Give it another half-hour and then call me again,' she said to whoever it was. Some night sister, no doubt, who'd trained less and earned more. 'If the blood pressure stabilises we're okay. Otherwise I'll come straight over.'

Well, it was what Dee had worked for, long and hard, bent over books, this responsibility for the lives of others, this abnegation of her own. And what Pauline had worked for too, to be able to afford at least a semblance of comfort and ease for her daughter: all the expensive business of keeping up with the rest: school excursions, text books, new trainers, latest fashions, eventually medical school, all to bring her to this underpaid, overworked end. At least these days Pauline got enough sleep, though her daughter didn't. And Pauline had a resident boyfriend and her daughter didn't.

Pauline's Dee, always pretty and pleasant and kind and smart, the pride and joy of the Estate mothers, not only Pauline's. Dee was the one who would go far. The mothers had been a good lot: Pauline knew she'd been lucky, she wasn't complaining. Reading groups, and campaigns for this and that, and baby-sitting clubs and mutual help and assurance. Another relationship for Pauline, when Dee was twelve, which had lasted eight years until she had an affair and he found out and after that it just didn't work: the union had produced no children: its dissolution didn't seem to matter much: it was rather a relief, in fact. Life for Pauline, not in the least dismal, just always dictated by the fact of her daughter's existence.

'Yes, I know all that,' said Dee, on the edge of irritation. 'I'm thirty-four and I'm not in a permanent relationship and I don't have any children and I work too hard and this is the way I like it and it worries you. But all those women you work with, all those other people's children, aren't they enough to make up for it?'

These days Pauline worked for a Catholic charity, Mums Plus, which looked after women who had so many children they didn't know what to do: a shrinking number, now that so many of the religious found their way round God's wishes. She loved her work but it had never occurred to her that employment could be a replacement for life, as it seemed to be for Dee. 'No they're not,' said Pauline, 'and that's old stuff between us.'

Dee's bleeper went again. This time she said, 'Okay, I'm on my way.' She turned to her mother, and said, 'Then what is it? You have to tell me or I'll worry about it and then I won't know what to do for the best for the guy with the brain tumour and it'll be all your fault.'

She had affairs with men, Pauline knew, and sometimes she brought them home, for a time, but mostly she dismissed them as soon as they came into her life. Freeze eggs, girl, freeze eggs, she wanted to say, so if the social order convulses again we won't have lost a generation, and me my grandchildren.

Dee had two abortions, Pauline knew that for a fact. Her grand-children, down the drain. She doubted that Dee had considered that. Dee just knew her exams were coming up and she hadn't done all those hours of studying through sleepless nights and giving up holidays and living on a low income just to have to stop now. That had been when she was twenty-two and twenty-three. She'd put children off until she was established in her career. In Pauline's view every baby a woman has keeps out the next one. If she hadn't had Dee so early she might have ended up with three or four children, who was to say? Women end up with as many or as few children as they can afford: emotionally, physically, and practically. Often these days it was only one, sometimes it's none. And Dee, Pauline could see, was heading none-wards fast.

'Your mouth's still going,' said Dee, on her feet, putting a tenner on the table. 'Tell me! Please! Because I have to go right now.'

When Dee had been fourteen and going out to an all-night party Pauline had tried to tell her about contraception and Dee had flushed and burst into tears and locked herself in her room, shocked, horrified, embarrassed. The thought of it! How revolting! Don't you trust me? What sort of person do you think I am? You had to be so careful, tread so gently. But that was then and this was now.

'Okay,' she said. 'It's this. I think you should have your eggs frozen, as the new technology permits. What you need is what you haven't got – time. This way you've got an extra twenty years to change your mind, to find a man. You'll never get it in before you're forty, the way things are going.' The volume of noise around seemed to diminish as if everyone was listening, not just Dee, but that was probably Pauline's imagination. Dee's face didn't harden. She laughed, she seemed entertained. It was okay. Dee bent and kissed her mother.

'Oh, Mum,' she said, 'don't worry. The new technology isn't quite here yet, another couple of years before it's perfected, but that's what I mean to do. We all of us do. I think you're sweet and I'm glad you care.'

Freeze eggs, girl, freeze eggs. Oh brave new world, that has such daughters in it, whose inheritance should not be lost. Dee left. Pauline paid the bill, an impossibly large sum. If they'd gone straight home and not to the tapas bar it would have saved £13.60. If Dee had booked cheaper theatre seats they could have saved £14. If they hadn't have gone out at all they could have saved £63.60. If you didn't choose to spend £63.60 after tax, that is to say about £90 before tax, Dee wouldn't have had to work seven hours to earn it, and could have slept instead. But that wasn't the way the world worked any more, let alone careers. Freeze eggs, girl, freeze eggs. One day we will live in a perfect society when there will be time to work and live as well. Then will come the day of the Big Thaw and National Rejoicing.

She called the waitress over as she left.
'Tell the chef,' she said, 'to scrape the peppers properly. Otherwise the pips can lodge in your appendix and kill you.'

Cold, Wet Nose

A leading genetic scientist of my acquaintance argues that horses, dogs, cats and other higher animals – that is to say those who have longer memories than the rest – don't have emotions. What they display, and what we anthropomorphise into emotion – love, hate, fear, hope, gratitude, joy, guilt, anger, resentment – is just behaviour which they know will get them what they want. Dewy-eyed nuzzling gets a horse a handful of oats, growling scares a dog's rivals off: snuggling up gets a cat a plateful of food. Once, being a stern realist myself, I would have gone along with it: these days I'm not so sure. And anyway my friend the scientist has done animal experiments in his time, so he would think that, wouldn't he. Whatever is most comforting, is what people like most to believe.

I'm a cat person myself: Millie and I live at a respectful distance from one another. I can't abide dogs: they crowd in upon you – noisy, messy, effusive creatures. But Millie and I, two tidy females, occupy the same space easily enough – my small, desirable, very expensive house in Westminster, London, in a new development overlooking the Thames. We circle one another: I feed and stroke: she preens and stretches and occasionally honours me by curling up on the end of the bed at night. I like the heavy warm weight of her: there's something sexy about it, especially now I have my bed for the most part to myself. Millie's a sleek Siamese: fastidious and fashionable: people say she and I resemble each other. I am perfectly prepared to face the fact that her reason for curling up against my feet at night is that they keep her warm, not that she feels any over-flowing affection for me.

When I was married to Halid he would not allow her on the bed. I resented that. He was an Iranian, a diplomat, as sleek and beautiful as Millie: he was jealous, but had nothing to be jealous of. He wanted to put her out at night.

'It's her or me in your bed,' he said.

'Then it had better be her,' I replied. It was the best thing I ever said. The break was not really about Millie, of course, but she served as an excuse. I think I am not very good at living with other people. What I liked most about Halid, after his looks, after his house, was his money, and it seemed to me I could keep more than enough of that without having to put up with little short black hairs in the soap after he had shaved. I slept on my own for a time, or at least with Millie, and he took to lap dancers and so forth and I was able to divorce him.

But then some months after Halid had gone, and I finally had his house to myself, I gave a fireworks party in honour of Guy Fawkes. I am the political correspondent for a leading broadsheet: I don't often give parties, but the idea of Guy Fawkes, anyone, trying to blow up Westminster always rather attracted me, and the occasional party is useful: an important part of the networking you have to do to stay at the cutting edge.

Early November is a good time of year for parties: before the Christmas overkill, when the nights are drawing in, and the sun-sets are red-streaked and hazy over the Thames, and the trees in Westminster Square are bare, stark and beautiful. When the river runs thick and cold and strong, biding its time before one day it bursts its unnatural banks and overwhelms all low-lying London. At neap tides, in stormy weather, I've known the water come just a couple of inches below my wall. Once they even wanted us to evacuate but I wouldn't.

*   *   *

November is also the time of year when I'm busiest, of course: everyone is: the House is sitting and reckons it's the month it gets its best work done; reports flow out of a host of commissions and enquiries and all need comment. A good headline can so easily tip a wavery public opinion one way or another.

'Nancy,' said my friend Ruth over lunch, 'a November party is simply perverse.'

'All the better,' I said. Ruth is an MP and has the ear of the PM, and he has hers. She is a useful political contact, and I take care to lunch with her from time to time. She is at least two stone overweight and I can't bear to see her sitting guzzling from overloaded greasy plates, and slurping rich red wine. Drink sparkling water and nibble at salad as I may, she will never take her cue from me. I always take care to book our table at the back of the restaurant.

'People won't come in November,' she said. 'They're too busy.'

'Of course they'll come,' I said. I am more of a power in the land than she realises. She thinks well of herself and tends to patronise me: I am 'only' a journalist: she is a politician. She is a mother of three and for some reason believes this gives her some advantage over me, who have none. If she'd forsworn the kids she'd be in the cabinet by now. I point this out and she shrugs her fat shoulders and laughs and orders sticky toffee pudding.

I was quite right. I invited a hundred and eighty accepted. I went to a lot of trouble, if only to show Ruth how wrong she was, how dull the domestic path she had chosen: and besides, what else am I to do with my money, but be stylish? Not ostentatious or vulgar: just, somehow, *perfect*. I had the house refurbished and refurnished (minimally) to get rid of the peculiar feel of gold leaf and cosiness mixed, which had been Halid's notion of how a sophisticated royal diplomat should live – and I booked the best in-house caterers around. Choosing a caterer is rather like choosing wine: best not to go for the most expensive on the list – it's usually a rip-off – two or three from the top usually offers better value. There were to be fireworks, of course, many thousands of pounds' worth, and a team hired to set them up and set them off. I had the garden redesigned – the soggy lawn taken up and gravel put down, with hot pipes for warmth running underneath. The Romans couldn't have done better. They say the site on which this fancy housing development was built was once a Mithraic temple. Mithras was the Sun God, worshipped in particular by the Roman soldiery, those by whose courage and tenacity this city of London was founded. As the sun dimmed and disappeared with the season they'd sacrifice bulls (lambs came later, in a more timorous age) and light defiant fires, to ensure their God's return to power with the spring. Our Guy Fawkes Day is of course the corruption of this early pagan feast, and who knows what deity was worshipped, propitiated, shamed and blamed before even the sunny Mithras? Our current God is money, and we sacrifice large sums of it to the deity in the form of fireworks. That's okay by me. A pity about the animals: at least they stay alive: we just shoot their nerves to hell.

For the occasion I shut Millie in my bedroom, which overlooks the street and which on November 5th is the quietest part of the house; the windows are triple gazed and the curtains thick. I stirred a spoonful of sedative from the vet into her cream – Millie is allowed treats I never allow myself – and went down to receive my guests. *Hello!* had wanted to come along but I had said no: in the circles in which I move no-one ever quite knows whom, a year hence, they'd rather not have been snapped chatting happily with. And besides, *Hello!* tend to move things round and set up lights and bring along their own pots of fern, which can quite upset the aesthetics of a properly organised occasion.

I can't say I have ever actually enjoyed parties, but, though I say it myself, I was at least quite impressed by this one. It was a black tie event, of course, and for once the suits seemed to fit and didn't look as if they'd been hired in a hurry earlier in the day: the women managed to look, on the whole, both beautiful and intelligent, and because of the under-patio heating, bare arms and shoulders were for once free of goose pimples. The caterers were behaving flawlessly: from time to time the night sky would erupt into colour as fireworks night took off up and down the Thames. The rather good-looking Australian in charge of the fireworks was on target for a nine p.m. liftoff and there were only ten minutes to go. The oblations were going well. I was pleased. The new Mithras was being well and truly served. If enough money were spent the Sun God would rise again, one day soon, in all his glory. Even Ruth seemed less patronising than usual, but then her husband, newly in the House of Lords, was chatting me up quite assiduously. Perhaps this, if nothing else, would persuade her to lose weight. Women do have to learn to compete. I was of course looking rather good. Diamonds always add lustre and in his time Halid had tried to woo me back with many a chunky bracelet and necklace, so I was not surprised by his new Lordship's attention. You can only of course wear one piece at a time, which is something of a pity, for fear of glittering like a suburban Christmas tree.

'Poor bastard,' Ruth's husband said now, of Halid. 'Look at those rocks, and all for nothing. But I don't blame him. Men always want the unattainable.' Poor Ruth, so totally attainable, by anyone who cared to take an interest (but who would), watching us from across the courtyard. I was glittering up at his Lordship as only I know how, when I felt something strange in the palm of my left hand, the one not carrying a champagne flute. It was cold, wet and nuzzling. And I remembered how often, in the past I pre-ferred not to think about, I had felt that very same thing: the cold wet shock of a dog's nose trying to prise open my innocent hand.

I looked down and saw not the Rex of the past, who though boisterous, had at least been a handsome, muscular, shiny, well-bred Labrador, but a revolting little fawning cur, come to plague my present and spoil my perfect party. He had a starey under-nourished brown-and-white patched coat, wriggling, grovelling rear quarters, a body out of all known proportion which he was now trying to wind about my legs, shedding dust and fleas on my Blahnik shoes the while, and soupy, dribbling eyes with which he gazed up at me. Worse, he trembled. He was scared. November 5th was, it was true, beginning to bang and crash from the neighbours around us, but so what? The creature was collarless, he had no business here or anywhere. He had somehow crept in with the guests or managed to scramble over the garden wall to the comparative, if temporary, peace of my patio. Why he had chosen me of all the assembled company, how he guessed I was in charge, I did not know. I didn't exactly kick him away in disgust but I certainly stirred my foot enough to keep him off me.

'I'm glad I'm not a pet of yours, all the same,' said the newly elevated peer, observing my response.

'This cur is nothing to do with me,' I said, shocked that he should assume a connection between us. 'It is a gate-crasher of the least welcome kind. Some wretched stray. See, the thing has no collar. And I have, as it happens, only one pet, and her name is Millie and she is a very expensive Siamese and extremely well treated, thank you.'

I think I spoke a little heatedly for the noble Lord stopped fingering my diamonds and the flesh beneath and put the dog on its feet again. His wife Ruth then bent over the creature and said, 'Poor little thing, she's terrified,' in spite of the fact that the animal was all too obviously male, while other more sensible guests carefully skirted the thing. No-one wants to be fawned and slobbered over by a pathetic, over-excited, ugly runt. The Australian signalled to me that the computer countdown had begun. He would stay the night with me if I wanted him to, obviously, but I wasn't sure that I could afford the time for sex. I had to get back to work next morning. Neglected deadlines were looming. With this in mind my champagne flute held delicately tinted fizzy water, not alcohol.

*   *   *

And again the animal lurched over to me and thrust its cold wet nose into my palm: dogs have a great capacity for forgiveness. And I have a reputation for toughness. I could drop the wriggling thing over the wall and into the Thames, I supposed, and let it swim to safety in someone else's back yard, or not, as the case might be. But even I could not go that far, and besides, there were too many witnesses, and I looked up and the noisy heavens were cascading and exploding in flakes of colour all around me and I felt dizzy. So I hesitated, and in hesitating, was lost.

I remembered all kinds of things. I remembered Rex and wondered what had become of him. I had not spoken to my parents for fifteen years. They kept a pub in Essex. As a child I'd wake to the smell of stale beer and vomit every morning. I'd got out of there as soon as I could. And I remembered the Guy Fawkes' parties we'd give each year in the pub garden. Drizzling damp, guests wrapped up in coats and mufflers, a makeshift bonfire, a vague effigy of the Prime Minister to burn, a rain-spotted barbecue with sausages and steaks, hot punch handed round, and a general feeling of mess and disarray. Squalling children, drunken men in charge, rockets zooming into the crowd, not into the heavens. Here a weeping wife, whose husband had disappeared into the bushes with her best friend; there a violent young man, who thought his girlfriend was two-timing him under cover of darkness: the sirens of approaching fire engines, or police cars, or both. They were famous, those parties, and everyone loved them but me. I'd go with Rex into the coalhouse, and he'd dig his cold wet nose into my hand and we'd do our best to sleep undiscovered until morning. Rex wasn't allowed into the house and he'd get beaten if he did. I didn't want that for him.

'Oh all right,' I said to the cur, 'you win.' And I signalled to the Australian to delay the onset of my oblations to the Sun God, and I took the dog into the kitchen and threw off my Blahnik shoes and fed him, and watered him. And then I went out into the patio and told the Australian to cancel the whole proceedings, and he said he'd still have to charge me, and I said fine by me, and then I told the guests there had been a flood warning and we all had to evacuate at once. And they fled. I really could not stand this kind of life a moment longer. It was just not me. Perhaps I would give Halid all his property back, perhaps I would not. Perhaps I would say sorry to Ruth, perhaps I would get in touch with my parents again, perhaps not. All I knew was that things would henceforth be different. And that if anyone was guilty of simulating emotions in their own interests, as do dogs, cats, horses and other higher animals, according to my friend the scientist, it had been me. I would do a minimum to find the dog's owners, and if I could not, why then he could yap and grovel at my heels for ever, disgracing me. I only hoped he would get on with Millie. I didn't think so.

Wild Strawberries

It was my fault their cat was pregnant. I'd left the back door open while we were clearing the flower garden and she'd slipped out and met her fate. Now it was high summer and we had moved on to the vegetable patch, and Strophe (rhymed with Sophie) looked startled, offended and reproachful. She was a Siamese, born to be sleekly elegant, and here she was, weighed down by this swollen bellyful of kittens. She, who was accustomed to being envied, was no longer enviable. It was a great shock to her. She sought out the shade rather than the sunlight of the long hot summer, and watched us garden.

The vet said it was a litter of five. He knew, because Strophe had had a CAT scan. (Well, what else?) Elaine spent more on the vet than most of us would spend on cosmetics in a year. Women like us, at any rate, smart media people, who mean to stay beautiful for ever, flat-stomached and childless. Or look at it like this: what most couples spend on school fees, Elaine and Felix were managing to spend on Strophe. She'd been about to go off to some kind of cattery to receive the expensive sperm of some lordly male creature when she'd slipped out of the door. Now God knew who the father was: some one-eyed ginger tom, some measly tabby. They'd be country kitchen kittens at best, half-breeds. Out of control. Elaine and Strophe both hated being out of control. And all my fault.

People like us. Elaine and Felix, myself (Rachel) and Kevin. Between us, we'd started Channel 8. Felix was head of programmes,

Elaine was head of marketing, Kevin ran PR, I was commissioning editor. We had a staff of fifty-two and rising. My, we were clever people, and busy, and pretty much perfect. Felix was going a little bald and even his No. 2 haircut didn't quite disguise the fact. And perhaps Kevin drank a little too much. Elaine and myself only ever drank sparkling water, and our diet was mostly salad and a little skinned chicken, with the occasional terrible fall from grace. Our hair was as glossy and shiny as our legs were long. That is to say very. The money was piling up in the bank, and the critics had stopped slagging off our offerings and we'd even had a few of our sexier programmes sold off to Channel 4, which isn't bad going for an extraterrestrial. But then we'd gone all out for high production values.

I did think Elaine had been behaving a little out of character of late. She'd bought the country cottage, for one thing. Everyone knows country cottages are insanity for busy people. Something always crops up and you hardly ever get down. And why? We live on a river as it is, next door to each other in a new development up near Canary Wharf, and if you want nature, watch water. The Thames can put on a quite a show of turbulent and untrammelled behaviour, from time to time, especially when the neap tides and the full moon coincide. We hope the Thames Barrier keeps doing its stuff – otherwise, believe me, Kevin is suing.

But Elaine had weakened and bought the cottage on the spur of the moment. We'd been filming in Oxfordshire and she'd fallen in love with the set, never a sensible thing to do. Worse, it hadn't been lived in for five years or more: the wallpaper was peeling and the garden was hopelessly overgrown. It was going to be work, work, work and little else. But she'd bought it, so we stood by her.

Every weekend this summer Kevin and I had neglected our normal networking party life and come down to stay and help Felix and Elaine strip walls, clean up, expose brick and clear the garden.

The garden had, I must admit, been rather fun. As you cleared away weeds, and the season advanced, nature sent things shooting up as if in acknowledgement of your help. A great bush of peonies would appear out of bare earth: thick hollyhock stalks would creep up the dry stone wall behind the ivy: clear the thistles and find wallflowers and delphiniums.

And then on to the vegetable garden: look here, an asparagus patch, with green stalks showing! Were those tomatoes, beans? Someone in the past had really gone for vegetables in a big way. We worked by hand: using spade, fork, hoe and trowel. No weedkillers or pesticides for us: later, when Elaine knew exactly what she had, and her plans were focused, she'd employ a local gardener and instruct him in organic ways.

Felix was currently dealing with a clump of nettles in the side garden where the old fountain was, just the other side of the iron gate. He was stripped to the waist: he wouldn't use sunscreen: he worked out: he had good broad muscular shoulders. I thought of him like a brother. He loved clearing nettles: he said it was like dealing with some sinister underground conspiracy of roots, a network of interconnections which he claimed reminded him of the Lottery Board. Elaine wanted him to leave enough nettles to encourage the butterflies but he was ruthless. He liked a clear field in which to operate.

Kevin was sitting on some mossy marble bench, his back to a wall. He was on his mobile phone again. It was not surprising, the Middle East doesn't keep Sundays and we had this big conference call the next morning at ten, back at the office, with Gerard Saudi Network TV. There was a lot at stake. Elaine had wanted to ban mobiles at the cottage altogether but that was obviously impractical.

And Strophe, awaiting her shame, the birth of her uncalculated offspring, lay stretched on her side near where Elaine was pulling out bindweed. You could see the shapes of the kittens moving inside. It was strange that Elaine hadn't had them removed in an early stage of the pregnancy – vets are accustomed to doing that kind of thing, I believe. But then as I say, she'd been behaving a little out of character lately. She'd had a great argument with Felix – and they never argued, usually they thought, moved and breathed as one person – over a sponsorship deal. A chemical firm involved with GM crops had offered to come up with money for our one drama series, 'Bird in the Hand', about a young struggling scientist, and Elaine didn't think that was ethical. She'd lost that battle, of course, money is money and business is business, and we were all three of us against her, and she came to her senses soon enough. But all the same! Do it once and you can do it again.

Then I noticed that Elaine wasn't wearing her gardening gloves. 'Elaine!' I almost shouted. 'What about your nails?'
She looked at them. So did I. Varnish broken and chipped: nails torn. I had never seen her hands like this before. I don't wear red varnish, only clear, in case I get run over by a bus and have to go to hospital with chipped nails. I put down my trowel.
'Are you mad?' I asked. She said she liked the feel of raw earth on her hands, without the barrier of the glove. I said she sounded like a woman talking about a condom, and just as rash. She said she didn't know about me but she had been married to Felix for twelve years and it was a long time now since she'd felt a condom. She had a contraceptive patch and there were no passing strangers in her life, she had Felix. I retorted that there were none in my life either. Husbands were fine: one needed them for parties and company and fixing the salad, but 'men' were quite another. Men were for sex and kept you up late so you didn't have a clear head for the morning: past thirty, and you were better off without them. Of course husbands were for sex too, or assumed they were, though I'd quite often have gladly exchanged the exchange, so to speak, for an extra half-hour's sleep. Or fifteen minutes, or ten – well, let's not go into that: Kevin was okay. I did have

dreams sometimes, in which other men somehow slipped into the bed, or I was having a romance with the plumber, but at least you can sleep through dreams. I wore a shady hat to keep the sun off my face and a long-sleeved muslin shirt to stop skin cancer. Outside is all right but you have to work at it. Strophe was half sleeping, half moaning. I felt great pity for her.

'Oh God,' I said. 'Those kittens. They're bound to be nasty squinty-eyed little things, after all this, and it's all my fault.'
'Shut up, Rachel,' said Elaine amiably. 'It was my fault. I didn't butter her paws when I should have, that's all.'
'Butter her paws?' I was mystified.
'You have to butter their paws,' she said, 'if you take them to a new place. Then they lick their paws and that makes them feel they're at home and they stay put and don't wander.'
'Strophe's too intelligent to fall for anything like that,' I said. If Kevin didn't get asthma I'd have had a cat too. A Burmese, I think.
'I know,' said Elaine, 'that's why I didn't butter them. But a cat's a cat and nature wins. I won't have you accepting the blame, because it's my fault.'
'If the cat gets pregnant because I left the door open then obviously I'm to blame,' I persisted. The truth was that I hadn't just forgotten and let Strophe out by accident. She'd been on heat and yowling and yowling to get out and I couldn't stand it and had practically shoved her out the door. I wasn't going to come clean about that. But the least I could do was take the blame.

'Elaine,' I said, 'tell me, what is the matter with you? What's going on?' Because something was. No gloves. Now taking the blame for Strophe. That was very un-her. She said nothing was going on; no, she wasn't going broody, anything like that. There were enough children in the world. If she and Felix had a baby you would look into its eyes and see Microsoft Windows. Everything was okay she said, except for Strophe now rolling over and over, pretending to be a sparrow a taking a dust bath. I moved on to a new patch of weeds.

'A strawberry!' I cried. 'Look. A strawberry!' It's odd how something like uncovering an unexpected berry can make you feel so jubilant. It was vast and luscious and amazingly red. And see another, and another. Lots! A whole hidden strawberry patch. I could almost have taken off my own gloves at that point: such fruit deserved a delicacy of touch. But I needn't have worried: they were not like the strawberries of my childhood; they were some new variety, bred to stand up to packing and picking. Elaine got up off her knees and stretched and said we'd have them for supper, she might even ask the farmer for some cream. She went inside to fetch a bowl. Strophe padded after her, stomach swinging.

I had to admit, looking after her, that it didn't matter much if her nails were chipped or not. I have to work quite a bit at being beautiful, Elaine doesn't. If a photographer was to mark us out of 10 for beauty she'd get 9.5 and I'd get 8.85. Above the 9 you can reckon it's inborn: beauty, a quality, an essence, a Platonic ideal. It stays with you for ever, from the day you're born to the day you die. What a beautiful baby, what a beautiful old lady! When I'm old people will just look the other way: my money will have to keep me warm. People will still be searching Elaine's face for the secret of goodness.

Strophe didn't go inside. Her attention was caught by something in the tangled vetch leaves by the path leading to the door. She pat-patted with her paw and nosed between leaves. I thought perhaps she'd found some wretched vole and meant to kill it, so I went to intervene. But all she was doing was investigating a bed of tiny little wild strawberries – the kind which once upon a time you'd find lining bridleways and footpaths, along with buttercups and cowslips and now so seldom do. They're tiny and sweet, and their flavour is more intensely strawberry than strawberry and their texture is slightly gritty yet they melt in the mouth. One of my great crude strawberries would make twenty, of one of these.

'We could pick some of those for supper as well,' said Elaine, coming to look. 'No,' I said. 'Too pernickety and bothersome.' But what I really meant was that I didn't want mine to be put to shame. I felt like crying.

There came a cry of triumph from Felix. He'd made the fountain work. A spire of water pierced the air and splashed down again to drench him. The pond and its central fountain were made of some soft ancient greyish metal: it looked like pewter to me, but I don't know. Felix stood barefooted in the hot dry basin of the pond and laughed. I didn't often see him laugh. A sculpted lion wove round the central pillar of the fountain, reaching for a cherub above him, and the cherub held an urn aloft and it was from the urn that the water spurted and stopped, and spurted again. Splashes began to make dark patches round Felix's feet and he stepped out of the pond and onto grass. Kevin came to see what was happening. It was his turn to be on the mobile. He looked at the fountain in wonderment as he talked. The birds seemed excited: there was an upsurge of twittering: they were everywhere. Something with a brilliant flash of colour under its wing dived over the pond and right through the spire of water and out again. Elaine and I stood open-mouthed. I don't know where Strophe was. Kevin's mobile was away from his ear: a tiny voice squeaked into space. Crimson roses clung to the side of the wall: a breeze got up and a mist of water from the fountain reached them, and you could all but hear the rustle of their gratitude. It was almost too much. I did my best to envisage the place in winter: muddy, cold, dank, windswept, a few black spotted leaves clinging on bare thorny branches, all that was left of beauty, and just about convinced myself.

Kevin was staring in horror at something stirring in the grass. A great big ugly toad was moving towards the pond. It leapt onto the rim and squatted on the hot pewter at the edge of the gradually encroaching water line. The pond was on a slope: whatever that was old was ever straight? The toad just sat there and stared at us. We stared at the toad and the toad stared back and the toad won. Someone spoke. Felix asked if it was a frog and Kevin said no, it had to be a toad. Too big and fat and squat for a frog. It just went on looking at us as if it were some kind of wise old judge who found us despicable, and I felt myself shivering.

Elaine and I went back to picking my big, firm strawberries. Strophe watched. She took to dragging her uncomfortable stomach along the ground. No way I would ever be pregnant.

Supper was at seven: we had to leave for London at the dot of eight. That meant, experience through the summer had shown, we would just catch the traffic gap between the waves of the ones who liked to try to get back 'before the traffic', and the ones who liked to get back 'after the traffic', both creating their own congestion. The salad was fine: our own asparagus was incredible: the strawberries were rather a disappointment. Not very flavourful, and hard rather than firm, almost woody. Elaine served cream and sugar with them and Kevin had both and Felix took the sugar but at least not the cream.

'Oh well,' I said to Kevin. 'If you want to die young that's your problem.' Elaine was staring at me. What had I said? It was true enough. Husband and wife are not of one flesh. You spent an awful lot of time making sure it was not so, keeping independence within marriage. Kevin's problems were not my problems. Elaine went out into the dusk and picked some of the tiny wild strawberries, just a teacup full, and put them one by one into our waiting mouths as if she were a mother bird and we were fledglings. 'I do love you all,' she said. The berries were so fragile, tender and sweet. Shy, almost.

*   *   *

Then she said, 'Strophe's lying in the airing cupboard, she's going to have her kittens soon.'

We trooped up to look. The cat was purring and padding, purring and padding on a nest of finest machine-washable linen. I could see we had a problem. Put her in the back of the car, and hope we got home before she popped. Or wait until the kittens were out and then decant the lot of them, and get back really late. We all turned to Elaine. It was her cat, even if the kittens were my fault.

'I'm going to stay here with Strophe,' she said. 'You lot get back without me.'

We explained that was no solution. There was a conference call with Gerard Saudi Network TV at ten the next morning. She was needed.

'Strophe needs me,' she said.

Felix came over all noisy and testosteronic and said she couldn't let a dumb animal stand in the way of a deal worth tens of thousands. What was the matter with her lately?

Kevin said something calming which failed to defuse anything. Elaine and Felix stared at each other and Elaine was unblinking. The toad was the essence of ugliness and Elaine the essence of beauty, but they had similarities: both were without doubt, and both were judgmental.

'I'm never coming back to London,' she said. 'I'm staying here for the rest of my life. You'll get on okay without me.'

And we did get on okay, and I'm with Felix now, and Kevin found someone else, but I do miss her. I can't eat wild strawberries without crying. Fortunately they're rather rare, these days.

I, Boadicea

Midnight, July 8th, AD *62*

I, Boadicea, am too restless to sleep. This is the eve of battle. The night is full of whisperings and murmurings. There are bad dreams about. One came to me and I cried out aloud but as I woke all I heard was a thin squeal from my lips. I didn't like that. It was ill-omened.

I, Boadicea, Queen of the Iceni, carry the anger of my people, and their rage and their vengeance should be full-throated. It was not. And now I can't get back to sleep. The night is hot, the tent is too enclosed, heavy with gold ornament: it weighs down upon me.

I go outside. The moon gives light. All around me men and women lie sleeping on the dusty ground, as they do tonight in all the thousand clearings of this great forest. Our camp fires still spark and smoke: the smell of charred meat catches the nostrils. I walk among my people, picking my way through sprawled and unwashed bodies. How heavily they sleep, how lucky they are. They've been drinking, of course; they will have headaches in the morning. For some, it will be the last one they ever have, poor things. But the deaths of a few are worth the pride of the many: all agree on that.

The people want their vengeance, so do I. Tonight the long scars on my back smart and sting; give thanks to the Goddess Adastre, for making sure I don't forget, that my resolution doesn't falter. Over there in the oak tree, see, her raven sits and stares at me.

159

Adastre, Goddess of Victory and Vengeance, has heard, and sent her creature as a message. But of what? Now it flies away, silently, dark wings flapping. Birds, like people, should be asleep. I shouted in my slumber and a mouse's squeak came out.

I, Boadicea, widow of King Prasutagus, who once went to Colchester to reason with the Romans, who claim to be so reasonable. He went to explain that the harvest had been bad, that we could hardly feed ourselves, let alone pay the tribute Rome demanded. Their response? To murder him, and come straight to our village, and flog me, and rape my daughters, to teach us the lesson: that you do not argue with Rome, you do as you are told. Well, how stubbornly argumentative we turned out to be; how shocked and surprised at our manners the Emperor Nero was.

In Rome the women stay quiet and good: they dress in fine white linen, and wash their hair with soap and dress it in elaborate patterns, and thread it with ribbons, and shriek at the sight of a spider. They do not go to war: they don't fight side by side with their men as we do. They are men's prisoners: so they grow sly and secretive, and if their husbands displease them, or they are ambitious for their sons, they put poison in the wine and kill that way. Everyone knows.

I, Boadicea, wish this night was over. In this female body of mine I have a man's heart. It passed to me when my husband died. That's what I'll say to the warriors when at last dawn breaks, and we gather for battle. A man's heart in a woman's body. It has a good ring to it, so long as my voice doesn't tremble. Sometimes I think it is easier to fight than speak. But the tribes are well enough accustomed to women commanders. And I will speak a self-evident truth, that I lead them not for my crown or my wealth, but as an ordinary person, as one of them: that all of us fight for our lost freedoms, our scarred bodies, our robbed homes and our outraged daughters. My woes are the people's woes: in the reign of the Romans not even their Queen is exempt

from humiliation. They will win this battle or perish, I will tell
them so loud and clear and my voice won't falter. I as a woman
mean to fight and win: let the men live in slavery if they will.

The enemy, the Romans, sleep just half a mile away, the other
side of the hill which tomorrow will be a battlefield. They sleep
neatly, no doubt, and soberly, organised even in slumber. A mere
ten thousand of them, my spies say, the frightened remnants of
their once proud and cocksure armies. We number eighty thousand, or more, and we are angry, and the Gods are on our side.
He is a brave man, this general of theirs, this Suetonius, and
foolhardy, to stop running, turn and face us and think he can
win. All Rome's logic, all its rules of battle, all its discipline and
drilling will be to no avail. So many of us, so few of them. We
will rush them and in the face of the din, the roar, the shock of
our onslaught they will take to their heels and run, as they did
at Mona, and we will cut them down. Their Roman blood makes
our British soil rich – that is the tribute we demand.

This is our land, not yours. You think you can sit round in your
villas in your fine clothes, and plant your outlandish veterans,
strangers even to Rome, the scum of the Empire, among us, to
insult and vilify us. We won't let you. You call us savages. Yes,
we women go bare-breasted, we mark our bodies with woad, our
warriors would not step into a steam bath if you paid them, but
we are not savages. What are you doing here? This is our country.
It is not to bring us the Pax Romana, as you claim, or the fine
straight roads to places we have no interest in going, or the rule
of law, or the skills of the marketplace; no, you come simply to
rob, to steal. To demand money with menaces to keep your
Emperor Nero in the style to which he is accustomed. You are
the savages, not us.

You come to loot and pillage, you take our wise men and enslave
them to teach your children, our doctors to cure you, our beautiful girls to bear your sons: our strong young men to join your

armies. You will die for it. My spies count up to seven times a thousand of your deaths to date: and one ten thousand more by the time the sun sets tomorrow. We are the Iceni, I am their Queen: we are not to be despised.

I, Boadicea. What will the future think? Will there be a future? Does the world just go on and on? Will the forests still grow and the sun still rise? Will bad dreams come for ever and stop good men and women sleeping? Who in future generations will know about this night? The Romans have historians they say, who write these things down, but why should any Roman want to remember shame? I'm sure I wouldn't write it down. How the barbarian horde they so despised and mocked rode in and sacked Colchester, their fine garrison town, which they guarded so badly we laughed as we swarmed over the walls. And how we slaughtered the lot of them, women and children as well as warriors, because all were tained by Rome, even those born here in the forest, who'd chosen the paved streets and the lazy life above the fate of their begetting. Let just one of the enemy's children live, it grows up to kill you.

And then how we chased on to Londinium, city of trade, and we burned the place down, even to the ships in the docks. Suetonius was there with his battalions, but when he heard we were at the gates he took his armies with him and fled, leaving the city without protection. So most fled with him, except those too ill or old or weak or stupid to venture it. These too we sought out and killed; they were better dead, and besides, they worshipped false Gods. Our people took the spoils of war, and more, and marvelled at what they found. There were merchants in that place from distant nations I had never heard of, spices and dishes and colours unthought of. Silks and jewels and delicate silver earrings. How great is this world, how small we are, for all our blood and murders and vengeance. The world outside the forest. When I am Queen of a land cleansed of Rome, I might build my own kingdom. I might guide my people out of the woods, away from the mud, teach them to wash and to read and write, to sew silks as well as furs, to prepare foods and eat at table and not crouch on the ground and tear with their teeth. Yes, I would quite like to do that. It shall be done. Now I think I can sleep. There is a breeze getting up. The leaves of the forest are stirring. That promises well for the morning.

Midnight, July 9th, AD 62

I, Boadicea. Tonight I will sleep well. I will sleep so soundly I will never wake. What was that story, Prasutagus, husband, of Cleopatra Queen of Egypt, who fell in love with Antony of Rome, and when he betrayed her, as Romans will, put an asp to her bosom and killed herself? There will be nothing so grand for me: I am a woman of the forests, Queen of the Iceni, a Warrior Tribe, and I take the poison of the forests. I join my people, so many dead, so very few left alive. How strong they were, those Romans. They fight for glory, not for vengeance. It is more powerful. They used their javelins to halt our charge, their shields to fell us, their swords to kill us. Each man was as three. They didn't stop to plunder the dead, as we did: there were as many women in our ranks as men, bare-breasted too, this seemed not to moderate their ruthlessness but to increase it: they killed us coldly, as if we were a kind of vermin not worth the effort of their endeavour. And those of us who tried to flee were trapped, we could not get out of the valley into which the Romans had driven us: our ways of escape were blocked by the carts of our own people, who had turned out in their hundreds to see the fun, and brought along their children too. They came as sightseers to watch Boadicea, Warrior Queen of the Iceni, whose fame had spread through all the tribes, cut down the Romans. So, husband, I was defeated by my own success, my own glory; I was punished for it by the Gods. They have no liking for mortals who rival them in renown. The uprising of the tribes of Britain fails, and be sure the Romans will write that in their history books.

*   *   *

And I know what comes next because I am a woman, and I know how the household goes. We've been so busy with our hate we haven't planted the fields, and now there is nothing to harvest, and there will be famine in the land, and Roman rule will be harsher than ever. For a time, that is, until our bitterness and reluctance begins to affect their profits, and then they will lighten the yoke and claim credit for their mercy. And one day they will be gone altogether because the centre cannot hold, but I will not be there to witness it. I, Boadicea, Queen of the Iceni, joined to my husband in the afterlife.

HOW WE LIVE NOW

Nothing to Wear

Heaven Knows

Living by the Small Print

Queen Gertrude plc – a radio play

Nothing to Wear

It was at half past four on Tuesday June 6th that Charles realised he had a problem. They had plans for the evening. Emily and he were to have tea at the Ritz – he'd booked it for five – and after that they'd go on to the Summer Exhibition at Burlington House.

Tea at the Ritz was mostly for Charles, for when he visited his old mother in her nursing home on Sunday afternoon and gave an account of his week. Tea at the Ritz was a useful talking point, being a concept the old lady could still understand, and there were allied subjects to discuss, such as how no-one knew how to make cucumber sandwiches any more, let alone how to blanch cucumber. And Emily quite liked the Ritz. She said she found it relaxing.

Then they'd go on to the Private View across the road, and if they got there early, he might well meet up with his friend Marlowe. Then he could casually mention the good studio property about to come on the market in South Kensington, a snip at two and a half million. He knew Marlowe was looking. If it worked there'd be a good commission in it for Charles.

But it was already half past four and here was Emily not even dressed, and not quite sitting, but somehow crouched, folded, on the bedroom carpet, wailing, 'I've nothing to wear.'

She crouched in her silk slip, pretty as a picture by a slightly astigmatic painter, her legs so long and her hips so slim that for the first time it struck him that there was something unreasonable about her looks. Other girls were pear-shaped, or had shorter necks, and complained of not being able to find clothes to fit. But Emily was the one designers liked to lend clothes to for grand occasions, because she showed them off so well. She catwalk modelled sometimes when she could be bothered, which was not often. She gave the impression of having sprung to life not from between human thighs but from a sketch in some couturier's notebook. Yet her mother was dumpy enough.

'I've nothing to wear,' she repeated, 'not a thing.' They had been married for five months. He realised by now that she had dressing problems the way other girls had eating problems, but he loved her and he indulged her, or at any rate had until now, when he suddenly found himself irritated. She sat surrounded by Blahnik shoes, and Ferreti dresses, and Etro jackets, and leather skirts by Versace, and Westwood corsets, torn from their hangers and flung anywhere on the floor, and the price of them added up was beyond belief. His pocket was not bottomless: he had to wheel and deal like anyone else and it was not easy.

'I don't want us to be late,' he said, rashly. 'Just put on any old thing. You always look fantastic.'

'Men always say that,' she said. 'It isn't true. I look absurd. For one thing my head is too small for my body. Haven't you even noticed?'

'I think it's about the same as anyone else's,' he said, but he could see what she meant. She went to the gym every morning: exercise developed her shoulders, but not her head, so she did seem a little out of proportion.

'I'm a monster,' she said. 'A freak. My eyes look like that alien's in *E.T.*'

'You could eat more,' he suggested and she threw a boot at him and laughed. He loved her laugh. 'Seriously though,' she said, 'I haven't a thing to wear.'

He picked up a filmy silk thing without much top. 'How about this? It's a nice colour.'

'Don't be absurd,' she said. 'It might work for the Summer

Exhibition but then there's tea at the Ritz as well.' He could see that it had become his fault that she had nothing to wear, because of his mother.

'People will be looking at their sandwiches and the paintings and not at you,' he said, though it wasn't true and he knew it. He just didn't want to miss Marlowe. It would be difficult enough finding him in the crush.

'That thing you wore to Ascot,' he suggested.

'That's the whole point, I wore it to Ascot. And it's no good without a hat anyway. And nobody who isn't weird or my mother wears a hat to an art show.'

'I just wear a suit,' he said, 'and it could be any old suit.'

'That's simply not true. I married an Armani man. Don't go and change on me.'

Her wardrobe took up the whole wall. Scarcely a day went by that she didn't buy something new. Sometimes she just shoved the bags at the back of the cupboard to open later, and forgot all about them.

'I've nothing to wear,' she said again.

'You're turning into a weirdo,' he said, losing patience. 'Just put something on and hurry up about it. I'll order a taxi now.'

Tears from the enormous eyes rolled down her thin cheeks. She was not accustomed to harsh words. He felt bad and after he'd ordered the taxi he sat on the floor with her, to be companionable.

'But I'm not being unreasonable,' she said, snuggling into him. 'It's just the shoes are doing my head in. I'm going to have to walk from the Ritz to Burlington House and you can never sit down at Private Views, and supposing my feet begin to hurt? If the rest is right the shoes aren't and vice versa. And Genia Marlowe will be there and Marlowe's made her pregnant, and she'll stand there with her six-month bump in stretch Versace being mobbed by the media. Babies are chic and everything, but personally I think she looks totally yuk.'

'Look,' he said, 'if you want a baby I'm not all that set against it.' He had been married before, and had two almost grown-up children, and was well into his forties. Emily was not yet thirty.

'Are you crazy? What makes you think I want to have a baby?'
'But you said you did,' he said, taken by surprise.
'Did I? That must have been a long time ago, before we were married,' she said. 'I've changed my mind. Genia Marlowe says she's going to breast-feed. I think that is so completely disgusting.'
'The taxi's here,' he said.
She uttered a shriek and stretched her long limbs out on the carpet and thrummed her pretty little fists into the white pile. She was a having a tantrum. He hadn't seen this before. He was afraid she would damage her feet as they banged against the floor.

He called up her mother in the country to ask for help. He'd never done that before, either.

'Oh dear,' said Mrs Julia Forresther. 'Not again! She used to do that all the time when she was little. The church bell would be ringing for morning service and there'd be our little Emily, throwing a tantrum because her ankle socks had frills, or didn't, I can't remember which.'

Julia and her husband had recently downsized, perforce, and the big house was gone and now Julia grew roses in her cottage garden, and her husband read all the books he'd never had time to read when he was something in the City. They seemed happy enough. Emily's income fortunately came from a trust fund, but the expected inheritance would never come, which made it all the more important that Charles got to drop a word in Marlowe's ear.

'Perhaps it's because she's a younger sister,' Julia offered. 'She never quite thinks she has enough, and what she has will never quite do. Or perhaps it's me. I never wanted to wear anything other than a comfy jersey and an old skirt. I never liked being noticed and I never cared what others thought. I expect Emily likes to make up for what she sees as my shortcomings.' There was a tinge of acid in her voice.

'But what do I do with her?' asked Charles. 'I hate being late for things.'

'You're just like her father,' said Julia. 'A stickler for punctuality. I expect that's why she married you. Now Katherine takes after me. Very relaxed. Sit it out, is my advice, and she'll be good as gold for the rest of the day. That's what I used to do.'

Charles called Katherine. Emily was still thrumming and still in her slip and outside the front door of the pretty little Chelsea house the taxi meter was clicking up. Katherine was older than Emily by two years. She favoured a neater and more expensive version of her mother's clothes, and changed her style only as Marks & Spencer did. She was married to a barrister and had three children. She went to Ascot, not to be seen, but to look at the horses and meet up with her sister. They were quite affectionate with one another.

'Get her to talk to me,' said Katherine. Emily consented to take the phone. She'd calmed down though she still gulped air. Charles listened from the other side of the door.

'It's Charles's fault,' complained Emily. 'He's so weird. He only wants to go to the Ritz because of his dotty old mother and I'm the living sacrifice, and he expects me to wear the same thing to both of them, and I've nothing to wear anyway.'

There was pause while Katherine spoke.

'That spotted la Croix thing? Are you joking? It's head to toe and last year's, and makes my bum look large, and nobody's wearing spots, and I have to show some flesh,' said Emily. 'Everyone will be showing flesh. Genia Marlowe will have a naked belly, I bet, with the navel pierced, if she can find it to pierce.'

Again Katherine spoke.

'Suede's cruel,' said Emily. 'You really are weird, Katherine. And it's far too solid, not in the least floaty, and floaty is in. I know you wear the same T-shirt three days running, but you live in the country where nobody sees you except kids and animals.'

Charles gave up and was about to send the taxi away when Emily came dancing out of the house wearing a pair of jeans, a lilac beaded chiffon blouse with frills, and pointy gold shoes cut so low they showed her toes, and so insubstantial he didn't see how they could carry all six feet of her. The secret no doubt lay in their cost. Her eyes were a little pink and she sniffed but she leant up against him trustingly in the taxi. At the Ritz she ate a whole plateful of tiny cucumber sandwiches, and looked so lovely, fresh and happy people stared, and there was an incident when a Japanese guest tried to take a photograph of her, and security appeared out of nowhere and confiscated the camera. He hadn't even known she was celebrity, being a tourist.

'I must tell Genia Marlowe about that,' said Emily. She had been to school with Genia.

They crossed the road to Burlington House. Emily stepped into the bus lane without looking, and Charles had to pull her back or she would have been run down.
'It was coming from the wrong direction,' complained Emily.
'You should have read the signs,' said Charles. 'It wasn't the driver's fault, it was yours.'
'Why do you always take my enemy's side?' she asked. 'You're so like my father I can't bear it'. She looked at him for a moment almost as if she hated him, but quickly composed her face again, and took his arm. She limped a little but denied that it was anything to do with the shoes.

They arrived at the Private View half an hour later than he had hoped, and the Marlowes had been and gone. There was a painting on the wall of a naked Genia, however, proudly pregnant. Journalists crowded round it, and guests mobbed the painter, a burly, bearded young man in a tattered green jumper, which looked as if he had slept in it. Certainly he had spilled soup down it. Charles caught a glimpse of Tattery Abel the art dealer, a man reputed to be rich as Croesus, with four Edward Hoppers, three Jackson Pollocks and five Andy Warhols to his name, who liked to dabble in painting himself. So failing Marlowe Charles fell into conversation with Tattery, and mentioned the fact that one of the best of the original studio houses in South Ken was coming onto the market soon, at about three mill. Tattery was undoubtedly interested and took his e-mail address.

Charles looked for Emily and found her deep in conversation with the painter in the green jumper, while photographers from the gossip columns and the arts pages snapped away. She'd like that: no-one seemed to take pictures of Charles any more, not since he'd taken a wife and stopped being the most eligible bachelor in town, even though it was Emily he had married. Charles wandered off to look at the paintings on the wall. He imagined Emily was persuading the artist to paint her portrait, and didn't doubt that she'd succeed.

Fifteen minutes later he came back to see how she was doing and found her sitting on a little gold chair while Green Jumper, on his knees, took off her shoes for her, and put one in each pocket of his trousers, little heels sticking out. The artist helped her up, tucking her arm under his, and took off his sandals to keep her company, showing dirty toes, and the pair of them went round happily in bare feet, he deriding the paintings, and she enthusing.

When next he went to look for Emily he couldn't find her. Marlowe turned up and said he'd seen her leaving with a weird-looking slob in a green jumper. They'd called a taxi. Charles mentioned the studio house in South Ken and was gratified by the other's eager response. Now he could play Tattery off against Marlowe, and the price would go up. He went home on his own.

*   *   *

The next time he saw Emily was when she opened the door to him a year later. She was living with Green Jumper in a dilapidated barn conversion in Essex. There had not been much to discuss in relation to the divorce; she'd left it to his lawyers. Charles had claimed alimony and Emily hadn't argued, to the extent of leaving herself with barely enough to live on. She hadn't bothered to come back to collect her clothes.

Green Jumper hovered in the background while Charles got Emily to sign a few necessary documents. Charles stayed on the step and was not asked in. The house smelt of garlic, oil paint, dogs and turpentine. Emily was wearing a frumpy jumper like her mother's and a soiled suede skirt of an unflattering length, and she was pregnant. If you hardly had anything at all to wear, he could see, having nothing to wear wouldn't matter too much, and the pain of it would be greatly eased. He was happy for her.

Heaven Knows

A Christmas story

'This baby is not going to be born on Christmas Day,' said Carol to her husband. 'It happened to me, but it shall not happen to a child of mine.' Her husband, as it happened, was also a Christmas Day baby but being Jewish had managed to escape with the name Linley, which heaven knew was bad enough.

'Do remember,' Linley said mildly to his wife, 'that all kinds of things have come about which you were determined should not happen. You are married, which you never meant to be, disapproving of the institution as you do. You are pregnant, which you never intended. And this house is strung with Christmas decorations, of the kind you claim to most despise.'

It was true enough that this year their normally elegant, minimalist loft space was gaudy with traditional decorations of the Woolworth kind, not the discreet and burnished kind that come from the Designers Guild. Crudely coloured glass balls hung higgledy-piggledy from a real Christmas tree which shed messy spikes from the moment it was in place. Shiny stars, bright as an Indian elephant in processional dress, glittered above them as they ate their low-fat, calorie-conscious, delectable meals.

'Victorian decorations are in this year,' said Carol, a little pathetically, by way of explanation, seeing his censorious gaze. 'It's called the Prince Alfred touch. I do seem to have gone rather too far.

It's nothing to do with being pregnant,' she added, before her husband could say anything. 'Nothing whatsoever.' She could not bear to think that her moods, her decisions, or her judgement were in any way affected by her condition.

'What's the matter with a Christmas baby anyway?' asked Linley, but then he would, wouldn't he.

'Firstly,' said Carol firmly, 'it's not fair on the baby. I hardly ever got a decent birthday present when I was a child; mine were all subsumed into the Christmas gift frenzy. Whereas my younger sister Claire, whose birthday was on June 1st, always got a proper present and had a birthday party as well. Secondly, supposing the baby were born on the stroke of midnight, or near it, and TV news crews came to the hospital to take pictures of mother and child, as they do? One would simply not look one's best. It can't be risked. And thirdly and most importantly I think my will should take precedence over the baby's. Let us begin as we mean to go on. No spoilt brat for me. I shall keep it inside me until January 6th or thereabouts. That was the original prognostication and fits in well with my plans at work.'

Carol's earnings as a systems analyst in a City bank were into six figures and Linley was a design consultant whose income plunged and soared in an unnerving way but seldom fell below the point where they had to think twice about anything they chose to spend. Carol intended to work until the last moment and return after three months of intensive child care, thus giving the child the best chance in life, nutritionally and emotionally.

Carol was happy as she was, to tell you the truth, without a child, and perfectly in love with Linley, and very much afraid that if two were company, three might be none, but she would do her best by this baby, as she did her best about everything. She dreaded the limitations on freedom, not to mention income, which must of necessity accompany a baby, but a baby had come along, as babies do, if only by accident. Undoing that accident turned out on investigation to be such a shockingly messy and crude business it seemed preferable to leave things as they were, and simply give birth, and cope. Other women managed, so surely she, Carol, famous for her clarity of thought, her energy, her efficiency, her earning capacity and logicality, would manage better.

'You'll have to ask Sister Kelly about that,' said Linley. 'But I have a feeling a baby's wishes in this matter are hard to withstand.' 'Bother Sister Kelly,' said Carol. 'I'm the mother. She's only the midwife. What does she know?' Pregnancy flushed her dark cheeks and made her eyes sparkle, and also, Linley thought, made her petulant, like a charming child. These days she made him laugh.

Sister Audrey Kelly was now saying, to Carol's dismay, that the baby was more likely to come along in the last week of December than the first week of January. She didn't care what the scans said, she had been delivering babies for forty years, and she had a feeling for these things. Audrey Kelly was in her late sixties and broad and robust in her looks as well as her opinions. She was too heavy and had thin hair and wore no make-up but could make you laugh. She was a heretic, and a hoot, Carol and Linley agreed. She should have been retired by now but there was such a shortage of midwives in the land she had been asked to stay on. Carol liked Audrey Kelly and felt safe with her, as if finally she had a proper mother, who could be relied upon and knew what she was doing. Carol's real mother had been awash with hopeless sentiment and prey to a slovenly inefficiency, and had managed to lose one husband after another in her life, culminating in Carol's father, which Carol held against her.

'At least,' Linley had said when they married, 'you'll do your best not to lose me. Getting rid of me would make you look too much like your mother.' They had resolved early on not to marry – the legal implications were so horrific – but had weakened after

Carol became pregnant. Now here they were, the Mr and Mrs they had never thought to be, Linley's family upset because he was marrying out, her principles compromised, all because of a baby.

They had purchased the apartment below theirs and were having it converted to a nanny-and-baby unit but the builders had let them down and the conversion might not be finished until March. Dust crept up from down below and distressed them. They were such a clean and tidy couple, neat, small-boned and handsome. They liked everything planned and in order. Normally they went to a country hotel for the few days around Christmas, which was deathly dull but could be relied upon to provide the rest they always so badly needed. This year, just in case Sister Kelly was right, they'd decided to stay at home, to be near the hospital. Grit seeped up through the floorboards and got everywhere, even into the crème brûlée, for which Carol had developed a demeaning craving.

'Many first babies are born into builder's rubble,' Audrey Kelly had consoled them. 'Parents feel the need for change but builders seldom share their sense of urgency.'

Meanwhile the Christmas season closed in upon them, with its peculiar sense of foreboding and excitement mixed: the weather was cold and clear and still: you'd scarcely had lunch but it was dusk and lights sprang into brilliance all around. People rushed about at twice their normal speed, Carol said, but everything had really gone on hold: you had to spend and spend and spend the better to give the material world validity. You couldn't blame people. Real work stopped, regardless of office policy, and it was unnerving.

She had become fanciful, even superstitious, Linley thought. She wouldn't walk under ladders, and gazed at the full moon and denied that men had ever landed on it (it had all been faked in the studio) and wondered whether her grandmother's soul – her grandmother had died early on in the pregnancy – had passed into the baby, and what did happen after you died if the birth rate was falling and there were no new babies available – idle thoughts, idle questions, of which no-one would ever know the answer so what was the point of asking?

As they ate their chicken in lemon sauce from Marks & Spencer a week before Christmas, Linley noticed that the glitzy streamers which criss-crossed the ceiling had been fixed to the wall with Blu-Tak, which was bound to make a mess of the plaster when removed. In normal times he would have protested vigorously but his wife was so pregnant, and his heart filled suddenly with such great tenderness towards her he could forgive her anything, even Blu-Tak. He found himself worrying more that she must have stood on a chair to fix the streamers and could have fallen off it and hurt herself and the baby, than about any offence to taste. He could see that he too was changing.

That evening Sister Kelly called by mid-meal to see how Carol was getting on. Working mothers had to put up with being called upon at inconvenient hours. The midwife and the mother had an unusual little tiff. It was about the date of the birth.

Carol said she didn't want the baby until January 6, Audrey Kelly was quite sharp in her response, echoing Linley. 'Babies do what they want, not what the mother wants,' she said.

Linley had offered her tea and made a pot of delicate Chinese Oolong, and Audrey Kelly drank it, though Carol thought perhaps she would have preferred traditional English. But Linley could never understand that his own taste was not universal, and in these days of late pregnancy Carol went for an easy and not an improving-of-Linley life.

'There's medication to bring childbirth forward,' said Carol. 'Surely there's medication to delay it?'

'No there isn't,' said Audrey Kelly, 'or not for the likes of you, anyway, and not when you've arrived at term. What are you, a control freak?'

That hurt. It was what Carol's family accused her of being, when she attempted to improve their sloppy lives: persuaded her sister Claire of the need to lose weight, or her mother to let a room in her house, with which she could pay off her mortgage before old age set in.

'It's for the baby's sake,' said Carol plaintively. 'I was born on Christmas Day and I know what it's like.'

'It's a small price to pay for being on time,' said Audrey Kelly. 'Not overdone, or underdone, just right!'

But Carol was not to be persuaded. The next morning she went behind Sister Kelly's back and arranged with a private hospital to have a Caesarean on the sixth.

'But darling,' said Linley, 'if Sister Kelly is right the likelihood is that the baby will come before then. We'll lose the booking fee at the hospital.'

'She isn't right,' said Carol bleakly, 'and we won't.' Suddenly she was at war with the whole world: with the shoppers in the streets, with the storm clouds now building massively in the east – a cold snap was expected for Christmas – with carol singers and chestnut roasters and mostly with her own body. How could it have betrayed her so?

She bought rosy red apples from a street vendor to complement the Prince Albert motif, but didn't look closely enough and when Linley took them out of the bag his finger went right through one. It was rotten. She made him take them back and demand the return of her money, and Linley did, though it went right against his non-confrontational grain. The vendor's rage if he did it was less than Carol's rage if he didn't.

*   *   *

At the office Christmas party someone brought Carol a chair to sit on and she said crossly, 'I am not an invalid,' and stood for three hours and twenty minutes and then fainted.

'I did not faint,' she said.

'Then why are you lying on the floor?' her boss asked her. She had no reply to that. Her boss said he hoped she'd have her sanity back in three months' time and why didn't she go home right now and put her feet up until then? She went, appalled, while her drunken fellow analysts sang a ridiculous if affectionate song after her; something about 'Cleopatra, Queen o' de Nile' (Queen of Denial – someone explained). It was beginning already – life as a mother – while Linley hopped and skipped about, unburdened by this terrible weight around the middle.

She went to a department store to buy last-moment toys for Claire's three spoilt brats, and saw the line of children waiting to go into Father Christmas's grotto, and could see no charm in them, only grotesque, wizened, greedy, grey little faces. Babies were bad enough but this was what they grew into. A total stranger patted her stomach and said what are you going to call it? She shrieked and ran.

'A good question,' said Linley. 'What are we going to call it?' Carol said it was unlucky to name a baby before it was born, and Sister Kelly said that was ridiculous. In the first three months perhaps but at eight months and three weeks – one week, corrected Carol, tight-lipped – that was going a bit far. They had elected not to be told the gender of the baby, but Linley reckoned from a glimpse once when it turned mid-scan that it was a boy. He wanted to call it Joseph. Carol said he wanted to return to his Jewish roots, and had only married her because he felt sorry for her, she was so unattractive, and now he regretted it. He flung his hands in the air and said yes, of course, and she should convert and could shave her head and wear a wig and punish herself some more if she chose, but she wasn't going to punish him for a decision she had made more than him, namely to go ahead with the baby.

Sister Kelly interrupted them mid-row. 'It is perfectly normal for couples to fight at this late stage,' she said.

'What do you mean, this late stage? This baby is not coming until January the 6th,' shrieked Carol, 'and that is that.'

Sister Kelly murmured that there were some safe sedatives she thought perhaps Carol could take, but Linley was worried about that. Supposing it harmed the baby?

Carol thought Mary Anne would be a nice name for a girl. Plain but kind of cute and old-fashioned. Girl-next-doorish. 'I don't want a baby who's a girl-next-door type,' said Linley. 'I want a cool sophisticate. How about Erica?'

'Yuk,' cried Carol. Suddenly there were pains all over her body. Her sciatic nerve gave her hell and her back had a permanent ache and she couldn't even do squats any more. Nurse Kelly said *she* couldn't do those at the best of times.

'Leon,' said Linley. 'Or is that too Jewish for you?'

'You forget,' said Carol acidly, 'I'm converting.'

They slept away from each other at night. Such a wide, wide bed they had, costing so much money, it could be easily done. Carol could see that it was better to be very pregnant rich than poor.

Carol broke it to Sister Kelly that it wasn't going to be a natural birth on the State, but a private hospital Caesarean to order on the sixth, and the midwife was fired.

'If you don't mind,' said Audrey Kelly, 'I'll continue coming on a daily basis as before. You are quite a nervy mother.'

'I am not,' said Carol, trembling with passion. 'There's not an unsettled nerve in my body.'

'I suppose if it's a girl,' said Linley, 'which heaven forfend, we could call it Maude, to fit into the Prince Albert theme.' A few friends had been round with good wishes and had raised their eyes at the decorations and Linley had apologised for them.

Carol's doing, Carol's condition. She didn't even wait for them to go before attacking her husband with nails and fists. Her house, her home, her money, he would be nothing without her, nothing.

And how she spent, as if there would be no spending tomorrow, which perhaps there wouldn't be, if her heart melted in the face of the baby, not that that seemed likely at the moment. Linley was so obstreperously lively on his feet, Carol so lumbering and scowling, her fingers easy enough with the credit cards all the same, he noticed, in the great general final Christmas spend. She bought a whole heavy ugly cutlery set for £1200 before the sales even began, and some Georgian silver tongs to pick up asparagus, as a gift for her sister Claire who hated asparagus. Part of the community as never before, the pair of them.

Six o'clock on Monday 24th and a great peace fell on the land. The shops shut. Doors closed. The nation holed itself up for its holiday. Too late now. All the passion and rage and doubt fell away as if by magic.

'Darling,' asked Carol, 'is that you? What's been happening? I love you.'

'Is that you?' asked Linley. 'Where've you been? I've really missed you.'

They opened a bottle of wine – she thought she could have a couple of glasses, at this stage – and the tin of Marks & Spencer chocolate biscuits Claire had given her – as fat people will, in the hope that everyone will join their club – and looked at each other with love. At nine o'clock Carol felt the first pain and claimed it was indigestion. Two minutes later there was another one and Linley called for Sister Kelly.

'Not much time for anything here,' said Audrey Kelly, 'not even hospital. But lightning births are the safest.'

She cursed the concealed lighting but Linley managed to twist one of the spots to ease the problem and at twelve midnight precisely the baby let out a cry of delight, or whatever it was, and Carol let out one that certainly was and Linley enfolded wife and son in his arms.

'Christmas baby,' said Nurse Kelly happily. 'I knew it would be. These things are inherited. As for the name, that's obvious.'

'What's that?' they asked.

'Noel,' said the midwife.

'Okay,' they both said, relieved.

Living by the Small Print

I like Christmas Eve. The office closes at midday. I reckon to get all my Christmas shopping done in the few hours available before the big stores shut. That's usually around four or four-thirty. Colleagues marvel at my efficiency, but I explain it's just a question of being organised. It's not that I'm so great, I say, it's just that you lot are so inefficient: you worry and fret and get neurotic. All you have to do is forward plan, know exactly what you mean to buy, and go to any big department store of which you have previously obtained a floor map. By leaving it to the last moment, too, you can save money. By December 24th the stores are setting up for the post-Christmas sales, a lot of stuff is already marked as reduced, and sales staff are too exhausted by the seasonal long hours to keep up any argument that everything is meant to be full price till Boxing Day. Marked down is marked down, say I, and they capitulate.

It's not that I'm mean, you understand. I just don't like spending money unnecessarily. I see so much of it. I work for a large insurance company, monitoring claims. This year I was promoted to Head of Department: I take the responsibility seriously. People waste so much money just because they can't be bothered to read the small print. It appals me. I'm sorry for them sometimes but what can I do? So an owl flies in an open window and leaves a nasty trail across the wedding feast, including the cake, and you put in a claim. But bird damage is specifically excluded in your agreement I say. You get nothing. There it is, bold as brass. Well bold might not be quite the word, but there it is all the same. 'But I've spent £900 a year for the last fifteen years on insurance, and never claimed a thing,' comes the response, 'now my daughter's wedding is ruined, is this all you can do for me?' And all I can say is, 'Sorry, you should have read the small print.' I think before my promotion I might have stretched a point – we do have some discretion – but not now. I see my duty as being to my employers.

Mind you, the toy department can be a bit tricky by Christmas Eve; things do sell out, and one may have to revise one's list pretty quickly, but there's always the educational toys to fall back upon. If staff act reluctant and say, 'But it's so late, Parcel Collection in the basement must just about be closing,' I remind them of their Christmas ads, and put it to them that they don't want to be in contravention of the Trade Descriptions Act. The whole store is advertised as open, not just bits of it. They soon enough find a messenger to take whatever it is first to gift wrapping, then down to the basement to await collection.

A ceiling of £10 a present and ten presents to buy and that's exactly £100 for Christmas, plus train fares home to my parents for the family get-together. Not bad. I book the train well in advance to make sure I get a good reduction. If there's any nonsense I demand that they call Head Office and get management to read them the small print on discounted fares. Best to book such tickets in person, in the rush hour. A long queue behind, pressing for attention, usually brings results.

Anyway, at four-twenty-six – gift shopping complete, and only £89 spent – it was time to turn my attention to me. I went on up to the Bargain Bin on the third floor – that's Fashion – to look for some glitzy top to wear with my jeans for the New Year's party. I have just about a perfect figure – 34, 26, 34 – which I've dieted and exercised and liposucked to achieve – so most things look okay on me, they don't have to be expensive. I found a piece of really agreeable glitter, low-cut to make the most of the

34. It was reduced from £90 to £8 – not bad at all. I do rather rely on the New Year's party to find my escort for the year. Around September I tend to get fed up with them and say goodbye; then I give myself three months solo in which to firm up the girlfriends; that done, my bed begins to feel a little empty and by Christmas I'm quite looking forward to filling it with someone new. I'm only twenty-eight, too young to settle down. As it happens, last year's escort actually dumped me before I could dump him, and that's made me nervous. His name was Corin.

'I don't know what's the matter with you,' said Corin, as he walked out. 'Every day you seem to get meaner and tougher. Perhaps it's your job.'

I am not tough, I am not mean, I am just practical and hate waste. If anything I'm too soft. I even trained as a nurse. My heart bled for humanity: so much so I had to give up because of the stress. Now at least suffering humanity only comes to me through the post or at the end of a phone, if reception slips up and lets the calls through.

I should be feeling happy and relaxed, here in the bosom of my loving family, in the time of year I most love, in that blissful torpor which descends on the land between Christmas and the New Year, when the office is closed and the streets are empty and you have time to have baths and read books and think about yourself. I don't often do that. There isn't time, is there? I often work a twelve-hour day.

For some reason I feel like crying. I've turned soft and gentle. See what just five days away from the office can do for a girl? I sit in my childhood bedroom looking out over the bare garden, and think of Corin. I miss him. I can hear my mother pottering about in the living room below doing her annual lament at the too early falling of the Christmas tree spikes, and my father tangling with the streamers as ever, and my twin nieces and one nephew arguing over their toys. I don't know how my sister Effie had the courage to have children: I don't know how any woman has. You have no control whatsoever over what comes out, and no insurance. If ever I have children I'll have them by cloning, thank you very much. Fortunately Effie's kids seem just about okay and I love them and they love me.

But anyway, my gold top. I had quite a tussle with this particular sales girl. She had greasy blonde hair with black roots. She said the top had got into the Bargain Bin by mistake, and was a designer piece and the asking price was £90 and I had to pay the shelf price. That was absurd. Blackroots was temporary Christmas staff: they can be greater sticklers than the regular girls. I noticed her hand was trembling: I knew then I would win. I demanded to see the Manager, and when Blackroots claimed she'd already have gone home, inasmuch as the store was now closed, I said oh no the store wasn't, while my stuff was down in the basement waiting for me to turn up it couldn't close. First I made her call down to the Collection Point to confirm that they understood this. Then I made her come with me to the sixth floor on the Managerial Level and we banged on doors until we found some woman still packing up, who after I had explained the situation in detail said, 'Oh give it to her for £8, for God's sake just give it to her,' and we went downstairs. When I said I wanted the top gift wrapped Blackroots began to cry and I relented, and said, 'Okay just shove it in any old bag,' and she did. I do have a kind heart. I even said, 'I do hope you get to the hairdresser before tomorrow, so you can get your roots done.'

It was ten past five by the time the janitor had unlocked the Collection Point – can you imagine, they'd just shut up shop and gone home, their business unfinished? I would never have done a thing like that. As a result I actually missed my train, and had to get the next one and you can imagine what happened then. The conductor said my ticket wasn't valid on the train, I argued that it was the crowds on the platform as a result of a

couple of their cancelled trains which had held me up, so it was
the Railway Company's fault, not mine. I got my way, but only
after a short unscheduled stop while the Railway Police were
called, and somehow I didn't feel the normal stab of triumph,
in fact I felt rather depressed. Why is everything always so uphill?

If I go on getting value for money like this I will have the deposit
of a house saved within a year. But who will there be to help me
with the mortgage? No lovers in sight, and friends pretty thin
on the ground. My bright idea for giving up smoking was never
to buy cigarettes but always to ask others for them, and let social
embarrassment stand between me and the wasteful, unhealthy
habit. But I think my s.e. threshold is rather high; it must be. I
smoked just as many cigarettes and ended up with fewer friends.

Downstairs someone opens a window.
'Now all the robots are broken,' one of the twins is saying, 'we've
only got what Auntie Bug Meanie gave us.' Me, Auntie Bug
Meanie?
'Hush. She'll hear,' says my sister. 'We don't want to upset her.'
'Why not?' asks the niece, in the manner of small children.
'She's upset enough as it is,' says my sister, and I suppose that's
true. Since Corin walked out I've been unhappy. I haven't seen
why other people should be having a good time when I'm not.
My father says I've grown obsessive about money, but he's a one
to talk. He's a gambler: he spends money obsessively, the way I
save it. And they even make him pay an entrance fee to get into
their bloody casino: I'd never stand for that. He's too soft. I
begin to cry. Time stretches forward and back in an odd way.
Forward to the New Year's Eve party where I just might meet
Mr Right, with the aid of a gold top which I should have paid
£90 for and paid £8. Back to Christmas Eve when I bought it,
and that poor girl with the black roots crying. I hope she got to
the hairdresser: bet she didn't. And then Christmas Day, and my
mother opening her diary, and my father his wallet – you can
get both in leather goods – and my sister her gardening gloves

and my brother-in-law his secateurs – both from gardening, the next section along – and the children their educational gifts, just down the escalator – and all their faces as they opened them: and how the adults seemed both polite and somehow concerned, and the children just plain unbelieving. It's true that once I was famous for the originality and extravagance of my presents, and would never, never, have had a store gift-wrap anything. It would be all wicked paper wrap and coloured string and tags and bows and glitter and so forth, done by me. And I wondered what was happening to me?

I call Corin on his mobile. I know the number by heart though it's six months since we split.

'I think you're right,' I said. 'I blame my job. If they pay you to be mean and tough that's what you become. If you get paid for reading the small print you get into the habit.'

There was silence at the other end of the phone. Then Corin said, 'You could try blaming yourself.'

So I put the phone down. He was a pompous prat: I'd quite got over him. But I thought I might call by the store and leave a box of chocolates for Blackroots, who put my wicked designer gold top in the Bargain Bin by mistake – forget about how you shouldn't reward people for being careless. She might even become my friend. I might even, who knows, chuck in my job and go back to nursing. Try living by the small print and everyone hates you. I give up.

Queen Gertrude plc

A radio play

Part 1

Morning:

1.

Exterior: Central City sounds. Joyous cathedral bells. People are on their way to work on a fine bright morning. We hear snatches of the news from the radio. 'This morning's inflation figures show a reduction of .2 per cent from 5.8 per cent to 5.6. Two years after the pound sterling gave way to the Euro, the new currency finally levels with the US dollar. "The success we anticipated," says Prime Minister.'

2.

Interior: The clip clop of high heels on marble floors beneath a vaulted hall, the splash of civic fountains, a murmur of mostly male City voices. The heels stop. A sigh. A woman speaks: firm, confident, soothing, in her middle years: a woman who knows best, accustomed to power. The voice of female politicians everywhere, profoundly reasonable. In public at any rate – in private it's different.

GERTRUDE: The office day begins. Thank God.

Lift doors open. GERTRUDE *steps inside. The doors close.*

3.

In the elevator, which is steel and glass and sleek, but nevertheless a box, soundwise.

GERTRUDE: Executive penthouse, non-stop.

ELEVATOR: Good morning, Miss Gertrude Hazlitt.
GERTRUDE: Morning, elevator.
ELEVATOR: And a very pleasant morning too.
Doors close.

ELEVATOR: On our way!
GERTRUDE'S THINK VOICE: Bloody personalised American lift, voice-activated. Artificial intelligence. Why should I want to converse with it? I don't want a conversation with anyone, let alone an elevator. Why can't it just do its job and shut up? It makes me uncomfortable – state-of-the-art, steel and silver and glass, hidden sensors, observing me. Supposing I want to pick my nose? All the same, if my friends could see me now. My own executive elevator, for my use and mine alone, to carry me non-stop to the highest level of all, the seventy-second floor, highest building in all Europe. Long live Britain and long live technology.

Problem: this is the age of equality. Should a chief executive, even one of my standing, have an elevator reserved for them alone? Who does she think she is, they'll be saying down below. They know who I am: I am Gertrude Hazlitt, top dog, top bitch, queen of all I survey. Chief Executive of the biggest, newest, government-funded public-private business enterprise in the UK. Britain at Work plc. I deserve my personalised, me-programmed artificial intelligence elevator, even though I do wish it would just shut up. I deserve my penthouse office at the top of the People's Palace. Top dogs, fat cats should never be seen waiting: someone might get ideas and come along and push them off the window ledge, down, down, down. Top job of top jobs: too bad, men, you've had it, now the women are on the march.

Up, up, up – hah, I love that feeling in the pit of the stomach as it really takes off after the twentieth. Reminds me of sex, that long-forgotten thing – not since Duncan left, too long, how long now, four years? Don't think about it. At least I have no children to wear me down, worry me to bits, like so many of my friends.

Friends, what friends? I've left them all behind. But there'll be enough people at my funeral, that's the main thing. They all come to see you when you're dead, happy to brush up against the famous. Dead. No, I don't believe in death, death is for other people not for me.

ELEVATOR: The time is 8.55, Ms Hazlitt. Early for work again. But all work and no play makes Jack a dull gay.

GERTRUDE: I didn't ask for your comments, you stupid cow, always mouthing off about something. Five to nine. Problem. In theory we begin at nine: the scale of this new building is such that nobody's at their computers until 9.05. Solution: work to begin at 8.45, spot check on punctuality levels, absenteeism. How I hate their excuses: they got lost, the building's too big, the children are ill, mother had a fall, the traffic, the pain in the stomach. Staff are either here or they're not here, the office is not a glorified home. Memo: consult Human Resources: suggest voluntary counselling services for persistent latecomers. If we can define unpunctuality as mental disability we can circumvent the clause in the standard employment contract that's costing us so much –

ELEVATOR [sings]: Happy birthday to you, happy birthday to you.

GERTRUDE: Shut up, you goddamn American thing.

It shuts up.

GERTRUDE'S THINK VOICE: I forgot it was my birthday. Did my mother send me so much as a card, did my sister? No. Fifty-four. Year by year it gets worse. These mirrors are cruel. I shall have them torn out: I will have this elevator refurbished, antiqued: done in burnished gold and red velvet. I shall put in softer mirrors, softer lighting, so I am cheered up, not cast down. I am still a woman. Men still look after me even if they don't know who I am. A replica of the Doge's closet in Venice. I saw that once when I went to Italy with Duncan, how long ago, twenty-five years? There was some fabric in a Bond Street window the other day, the real original thing, Venetian, £2000 the yard.

Wow, I thought. If the work were done over the weekend and I buried the cost in office repairs – no, it's not worth the risk, forget £2000 the yard, the press would have a field day, you can get imitation at £20 the metre.

ELEVATOR: The Penthouse Suite offers the finest view in all Europe. Housing more than 1500 staff and dedicated to the welfare of the worker consumers of Britain, the new People's Palace tops Canary Wharf to the east and pays homage to Big Ben to the west. At your destination, Miss Hazlitt.

GERTRUDE: I hate you, you brainless fool. I cannot stand people who state the obvious. But you are not of course a person, you are an elevator. I forgive you. It is not your fault.

4.

The lift doors open into GERTRUDE's *office, in the Executive Suite. This occupies the breadth of the tower at its pinnacle: there is considerable movement here as in all tall buildings. You can hear the wind outside the triple-glazing, stronger in* GERTRUDE's *office than in the outer one where* CUMBER *her PA works and, thanks to a quirk of wind currents on the north side of the building, you can hear the bells of St Paul's and other City churches as well.* GERTRUDE *walks through from the comparative noise of her office to the comparative peace of* CUMBER's. *Here the wind is fainter and there is a background noise, never obtrusive, of the clicks and hums of computers and the odd sneeze or cough to suggest the deferential presence of others.* CUMBER, *a senior civil servant in his late forties, pleasant, well-educated, self-possessed and competent, welcomes her. He is a little in love with her.*

CUMBER: Good morning, Ms Hazlitt.

GERTRUDE: You know that lift tried to sing 'Happy Birthday' to me?

CUMBER: It'll be programmed in, Ms Hazlitt. It's a very user-friendly elevator you have there. Very state-of-the-art.

GERTRUDE: Of course it's fucking programmed in, Cumber. Do you think I'm stupid?

CUMBER: I'll get you a cup of coffee. Happy birthday, Ms Hazlitt.

GERTRUDE: Hah! I'll make my own coffee. I hate to see men waiting on women. It's pathetic. If it's wrong for women it's wrong for men.

Clip clop clip clop into her office. Her door slams.

CUMBER'S THINK VOICE: It's her birthday, poor thing. I expect she worries about ageing. She shouldn't. She's so beautiful, how was it the folk song put it? Backed like a swan. The upswept hair, white since she was thirty, they say, the full mouth, the long neck, those eyes that can flash with fire. He must have been a poor thing, that Duncan, to have left her. Envy, I daresay. Difficult for a man to be married to a successful woman, they say, even in this day and age.

Alas, my wife found me not successful enough. Too boring, she said, too weak, always the sergeant never the officer, and then ran off with a general. You become the thing they say you are, you catch it lying next to them in bed. You osmose their bad opinion. I did better once she'd gone. Though Cecilia, the daughter she left behind, and I suppose she is my daughter, although it would take a DNA test to tell for sure, drove off all other potential wives as they stepped over the doorstep. And I have lived with an empty bed from that day to this. Poor little Cecilia, always angry, always trouble, ruined my life, and God knows what she's up to now.

They use you up and spit you out. Perhaps now Cecilia's grown and gone I should try a dating agency. But that's a humiliation. I'd rather sit and gaze at Gertrude Hazlitt and try to weather the insults and think of what might have been. Perhaps they'll give me a knighthood, one day, or at least a medal. Think about work, never think about home, that way sanity lies.

His phone rings.

CUMBER: Yes, Miss Hazlitt?

GERTRUDE'S VOICE: Cumber, if I've asked you once I've asked you a hundred times – get those church bells silenced. How can I be expected to work when I am persecuted by these mediaeval relics?

CUMBER: Oh dear. It does rather tend to happen when the wind is in the west.

GERTRUDE'S VOICE [outraged]: This is the twenty-first century. What can the wind have to do with anything?

A chair is scraped back, clip clop to the door, which is pushed open.

5.

A Probation Office.

Now we're in the waiting room of a magistrates' court, on the ground floor. A windy morning. Staff and public come and go through revolving doors. A dreary place, where people would really rather not be if they could help it. The door from the inner sanctum opens and Pol the probation officer pops out.

POL: Sorry, everyone. We're running a little behind schedule. Cecilia? Anyone here called Cecilia Cumber? Are you Cecilia?

CECILIA: I'm coming. Here I am. Don't panic. I was just leaning out the window having a fag.

POL: That was thoughtful of you. My, what a pretty nose ring. And you brought the baby along, how sweet. I hope we can hear each other think, if it cries. Do keep the smoke well out of baby's way, it's carcinogenic, you know. And this is a non-smoking environment. Shall we go through?

They go through to the inner office and POL *shuts the door, and with it a lot of extraneous sound.*

CECILIA: Mummy was off on a cruise this morning, or she'd have taken him. Anyway, I don't like leaving him.

POL [with distaste]: Darling little baby. Not that I'm a baby person myself. What's its name?

CECILIA: I'm still thinking.

POL: Well, sit down, relax. We only have a few minutes. We probation officers are getting to be just like doctors. We must keep to the clock. It's no way to work, of course, but what can you do? At least you're on time, for once.

CECILIA: What do you mean for once? I'm always on time. If it's in my notes that I'm late it's a lie.

POL: I'm afraid in our latest move your notes have been mislaid, Cecilia. We've been reorganised and re-sited three times in the last year.

CECILIA: Same old orange sofa though, pity that didn't get mislaid. I haven't seen you before, have I? The faces keep changing, same with the midwives. Only the voices stay the same.

POL: We can do without notes. I had a nice little chat on the phone with Susan, she's your senior adviser. She'd have been here for you today if she could be. She's ill. Actually, it's stress, she was assaulted by one of the clients.

CECILIA: That's terrible. That won't do them any good.

POL: It happens all the time, we don't make a fuss. She told me you're doing very nicely, Cecilia. One more week and you'll be off notice. Your file will go from current to reserve to closed. Hopefully never to be reopened.

CECILIA: What's off notice?

POL: You do ask a lot of questions. She told me you were an intelligent girl. How old's the baby? Lovely little thing. Itsy bitsy coo.

CECILIA: Three weeks.

POL: You're so brave. I wouldn't bring a baby into this nasty world, even if I had the time. Boy or girl?

CECILIA: Boy.

POL: Boys have such a hard time these days. Suicidal, ill, failing their exams, always in trouble. Better to be born a girl.

CECILIA: You still haven't told me what off notice means.

POL: It means you'll no longer be on suspended sentence, Cecilia. If you do anything silly you won't be taken off to prison for the original offence, grievous bodily harm – twelve months, wasn't it – plus whatever sentence it is for your new silliness. One more week and it's all over. No longer reporting weekly to me – or whoever – and free to go back into society like any other normal person.

CECILIA: It wasn't grievous, it wasn't harm, I was just trying to warn the bitch off.

POL: That's as may be, Cecilia. But it's easier on everyone if you can just sigh and say to society, well I did it, I was silly, I'm sorry, I learned my lesson, now I won't do that, or anything like that, ever again. So, how are you managing with baby?

CECILIA: Oh fine. Pity it's a boy, as you say. All those things to look forward to. Failing his exams, depression, suicide, all that.

POL: It's not always like that, Cecilia. I didn't mean to depress you. Good mothering and proper attention, no truancy, and keeping the right company, and you can turn the statistics upside-down. Still living with your mother?

CECILIA: I've got a flat of my own. It's well nice. And a garden for the baby. I love gardening. Daddy used to do a lot of gardening, but after Mummy walked out we had to move house. She left me behind, you know.

POL: Boyfriend still with you?

CECILIA [firmly]: *No.*

POL: Probably just as well.

CECILIA: How do you know that, if you've lost my notes?

POL: It was quite a thing in all the papers, wasn't it? Top civil servant's daughter in knifing brawl. You're just as pretty as they say. Rings and all.

CECILIA: I look like shit. It's the baby. I don't get all that much sleep.

POL: I really don't understand girls like you. How old are you? Twenty-three? Every advantage, good looks, good background, good education, well-spoken, and you end up in a nightclub brawl mixed up with a Yardie.

CECILIA: He wasn't a Yardie, he was just black. And I was not mixed up with him, I loved him.

POL: Trying to shoot his girlfriend. You could have killed her. What sort of love is that?

CECILIA: My sort. I wanted to kill her. Anyone would. I was fighting for everything I had. My baby, my home, my life, him. But I wasn't trying to kill her, just frighten her off. Is there nothing they let you do to look after yourself? Anyway don't want to talk about it, it's over, it's all in my notes only you've lost them.

POL: They're not lost. They're mislaid. They'll turn up.

CECILIA: Anyway he went off with her, and now she's pregnant he's left her too, so we're just the same except I've got this stupid suspended sentence and she hasn't.

POL: And your poor father lost his job.

CECILIA: No he didn't, he just got transferred: he works with Gertrude Hazlitt in the People's Palace. He shouldn't have had a gun anyway. Tucked away in his bottom drawer in case of burglars. Or so he said. Look, everything's okay now. I've got my flat, I've got a course lined up – computer studies, I've sorted all the benefit junk and the baby's okay and putting on weight, and if I get mixed up, as you call it, with anyone else, I'll be lucky. All my old friends, my proper friends, well, forget it. Once something like that happens, they turn their back. I'm on my own now.

POL [impressed]: Gertrude Hazlitt? Always in the papers. Such a role model for us working women.

CECILIA: Mummy says Daddy's not quite right in the head, he went to Eton and was emotionally crippled. A loner, Mummy says, and the gun proved it. In fact, the reason she had to leave me with him when I was small was because she thought that if she took me away he might follow us and kill us. You know, those terrible cases, blood everywhere and bits of bodies in the boots of cars? But perhaps Mummy just says that to let herself off the hook. She's not the maternal type, not deep down, the truth is she couldn't be bothered with me and just buggered off.

POL: Thank you for sharing that with me, Cecilia. 9.35 already. The People's Palace! Like a great city, they say, the city of the future. That's the business to be in: Power to the People, forget social work. All we get here is traffic fumes.

6.

The revolving doors let us out onto the city street, where it's noisy and dirty and busy and windy, and cars hoot in rage, and then we go up and up to where the wind is mixed with the sound of distant church bells and to our relief we're in CUMBER'S *subdued office suite in the People's Palace.*

GERTRUDE: I refuse to believe that the People's Palace, this great building, which is newly completed, and cost thirty-six-and-a-half million over the original estimates, is in any way vulnerable to the direction of the wind. I hear church bells because the wind is in the west? You use that as an excuse?

CUMBER: It's complicated. The sound engineers say it is to do with the sheer scale of the building, which creates a tunnel of air through the central well, as at Canary Wharf. But also, the extra height of the Penthouse Tower, which, frankly, exists only so we can claim to be the tallest building in Europe, tribute to the power of the nation at work and play, creates an unexpected design flaw, moving us from the linear to the non-linear dimension in which patterns will not settle and the unexpected happens. It's known as the pendulum on pendulum effect.

GERTRUDE: Don't blind me with science. There is no problem that cannot be solved: I want no truck with these civil service minimax games of yours, Cumber. In this office we're into zero sum games and the sooner you acknowledge that the better. We win, they lose. I will not be at the mercy of these miserable bells. Do you know how much I am paid?

CUMBER: All too well, Miss Hazlitt. It was in the *Daily Mail* only last week, as we know to our cost. Rich bitches and fat cats. But no one could accuse you of being fat.

CUMBER'S THINK VOICE: Rich she is, fat she isn't. All alone in her perfect Georgian house, with a maid to arrange the flowers, and nothing to do of an evening but think about her wheat intolerance. She is lonely and unhappy, and I could make her happy but she would never let me.

GERTRUDE: You can be so servile, Cumber, but thank you. Don't you then think we owe it to the taxpayer to create an environment in which I can work properly and give them value for that money?

CUMBER: Short of dismantling the tower and losing height and status, and the *massive* restructuring and disruption to the working environment involved, no.

GERTRUDE: If you can't stop the sound, stop the bells. Muffle them.

CUMBER: Tricky, Miss Hazlitt. There are various ancient rights involved: I've had the law department look into it very thoroughly.

GERTRUDE: Okay. Ear plugs. Three memos, Cumber. One, I want that elevator renovated. The lift with lip. I want that electronic bitch silenced. Get the designers in for a meeting.

CUMBER: Designers, not the electricians?

GERTRUDE: I am a woman, Cumber, perched in the air though I am, swaying for my own safety, bending so that I do not break. Designers. I want a patch of velvet, and gold and richness and gloom, I can't be doing with all this male minimalist modernity. The brightness in here can be intolerable. Two, I saw stragglers on the way in this morning. We need a new punctuality initiative. Investigate the feasibility of removing all mirrors from the restrooms, male as well as female. There are more men primping and preening in front of them than ever. Thirdly, I need statistics relating to the growing resentment amongst the workers of Britain at the ringing of church bells. We are not in the Middle Ages, we are not monocultural. Sundays are now just like any other day, and if the Christian Church wants to disrupt the working life of Britain it's going to have a battle with me on its hands. I'll bring it up with the Prime Minister under any other business at today's meeting.

CUMBER: Ms Hazlitt, we are already over budget on office renovation, a full punctuality survey is not practical at the moment, and there are no statistics available in relation to church bells.

GERTRUDE: You can be very negative in your responses, Cumber. There is nothing whatsoever to prevent an informal survey. Ask around. We have 1500 employees: oh come on, Cumber, I just need some figures.

CUMBER: I'll do what I can.

GERTRUDE: Not good enough, Cumber, do what you *must*. Are we set for this afternoon's meeting with the PM? What is it, new European directives on the length of the working week?

CUMBER: It's straightforward: you see eye to eye in this area. He'll need only your initial response and a few figures to back it up. We'll have the team together later this morning.

GERTRUDE: Is this dress okay for Downing Street?

GERTRUDE'S THINK VOICE: Now why did I ask him that? He's not a husband, he's an assistant. He gets paid so much less than I do it can hardly matter what he thinks. Duncan used to pick hairs off my collar, tidy my parting: ages and ages ago. So much touching in a marriage, so little in an office.

CUMBER: I hadn't noticed it so I expect it's okay.

GERTRUDE: Oh forget it, you're a civil servant not a man. I shouldn't have asked.

CUMBER'S THINK VOICE: I love that dress. She wears it when she means to impress. Pale grey to show off the figure, she could be a girl from her body: the little strappy sandals on the narrow feet. She's painted her toenails. Why couldn't Cecilia dress like that? Why did it have to be all body piercing and shaven head and drugs? She made life so difficult for herself. Only another week and the suspended sentence runs out. Stop it, stop it, you're at work. Mustn't think about home.

GERTRUDE'S THINK VOICE: Why is he looking at me like that? I can't stand men who fall in love with me. How can they be trusted to give me good advice? Wife ran off with a general, that business of the gun in the bottom drawer, the daughter up on a charge, they warned me against him, strongly, but this country loses too many able men to irrelevant scandal: I took him on. Broke my own rules, listened to my feelings not my head, gave in to the feel-good factor and rescued him. I bet I live to regret it. One always does. Good-looking, but not my type. I like young men with neat butts and you mostly find those on building sites, not in the office. Too much sitting. Now that soppy look on his face again. There are no real men left in the world at all.

7.

GERTRUDE's *office.* GERTRUDE *works at her desk. Wind and bells,* GERTRUDE *murmurs to herself.*

GERTRUDE: Of course, a shorter working week would be popular with some segments of society, but not necessarily those contributing most to the working, earning, spending economy, that is to say, working mothers . . . bloody bells.

ELEVATOR: The time now is 10.32. '*The bells of hell go ting a ling a ling for you and not for me. Oh death where is thy sting a ling a ling, oh grave thy victory.*' Song popular in the British army, 1914–18.

GERTRUDE: You again. Shut your doors. They shouldn't be open, I'll swear some of this noise is coming up your shaft. Shut up, bitch!

ELEVATOR: '*Today I pronounced a word which should never come out of a lady's lips, it was that I called John an impudent bitch.*' Marjorie Fleming, 1803–11, a child prodigy who died at the age of nine.

GERTRUDE: I'm not going to be spoken to like that by an elevator. Do you know who I am?

ELEVATOR: Queen Gertrude, plc.

GERTRUDE *laughs.*

GERTRUDE: Okay. Pax.

8.

CUMBER's *office. His phone rings.*

CUMBER: Cumber here. Well?

CECILIA: Daddy, it's Cecilia. Can we have lunch today?

CUMBER: How did you get through to this line?

CECILIA: I dialled the extension. The baby's three weeks old and you haven't even seen him.

CUMBER: You've been with your mother.

CECILIA: She's gone off on a cruise. You know what she's like. She says she withers if she doesn't get the light – like a rose.

CUMBER: What about that man?

CECILIA: He's gone. Of course he's gone. I'd have got rid of him sooner if you hadn't made such a fuss. I'm sorry, Dad.

CUMBER: That's okay, darling. Let's start again.

GERTRUDE: Personal phone call, Cumber?

CUMBER: Just my daughter, Ms Hazlitt.

GERTRUDE: Oh yes, the jailbird.

CUMBER: Cecilia, we've got an important meeting this afternoon so it's a quick lunch in the canteen for me, but give me a call tomorrow. Okay? We'll fix something up.

The phone goes down. CUMBER *decides to take a stand.*

CUMBER: As it happens, Ms Hazlitt, my daughter is not a jailbird. By the skin of her teeth, I grant you. A suspended sentence, but suspended nonetheless.

GERTRUDE: I know. Isn't she the lucky one. There's so much movement in my office today I can't think. My coffee tilts one way and when I look again it's tilting the other. It's driving me mad. And the elevator doors have stuck on open, it's self-educating, interactive, and learning fast. Someone must have told it I did English Literature and demotic language at university. I want those designers in fast, Cumber.

CUMBER: It won't be before next week. Your diary's full. Unless you want me to start making inroads into your thinking time.

GERTRUDE: Did you call your daughter or did she call you?

CUMBER: She called me.

GERTRUDE: And she got through? I thought all personal calls got passed to Family Matters and held over until after office hours. How very strange.

9.

Clip clop, clip clop: someone young is running and panting up to the top floor of the tower extension of the People's Palace.

KATE: Thirty-third, thirty-fourth, thirty-fifth, thirty-sixth, thirty-seventh, thirty-eight stairs and it's the seventy-second floor.

KATE'S THINK VOICE: Made it. Six floors in three and a half minutes. Should have got rid of last night's alcohol. Calorie wise, if not kidney wise. I hate it up here on the tower. I get agoraphobia, claustrophobia and fear of heights all at the same time. Dark glasses, that's the thing. I don't know how she stands it. If I got paid what she gets paid I'd move down to the ground floor, to be nearer the earth.

10.

CUMBER'*s office.*

KATE: Happy birthday, Ms Hazlitt. Morning, Mr Cumber.

GERTRUDE: How do you know it's my birthday? Have you been using my elevator? I didn't see you come in.

KATE: I couldn't use your elevator. It's personally programmed to you and your invited guests, tailor-made for your temperament and tastes and all that. The pride of the AI unit. I wrote all the PR stuff, I should know.

GERTRUDE: Then how did you get in here?

KATE: I used the stairs, I ran up. Good for the figure.

CUMBER'S THINK VOICE: She could have been a stalker, an assassin, anyone. There's no CCTV on that door. I'm right to keep a gun in my drawer. If someone bursts their way in here, they'll die. I'd have no qualms. She has to be protected.

KATE: Let me introduce myself, I'm Kate from Human Resources, staff morale division. They moved me from PR. It's a promotion.

GERTRUDE: I don't care who you are, how do you know it's my birthday?

KATE: I read it in *The Times.* It's in all the papers this morning: you're such a celebrity these days.

GERTRUDE: I don't want my birthday in the papers.

KATE: But age is something to be proud of, not ashamed of.

GERTRUDE: Go back to the lower floors where you belong and stop littering up my office. You're sweating, that's horrible. Next thing you'll say you need a shower in one of the new restrooms, and that's more of the People's time and money wasted. This is an office environment, not a gym.

11.

Door slams: back to the sound of the wind and church bells.

GERTRUDE'S THINK VOICE: God, these young people, dewy fresh from the nursery telling me how the world runs. What does she mean, age is something to be proud of? Is she mad? Bloody church bells, non-stop, is the world so very full of funerals? And the wind. How much movement is there meant to be in these towers? It's so erratic. What did Cumber mean, non-linear, the pendulum on pendulum effect? I'm not going to ask him, that's for sure. I hate it when he knows more than I do. Oh crack your cheeks, ye winter winds, do your worst.

GERTRUDE: I am Queen Gertrude, plc, lord of all I survey: the Lord is my Shepherd, though I walk through the shadow of the valley of death, though I dwell in the clouds, yet he is with me . . .

ELEVATOR: 10.35. '*And all our yesterdays have lighted fools the way to dusty death.*' Shakespeare, 1564–1616.

She lifts the phone.

GERTRUDE: Cumber, you can eat into my think time as much as you want. Just get the designers up here. I want this elevator refurbished and silenced.

12.

CUMBER'*s office.*

KATE: What she said was uncalled for, I don't care who she is. I don't sweat. Do I?

CUMBER: If you do, my dear, I haven't noticed it. Miss Hazlitt has a lot on her shoulders. You were a little tactless about her age.

KATE: Was I? I hadn't realised she'd be quite so sensitive.

KATE'S THINK VOICE: My God, she's a bitch. This man can only be suffering from Stockholm Syndrome. The one where the hostage falls in love with the terrorist. It happens in offices too. I must write a paper on it.

KATE: Normally I communicate by e-mail, so much safer. But e-mail's down throughout the building because of yesterday's hoax virus report. The search engines overloaded and the system crashed. It's had a feed-through effect on voice mail for some reason so if you get calls coming straight through from the outside world, be warned. We're on overcast security alert only, nothing extreme, just a nuisance. If you're the messenger of bad news you can reckon to have a hard time, you just don't expect to get it before you deliver it.

CUMBER'S THINK VOICE: Bad news. She calls that bad news. Technological hitches. Bad news to me is my wife's running away note, my daughter in a cell accused of attempted murder, or me being suspended the day I've got the public/privatisation Underground Transport partnership deal worked out. This silly pretty sweaty little girl, not a brain in her head and no idea what life is like. Pray God she never finds out.

KATE: I'm glad you take it so calmly. People can get quite agitated, they like things to go on the same from day to day.

CUMBER: Lucky old them. Don't worry about me. I've survived a lot of things in my life. I reckon we can manage a day without e-mail.

CUMBER's *phone rings.*

KATE: Careful. Find out who it is before you reply.

CUMBER: Who is this? Oh, the PM's office . . . Cancelled? I know, things are very finely tuned. An e-mail crash does mean delays. But are you sure? We are talking Gertrude Hazlitt here. Britain at Work plc. Oh, the devolution of Northern Italy to the US. I know overseas affairs are tempting but crisis points do tend to be on the domestic front, and working hours are in danger of becoming quite an issue. However. Get back to us when you can and we'll try and find another window.

13.

GERTRUDE's *office. Wind, bells and the elevator.*

GERTRUDE: It's like a bloody graveyard up here. Does everything stop because e-mail stops? I hate meetings being cancelled. There's nothing to look forward to.

ELEVATOR: 11.22. '*The grave's a fine and private place, but none I think do there embrace.*' Robert Herrick, 1591–1674.

GERTRUDE: It's getting spooky, I can't bear spooky.

The phone rings.

GERTRUDE: Cumber? Has that sweaty little ninny gone away? Is it safe to come out?

MARIE: Gertie, this is your mother.

GERTRUDE: How did you get through? You should have been put through to Family Matters.

MARIE: Surprise to me, too. Normally I get lost by accident on purpose on voice mail.

GERTRUDE: This is a big organisation, Mother, we're still having teething problems.

MARIE: With you in charge I'm not surprised. You should never have left Duncan. It's been downhill all the way since then.

GERTRUDE: I'm very busy, Mother.

MARIE: That's what you always say. You were always good at looking as if you were busy, leaving your poor sister to do all the work.

GERTRUDE: Mum, I am chief executive of Britain at Work, plc: I look after the workers of this country. Twenty million of them. I am the Trade Union and a caring Management rolled into one.

MARIE: Well, I've broken my hip.

GERTRUDE: Yes, I know that but you had the op and you're just fine.

MARIE: Gertrude, that is simply wishful thinking. I am not fine.

GERTRUDE: Mum, it's my birthday, please say something nice.

MARIE: And did you remember mine? No. More important things to worry about. I'll be surprised if you even turn up to my funeral, which won't be far away.

GERTRUDE: You're not ill or anything?

CUMBER'S VOICE: I'm sorry to interrupt this call, Ms Hazlitt, just to let you know the PM's cancelled for this afternoon. The e-mail crisis has hit those offices too.

GERTRUDE: Ah, shit. Mum, something's come up. I'll call you back, same number?

MARIE: No, actually, Gertie, it's not. I'm in an old people's home and I need you to get me out of here. It's called the Sapphire, in Okehampton.

GERTRUDE: I've made a note of that, Mum, I'll call you back.

Phone goes down.

GERTRUDE: Thank you, Cumber. I don't know how she got through.

CUMBER: In the same way my daughter did, I imagine. Voice mail's having problems.

GERTRUDE*'s phone again.*

CUMBER: I've taken the liberty of getting the design department to come on up.

ELEVATOR: '*Free from self-seeking, envy, low design, I have not found a whiter soul than thine.*' Charles Lamb, 1775–1834.

GERTRUDE: Cumber, I'm sorry if I was mean about your daughter. It's just that everyone loves her and worries about her and bends over backwards to help her, and all she is is a criminal. I bust my guts for the workers of this country and everyone hates me. Even my own mother. There's no justice in the world.

Part 2

1.

Exterior: Late morning. The sound of the Council Recycling Depot, tipper trucks tipping, clanging vehicles, warning bleeps as they manoeuvre, men's shouts and oaths, loudspeaker announcements. 'Clear glass is now to the north side of the depot, green glass to the south.'

2.

Interior: The sound muted inside CECILIA*'s flat, which faces out over the depot.* CECILIA *rocks her baby and sings a Schubert lullaby.*

> CECILIA [sings]: *When the dawn,*
> *Tips the skies,*
> *God will bid thee arise . . .*
> *Lie warm in thy nest,*
> *By moonbeams caressed.*

Little baby. You're not too young to smile, I don't care what they say, that was a smile. (*Bang, crash*) No, don't startle. Don't startle: that was just the garbage men: that's why we got this place so cheap. It's going to smell a bit come the hot weather, I expect, but we can put up with that. Sometimes the men shout and swear – perhaps they'd rather be doing something else, but I think it's a good job, a real job. I think the garbage men should get paid more than anyone else, more than my Daddy, more than Gertrude Hazlitt, swanning around. I want you to grow up to think things can be put right. I don't want you growing up depressed the way that Probation Officer said. It's all right out the back, there's a little garden: we'll grow roses, I can scrub the graffiti off the wall. The earth isn't up to much because of the cats and the soot but Daddy says roses are best, roses can survive anything nature throws their way. Only thing is, it's not so much nature, as mankind.

[sings]: *Dance for your daddy,*
My little Manny,
Dance for your Daddy,
My little man,
You shall have a fishy
On a little dishy,
You shall have a fishy
When the boat comes in.

Another thing: I don't want you thinking badly about your Daddy: I know he's gone, and we won't see him again, but he was big and strong and black and beautiful, and he had his A-levels which was more than I did, it's just he smoked a lot of dope and got angrier with people than he should, and his friends would have laughed at him if he'd stayed with us. And he thought the world of his friends.

[sings]: *Cannily cannily, bonnie wee bairnikee,*
Don't you cry now, my little pet.
Hush-a-bye now, your daddy is sleeping,
It's not time to waken him yet.

I wanted to have lunch with my Daddy today but he put me off. He thinks I'll disgrace him. But I'm not like that any more. I've only got one nose stud left and two bolts in my left ear and my hair's getting so long I can almost comb it.

[sings]: *Golden slumbers kiss your eyes,*
       Smiles await you when you rise . . .

I can't remember the rest. My Mummy used to sing it to me when I went for weekends but by the time she got that far I'd be asleep.

[sings]: *Sleep my child and God attend thee,*
       All through the night.
       Guardian angels God will send thee,
       All through the night.

When I was twelve I wanted to be a nun. An old-fashioned nun covered up with black and little bits of white, a bride of Christ and all spirit and no body. But they soon talked me out of that. And then suddenly it all went the other way, it's the hormones, they say, head-over-heels into hatefulness and self-destruct and bring the whole world toppling down on top of you: anything to be not what they wanted, not to fit into the mould they'd got ready for you. They wanted me to be happy and nice so what I was a little ball of body-pierced head-shaven hate. And then one day you see the pubs and the clubs and the drugs are as much a mould as anything, but by that time you've had so many men up the alleys and in the gutter you can't remember what that was all meant to be about, anyway.

[sings]: *I gave my love a cherry,*
       That had no stone,
       I gave my love a story
       That has no end,
       I gave my love a baby that's no crying.

       A cherry when it's blooming, it has no stone,
       A chicken when it's pippin' it has no bone,

The story that I love you, it has no end,
A baby when it's sleeping, it's no crying.

Then I met your Daddy and fell in love. Wasn't that peculiar? I thought that was all just in books. And then I was pregnant and he started seeing this other girl. I wanted to make a baby, something out of nothing, and him to share it. She was black and beautiful too and skinny and her name was Gloria. I hated her. And quick as a flash I was like someone out of Jerry Springer, from the lowest depths. (*Bangs and crashes from the depot*) Don't startle, don't startle. It's only the men.

[sings]: *Sleep my little one, sleep,*
           Fond vigil I keep,
           When the dawn tips the skies
           God will bid thee arise –

I said to her in her own language, bitch I said, bitch, keep away from my man. It was so stupid.

[sings]: *Frankie and Johnnie were sweethearts,*
           Lordy and how they could love,
           Swore to be true to each other,
           Just as true as the stars above
           He was her man
           And he was doing her wrong.

But guns are peculiar: you point them and pull the trigger and the bullet doesn't go where you think and instead of getting the bottles behind the bar it skinned her arm. How she shrieked, the cow. It was only a graze. And the police came and they put me in a cell and I thought I would die. And it all came out, where I'd got the gun, and my father was up in court too for keeping an unregistered weapon in his bottom drawer, not that he'd ever fired it, he just liked to have it there. To protect his family. And he was sent to work for Gertrude Hazlitt which is a kind of punishment post, I guess.

And then I felt you kicking inside me, hi, you said, it's me, I'm here, and all the nasty stuff just oozed away. Well, most of it. A butterfly out of a cocoon, that's me. And now I'm just like everyone else, picking myself up again. I guess I'll have to think of a name for you, soon. It won't be anything fancy, just after one of the old saints, to remind me of when I used to want to be a nun. (*Bang crash from outside*)

[sings]: *Go to sleep,*
You weary hobo,
Let the town drift slowly by,
Listen to the steel rails humming,
That's the hobo's lullaby.

I'll go to the People's Palace for lunch, perhaps I'll see my Daddy there. Time we saw each other again. You need to see this building, baby, so big, bigger than Canary Wharf, in the early morning it's like sun on mountains: so tall you know the day is coming when the spire begins to glitter.

Part 3

1.

GERTRUDE's *office: wind and bells and a male designer.*

GERTRUDE: I don't see that it's incongruous at all. Artificial intelligence – so called, that thing is just a joke, so stupid – can function just as well out of velvet and gold as out of glass and steel. I want it the way I want it. Antiqued. Gold twirly cues and crimson velvet. Softly lit.

DESIGNER: Like a French brothel you mean?

GERTRUDE: No I do not, young man. And you'd only know what that looks like by hearsay.

DESIGNER: Like a casino then, more for night living than for day? I'm trying to catch the gist.

GERTRUDE: Like the closet in the Doge's palace in Venice. They have some of the original fabric in an antique shop in Bond Street in quite good condition. Not very expensive.

DESIGNER: How much?

GERTRUDE: £2000 the yard.

DESIGNER: We like to measure in metres. In fact one of the directives from this very office, Ms Hazlitt, requires us to purchase only materials measured in the new metric system. And Ms Hazlitt, this building is a tribute to British design, it's won awards worldwide, we can't spoil the effect by dressing up your elevator like a Turkish harem. It's not as if it were for your eyes only, I imagine when the Prime Minister visits, or some VIP from abroad, you share your elevator.

GERTRUDE: Not if I can help it. Foreign dignitaries often smell, and sometimes they smoke. And believe me, if I want to spoil an effect, I will spoil it. Oh Lordy me, why do I always have to fight my own staff?

ELEVATOR [sings]: *Frankie and Johnny were sweethearts,*
Lordy and how they could love –

DESIGNER: What in God's name was that?

GERTRUDE: That's it, that's my personalised elevator. Now do you understand? It picks up key words from my speech and comes back with a quotation or a song. It keeps trying to have intelligent conversations with me. I can't stop it. I can't turn it off. I can't even shut its fucking doors. It sticks to me like glue: it tags along as if I was a school prefect and it had a crush on me. It's unendurable.

ELEVATOR: *They swore to be true to each other,*
Just as true as the stars above,
He was her man,
And he was doing her wrong.

DESIGNER: That's fantastic! I read about this only last week in *Technology Today*. Massive technological advance. Not quite artificial intelligence but then what is self, what is consciousness? Swallowed the dictionary did you, elevator? What was it, *The Oxford Dictionary of Quotations*? Or *The Archetype in Popular Language and Song*? Well?

GERTRUDE: I would be obliged if you would talk to me, young man, and not my elevator.

ELEVATOR: *This story has no moral,*
This story has no end,
This story only goes to show,
That there ain't no good in man,
He was her man
And he was doing her wrong.

The phone rings.

GERTRUDE: Yes, Cumber, we've finished in here. Designers will have drawings and costings by the end of the week.

RITA: It's Rita, Gertie. Rita, your sister, you remember? I'm sorry to bother you at the office. I called to leave a happy birthday message but they put me straight through. It's not my fault. Are you terribly busy? Gertie, my therapist says I have to come out with my feelings more, and I want to tell you just how hurt I am. Why is it, Gertie, that in all the interviews about your happy childhood I never get a mention? I begin to feel you're ashamed of me.

GERTRUDE: Yes, Rita, I am.

RITA: But what have I ever done to you? I love you. You're my sister.

GERTRUDE: You've done nothing whatsoever with your life.

RITA: I've got a husband who loves me and three children.

GERTRUDE: That's what I mean. You're a housewife. What is there to say?

CUMBER'S VOICE: A call for you, Ms Hazlitt. The Lord Chancellor's office.

GERTRUDE: I've really got to go, Rita.

RITA: It's about Mother. She needs money. She's in this nursing home in the West Country.

GERTRUDE: Goodbye, Rita.

She puts the phone down. CUMBER *comes into her office.*

GERTRUDE: Thank you for that, Cumber. My mother put away nothing for her old age, why shouldn't she live with the consequence? She never did a day's work in her life, she was parasitic on my poor father, she always loathed me anyway. The State is there to look after her, Rita has no business to come pestering me.

CUMBER: You must be quite fretted and tired, Ms Hazlitt. It's always disconcerting when the office routine is disturbed. But they say e-mail will be back online this afternoon, and I daresay voice mail too. Supposing we go down to the canteen for lunch?

GERTRUDE: The food's so awful.

CUMBER: Human Resources like you to be seen there every now and then, Ms Hazlitt. This is meant to be an egalitarian environment, for workers by hand and brain.

GERTRUDE: They all hate me, however they work. I don't see why I should be expected to face them. And Human Resources is going to be worse than ever now I've told their minion she sweats. Well, it was true. All right, we'll have a drink at the bar. I need one. Will you come down in the elevator with me?

CUMBER: Well, there's an offer! But will it let me?

2.

The sound of a bar on the tenth floor of the People's Palace. It caters for hundreds, and is very busy.

WAITRESS: This is a non-smoking environment. Could you put the cigarette out?

CECILIA [none too pleased]: Oh, all right.

WAITRESS: Such a bad idea for mothers to smoke, dear.

CECILIA: I'm sorry, I'm nervous. I'm looking for someone.

The bar noise closes round them again.

3.

The elevator closes its doors. GERTRUDE *and* CUMBER *are enclosed.*

ELEVATOR: Which floor, Ms Hazlitt?

GERTRUDE: Second floor, restaurant level.

ELEVATOR: Bon appetit, Ms Hazlitt, and welcome to your guest.

CUMBER: How does it know? Does it work out weights? It is an interesting debate, isn't it, just what constitutes consciousness, when a machine can be said to have intelligence.

GERTRUDE: It's monstrous.

ELEVATOR: *'The first blast of the trumpet against the monstrous regiment of women!'* Title of Pamphlet, John Knox 1505–72.

CUMBER: Perhaps we could get it for sexual harassment.

GERTRUDE: That's not funny.

ELEVATOR: *'Isn't it funny how a bear likes honey, buzz, buzz, buzz. I wonder why he does?'* A. A. Milne, 1882–1956. The time is 13.00 precisely. We are at the restaurant level. Bon appetit.

GERTRUDE: Fruitless thing.

ELEVATOR: *'To live a barren sister all your life, Chanting faint hymns to the cold fruitless moon.'* A Midsummer Night's Dream, Shakespeare.

GERTRUDE: Yes I know. 1564–1616.

CUMBER: You see, a conversation!

4.

The buzz of the canteen bar as the elevator doors open onto it.

GERTRUDE: They're only going to say she's too fond of a drink. Let me sit at the bar with my back to everyone.

CUMBER: The bar's not very peaceful. They do the food orders from here.

GERTRUDE: I was brought up in a pub. I bet you didn't know that. Don't tell my elevator. Are people staring?

CUMBER: Only in admiration, Gertrude. Perhaps one day when we have a spare minute we could go somewhere quieter.

GERTRUDE: Gertrude?

CUMBER: For out of the office use only.

GERTRUDE: I suppose I do have to remember sometimes that I'm a woman. People are staring. It will be autograph time next. I feel soiled, for fuck sake, get us some gin and tonics, Cumber, and we'll drink them down and get out of here.

Suddenly the twosome becomes a threesome. GERTRUDE *is not pleased.*

CECILIA: Daddy?

CUMBER: Cecilia. My darling child, how wonderful to see you. And is this the baby? My little grandson? Gertrude, you haven't met my daughter.

GERTRUDE: I haven't had that pleasure. She's smaller than I thought for someone who looms so large in so many people's lives.

CECILIA: I'm so glad you're being like this, Daddy, I thought you'd still be angry.

CUMBER: What's the baby's name?

CECILIA: I don't know yet.

CUMBER: You'll have to make up your mind soon.

CECILIA: Do you like my hair like this? Is it okay?

CUMBER: I haven't noticed so I expect it's okay.

CECILIA: Look at it as if I've been ill, Daddy. A bad case of behavioural flu that went on for six years. I'm better now. Can we order some food? I'm so hungry.

GERTRUDE: Cumber, you were getting me a gin and tonic. You really shouldn't bring a baby in here, young lady. I'm sure there's some regulation to do with infants in proximity to alcohol.

CUMBER: Sit down, Cecilia, next to Ms Hazlitt here. People are watching. Smile, Gertrude.

GERTRUDE: The baby smells of sick.

CUMBER: They often do, Gertrude.

GERTRUDE: And stop calling me Gertrude.

CUMBER: It's lunchtime. Loosen up. Now come on. People have cameras.

GERTRUDE: How can I loosen up? This simply brings it home to me. There must be a new government initiative. The current approach to pregnant women and mothers is far far too lax. A good fifteen per cent of women need to be sterilised, voluntarily of course. It would resolve so many of this country's problems, financial and social. No more sub-standard babies, no more sink estates, no more cycle of deprivation. We can hold up our heads in Europe.

CUMBER: You're joking.

GERTRUDE: Do I joke?

CUMBER: Sometimes.

GERTRUDE: Not on this subject. A grant of £1000 cash to every woman who wants to terminate, that's all it needs.

CECILIA: Daddy, I'm so hungry. Can I order some fish and chips? I'm breast-feeding.

GERTRUDE: Don't, please, take out any nipples in front of me. You know there's such a thing as a criminal gene? It needs to be bred out. Women just have to stop dropping babies as if there was no tomorrow. Because for the State, which has to pick up the pieces, there most certainly is. A very expensive one.

CECILIA: A criminal gene? Are you talking about me?

CUMBER: Smile, Gertrude, there's someone wants to take a photograph.

GERTRUDE: Cecilia, what are you eating?

CUMBER: I'm sorry to say my daughter is eating, with her fingers, the prawns out of someone's half-finished prawn cocktail.

GERTRUDE: That's theft.

CECILIA: Oh come off it, four prawns. Four cast-off prawns, in a half-finished prawn cocktail the waitress left on the bar. That is not theft, that is common sense. I'm hungry.

GERTRUDE: Your daughter is blind to principle, Cumber, it seems. She is a moral defective. The Victorians used the term for mothers whose babies were born out of wedlock. I take it yours is?

CECILIA: You mean did he marry me? Of course he didn't marry me. It's not in his culture.

GERTRUDE: So the baby's illegitimate. Wasn't that irresponsible?

CECILIA: It sort of happens, Ms Hazlitt, it's called sex.

GERTRUDE: Do you know what girls like you cost the State every year? £90 billion not just in benefits but counting in the loss to the labour market. Cumber, I want you to call the police.

CUMBER: Why?

GERTRUDE: Your daughter has just committed theft, and seems to have no idea at all that she has. Somebody has to point it out to her. The police are the appropriate authority.

CUMBER: This is a joke?

CECILIA: I'd rather she didn't call the police, Daddy, I'm still on probation. I could go inside for a year.

CUMBER: You heard that, Ms Hazlitt, I take it. You're not being serious?

GERTRUDE: But I am. These things must take their course. Your daughter has a suspended sentence conditional on her good behaviour for a year, this is not good behaviour. This is theft.

CECILIA: Four prawns. Daddy, she's going to do it. Daddy, they take the babies away.

CUMBER: I'd always take the baby, dear. But it's not going to happen.

GERTRUDE: I doubt if they'd allow that, Cumber. A single man – men and babies, come off it. You have a conviction too. Unlicensed firearms.

CECILIA: I don't understand you. Why do you hate me?

GERTRUDE: I can't stand the sloppiness, the sentimentality, the cost to the community. The law must take its course.

CECILIA: You don't know what prison's like.

GERTRUDE: I do. I went over one once. A glorified girls' boarding school.

CECILIA: No, it's not.

CUMBER: Surely the courts won't convict.

CECILIA: Daddy they will. It happens.

GERTRUDE: The girl is a thief. I saw her. I have been observed seeing her. Indeed, I think someone took a photograph. There was a decided flash. It is my duty as a citizen to report her. If you won't call the police, I will. Where is my mobile phone?

CUMBER: In the penthouse, Ms Hazlitt. Your top drawer.

GERTRUDE: You should have brought it down with us. Go and get it. Or else I'll borrow one from the plebs and there will be a scandal. Fetch it, Cumber.

CECILIA: Daddy, don't go.

GERTRUDE: You may use my elevator. It's quicker.

CECILIA: Daddy, don't leave me. Daddy?

CUMBER *goes.*

GERTRUDE: You see, Cecilia, how your daddy does what I say,

not what you say? Self-interest does tend to win over family feeling. Why else are our old people's homes full of neglected ancient mothers and senile fathers? Better to be obeyed as I am, than be liked, as you are. Liking's a feeble thing. As for parental love, it can be quite worn away by naughty children, as you see. Your father is loyal, principled and obedient to me, which is how it should be. Oh, and Cecilia, don't think of running away. I'll ask the police to be lenient, you never know, a word from me and they might decide to look the other way. But that's up to them. Waitress, some fish and chips for the young lady, now she has finished her stolen prawns.

5.

The elevator's doors close. CUMBER's *breathing is heavy.*

ELEVATOR: Good afternoon, friend of Ms Hazlitt's. The time is 1.15. I hope you had a good meal. The weather's overcast and a little humid today. Where would you like me to take you?

CUMBER: Executive penthouse.

ELEVATOR: *Carpe diem,* as they say. Seize the day. A latin tag. Males are more fond of them than females. We're on our way, sir!

CUMBER: Do you have anything to say on worms turning?

ELEVATOR: Worms turning? A minute, sir.

> *Oh rose thou art sick,*
> *The invisible worm*
> *That flies in the night*
> *In the howling storm*
> *Hath found out thy bed*
> *Of secret joy,*
> *And its dark secret love*
> *Doth thy life destroy.*

William Blake, 1757–1827. He lived not far from here, sir, in Paternoster Row.

CUMBER: 'Oh rose thou art sick.' Thank you. I know what to do. I see it clear.

ELEVATOR: As you say, sir.

CUMBER: Do you have anything to say on love? No, don't start.
I can see why you drove her mad. She is mad.
ELEVATOR: 'Mad, bad and dangerous to know', said of Lord
Byron, 1788–1824.

6.

The Penthouse: Wind and bells. CUMBER *walks through* GERT-
RUDE's *office into the comparative peace of his own, and opens his
desk drawer.*
CUMBER: E-mail's back up, I see. You have thirty-two messages
waiting. Well, they will have to wait. Where are you, you little
illegitimate weapon? Kept to save her: now must save her from
herself.

7.

Elevator doors open.
ELEVATOR: The time is 1.18. Where to, sir?
CUMBER: The restaurant floor. The bar.
ELEVATOR: The bar! [sings]

> *Ha ha ha, you and me,*
> *Little brown jug don't I love thee.*
> *The rose is red,*
> *My nose is too,*
> *The violet's blue*
> *And so are you.*
> *And I guess,*
> *Before I stop,*
> *I'd better take another drop.*

CUMBER: Thank you, elevator.

8.

The bar.
Elevator doors open on the noise of the bar. CUMBER *steps out.*
The elevator speaks after him, in warning.

ELEVATOR: '*Children hold on tight to nurse, For fear of finding something worse.*'

CUMBER: Too late.

GERTRUDE: That isn't my mobile, Cumber. You've brought the wrong thing. That is a gun. Is it licensed? Registered? No, Cumber, don't point it at her. Don't shoot her: that is too extreme. Please don't. Really. Such a nasty scandal, people are so sentimental about mothers and babies. I don't believe this. You are pointing it at me. But you love me, Cumber, I know you do. My God, you were my one good turn – I should have known it would happen – biting the hand that feeds you – don't do this –

CUMBER: One for you, Queen Gertrude, plc, to save the world.

GERTRUDE: But the world needs me.

CUMBER: No. Sorry.

A gunshot, and a whimper from GERTRUDE.

CUMBER: And one for me. I'm sorry Cecilia; this is very unpleasant for you. Just tell them I went mad. Your mother will be so pleased, vindicated at last. Don't mention the prawns, whatever you do.

A gunshot and a whimper from CUMBER. *Silence.*

CECILIA: Daddy?

The baby begins to cry. The wind gets up. Bar noises, City noises, tower noises, wind and bells and the elevator singing Ha ha ha Hee hee hee . . .

Fay Weldon

The Bulgari Connection

'A glorious, positively inspired romp of love, lust, greed, power and stonkingly expensive jewellery . . . She is a true original, completely of her time.'   *The Times*

Fay Weldon turns her gaze on London's super rich and delivers a thrilling satire on their world – charity auctions, commissioned portraits and exclusive designer jewellers. Not to mention adultery, attempted murder, bribery, corruption and more than a few tantrums.

'It is impossible for Fay Weldon to be dull. *The Bulgari Connection* is her at her most seductive. It winds you in, intrigues and grips you until the end.'   *Daily Mail*

'A wonderful comedy of modern manners. Weldon writes with her characteristic dry humour and wonderful economy of language. Witty, profound and whimsical by turns, this is a sparkling novel, showing the hallmarks of a master craftsman.'   *Literary Review*

'The thinking person's frothy read. It's intelligent and funny, with fully drawn and recognisable characters, both goodies and baddies.'   *Time Out*

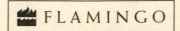

Fay Weldon

Auto da Fay

A memoir

'You can't put this terrific book down.' *Daily Mail*

'It is an astonishing, gripping story, lightly and deftly told, without self-pity. It will delight her many fans.'
LYNN BARBER, *Daily Telegraph*

Fay Weldon, one of the pre-eminent writers of our times, has crammed more than most into her years. From the 1930s to the 2000s, Weldon has seen and lived it all. As a child in New Zealand, as young and poor in London, as unmarried mother, as wife, lover, novelist, feminist, anti-feminist, there are few waterfronts that she hasn't covered, few battles she hasn't fought.

'Effervescently funny, honest and insightful. Transports us across years of sadness, brightness, chaos, triumph. An exuberant and thoughtful treat.' ANDREA ASHWORTH.

'Wonderfully fluent and entertaining, revealing a life crammed with more gritty drama than a tea-time soap. You can always trust Fay to be provocative – and this time she excels herself.'
VAL HENNESSY, *Daily Mail*

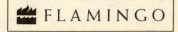 FLAMINGO

Fay Weldon

Puffball

A novel of urban deceit and rural passion

'Gripping'   *Observer*

Richard and Liffey haven't been married long. They are still
madly in love, and in lust, and so, when Liffey suggests
moving out of London to a country cottage in the middle of
Somerset, Richard puts aside his reservations; he wants his
young, pretty wife to be happy, after all.

But then the real world intervenes, and Richard must remain
in London during the week and see his Liffey, now pregnant,
only on weekends. And so that leaves poor Liffey, pregnant
and alone, burdened, confused and frustrated by biological
impulses which are suddenly overwhelming her. Can she
rely on Mabs, her seemingly kindly neighbour, and Tucker,
her rather over-friendly husband, for solace? Surely there
can't be anything sinister in their motives – can there? At least
she has no reason to doubt Richard's love for her – or does
she?

With wit, wisdom, and a little dose of witchery, Fay Weldon
reveals the conflicts that arise from the eternal struggle
between male and female.

'Magical – she lays out the ingredients of her brew with a
kind of manipulative glee, coolly moulding her characters
and then neatly skewering them with mockery.'   *Daily Mail*

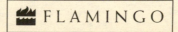 FLAMINGO

Fay Weldon

The President's Child

'Delicious: effervescing and overflowing with fun'   *Telegraph*

'Excellent.'   *London Review of Books*

Isabel Acre has lived on lovely Wincaster Row in Camden for
seven years, with her perfect husband Homer, her adorable
son Jason, and her wonderful career. But she has spent those
seven years guarding a secret – Jason is not Homer's son. And
when Jason's real father, a US Presidential candidate no less,
comes to London on a political trip, Isabel realises how ruthless ambitious men can be, and how easily the façade of a
perfect life can crumble.

'Weldon's acute intelligence focuses upon naked, flame-like,
fierce emotion. Its world seems all important, yet it is handled
with great deftness and a concentrated cleverness which is a
joy to read.'   *Financial Times*

'Delicious, far-fetched and enormously enjoyable.' *Daily Mail*

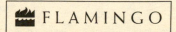 FLAMINGO

Fay Weldon

The Fat Woman's Joke

'Weldon oozes readability. She should be cloned.'   *Scotsman*

What *is* the joke? What's she laughing at? What in the world can she find to laugh about, fat fierce old Esther? Her husband's mistress going off with her son? Funny? Going on a diet and ending up with less waist and less husband that when she started? Funny?

It had, in fact, been Esther's husband's idea to go on a diet – they'd do it together. But sometime into their enforced starvation, Esther had a revelation. Suddenly she saw her life for what it was and found it all remarkably pointless. And so Esther left home, moved to a flat of her own, and began eating . . .

'Impassioned, angry, quirky and brilliant.'   *New York Times*

FLAMINGO